JEAN CHAPMAN

DEADLY
SERIOUS

Complete and Unabridged

ULVERSCROFT
Leicester

First published in Great Britain in 2013 by
Robert Hale Limited
London

First Large Print Edition
published 2014
by arrangement with
Robert Hale Limited
London

The moral right of the author has been asserted

A catalogue record for this book is available
from the British Library.

ISBN 978–1–4448–1892–5

Published by
F. A. Thorpe (Publishing)
Anstey, Leicestershire
Set by Words & Graphics Ltd.
Anstey, Leicestershire
Printed and bound in Great Britain by
T. J. International Ltd., Padstow, Cornwall

This book is printed on acid-free paper

Jean Chapman began her writing career as a freelance journalist before going on to write fiction. Her books have been shortlisted for both the Scottish Book Trust Award and the RNA Major Award, and she has been President of the Leicester Writers' Club three times.

SPECIA   **RS**

THE ULVERSCROFT FOUNDATION
(r
wa   BOOK LINK
resea   ROTHERHAM LIBRARY & INFORMATION SERVICE   .

4/3/14

Tel: 01709 815120

BOO

This book must be returned by the date specified at the time of issue as the DATE DUE FOR RETURN.
The loan may be extended (personally, by post, telephone or online) for a further period if the book is not required by another reader, by quoting the above number / author / title.

You
b
Eve
wo
re

Enquiries: 01709 336774

www.rotherham.gov.uk/libraries

DEADLY SERIOUS

When Jim Maddern — well-respected police sergeant and pillar of the local community — begins to act completely out of character, ex-Met officer John Cannon is concerned. As Cannon tries to find out what has got Maddern so spooked, he discovers that death threats have been sent to Maddern and his family via the local paper after Maddern stumbled upon the paper boy's criminal lineage — trouble-makers for decades, each generation has climbed the ladder of serious crime. And it is throughout Lincolnshire's waterways, woods, villages, and Cannon's own public house that the gangland rivalries, revenge and retribution will reach their bitter end . . .

To Richard Johnson, Landlord of
The Cock Inn, Peatling Magna,
Leicestershire for his help.
The pub may be in Lincolnshire but
the cellar is certainly in Peatling.

1

John Cannon had not liked the look of Jim Maddern when he had first walked into his pub early in the evening, even though the police sergeant was a friend, and in civvies. He liked the look of him even less when he was still there at closing time, slouched over a third untouched pint in one corner of the pub's dining area. He had ordered a meal, which he had never done before when on his own. He had an excellent wife, whose cooking had sustained him for the last twenty-six years, plus three lively teenage daughters, two at high school, one at university, all he idealized.

In ex-Met Chief Inspector John Cannon's opinion, Sergeant Jim Maddern was of the salt of the earth variety, a man respected, even loved, by the community he served. Big, warm-hearted, loyal, smart and upstanding. Tonight he had sat in The Trap public house with all the elegance of a down-and-out, all the conversation of a Trappist monk and the looks of a lost man.

'I'm not letting him go home without finding out what the trouble is,' John told Liz, his life and business partner. 'Keep your eye on him, make sure he doesn't leave without me seeing him.'

'Jim!' Cannon finally caught up with the sergeant, one of the last customers to leave, as he walked across the car park to his blue Peugeot estate. If he had not been convinced there was something wrong before, he was now. The smart military-style walk, like a guardsman's slow march when he was on duty, had become a slouch and the man appeared to have shrunk about six inches. Ignored the first time, he called again.

Maddern was unlocking his car door as Cannon reached him. 'Goodnight, John,' he said, a note of finality in his voice as he got in behind the wheel, his hand on the door handle.

'Just a minute,' Cannon said. 'Come on, I thought we were friends, something's obviously wrong and I wondered if I could do anything to help.'

'No,' Maddern said, and with a gentle but firm action brushed Cannon's hand from the door, adding as he closed it, 'not you of all people.'

Cannon stepped back, shocked and surprised by the remark. Then, as if he saw the hurt, Maddern raised his voice to call, 'Take care, you and Liz, look after each other.'

The car was driven away with a jerk and

grind of gears. Everything about the man: his looks, his manner, his remarks — his very driving — was wrong. Cannon's concern deepened as he walked slowly back towards the front door of The Trap. He could not just let this go. He paused on the step, turned and lifted his head to inhale the freshening breeze from the sea, and beneath that the heavy odour of fen marshland, drying a little, perhaps the February rains were finally over. His heart lifted at the thought of spring, new growth, the renewal of life, sap rising, the very opposite of the sergeant.

He went inside, locked and bolted both sets of doors and walked through to the bar. As always he had a sense of the lingering atmosphere of a busy night even when the last customers had gone, as if their presences and laughter still remained, echoing in his mind, needing time, and probably several cups of tea in the kitchen, to fade away, allowing him and Liz to relax.

Tonight, Jim Maddern's brooding presence was paramount — and there was something else. Cannon frowned, suddenly sure he had glimpsed something, something meaningful, seen but not registered, not remembered. He was not sure whether it had been in the bar, in the car park, or as the sergeant had driven away.

Liz had already cleared the bar and was putting the last of the glasses through the sterilizer. 'Is it serious?' she asked. 'Not one of the girls, is it? It's his Katie's second term at uni,' she said. 'Usually it's the first term if there's going to be trouble, or the first exams. What did he say?'

Cannon shrugged, still plagued by the mysterious something — something or nothing. He wasn't sure and Liz was chattering on.

'You know, I remember asking him some weeks ago if he was all right,' Liz said, switching out the last of the bar lights and leading the way to the kitchen. 'He wasn't quite himself then, seemed to have something on his mind, and tonight he looked worse than ever, dreadful.'

'When did we last see his wife and the girls?' John asked.

'Margaret came with him and the girls early January, before Katie went back to uni. Yes, you remember, it was Jim's birthday, we did a cake for him — '

' — and the girls brought those candles that were like sparklers, and the whole pub sang happy birthday to him.'

'Yes,' Liz laughed, 'he was embarrassed for a start, then got up and took a bow. He was quite a star!'

4

'A different man from the one that's just left, that's for sure,' John said, remembering the happy family, three daughters with long, shining blonde hair. The happy memory made the contrast starker.

'Can't believe he's got family problems he can't handle, even if . . . ' Her mind strayed to teenage pregnancies before she added, 'Whatever, he'd stand by his girls.'

Cannon nodded deeply and positively. 'I might go to see him at home,' he said at length. 'If he throws me out, at least I'll feel I've really tried to help,' then he remembered, 'but — '

'But what?' Liz asked.

'Well, apart from saying he did not want help,' Cannon straightened up and stood very still, 'he added, he didn't want it from me . . . of all people.'

'Oh, so . . . ' Liz stopped, watching her man as he still stood motionless, and her breathing suddenly became shorter, sharper. She had seen her man freeze like this in his Met days. It was what she had come to call his moment of epiphany, a moment of insight into a course of action, usually involving some act of indiscretion, (and indiscretion might be a mild description) to get to the truth in one of his cases. 'So?' she repeated.

'So, it's me he probably really needs,' he

said softly. 'He's involved in something he can't extricate himself from.'

'Something illegal, you mean? Hardly likely,' she said, rejecting the idea.

'No, not likely at all, unless his strict moral and legal ethics have become tangled with his private life.'

'That would be a matter he should take to his commanding officer,' Liz said. Then her face took on a new concern.

'Yes,' he said, following and confirming her thoughts. 'His immediate commanding officer, Chief Inspector Helen Moore is now Chief Inspector Helen Jefferson, on maternity leave, and Jones — '

'Inspector Jones is in charge.'

'Yes, Jones, who once pooh-poohed Jim's local knowledge and told him he did not believe in Fenland folk tales.'

'But Jones has been here a time now,' Liz said. 'He's got himself a partner, moved to a bigger house, and Jim says he excels at the paperwork.'

'Sure, that pleases head office, but policing's about people not paperwork,' John growled, scornful, disapproving, 'and as far as Jim Maddern is concerned, Jones is still as unapproachable as an African despot when it comes to needing a sympathetic hearing.'

Liz poured tea, the ritual of teapot, loose

tea, cups and saucers she had introduced on pretence of personal preference, but in truth to slow John down. He had tended to pace the kitchen with tea made in a mug with a bag, now he sat to talk. 'We could be on quite the wrong tack,' she suggested. 'He could for instance be physically ill himself.'

'He ate well enough,' John said, 'finished his steak, not exactly with pleasure, but he cleared his plate.'

'Yes, he did.' It was now Liz's turn to reflect. 'And for some reason he had me thinking the condemned man ate a hearty meal.'

'His parting shot was for us to look after each other,' John told her, 'the kind of remark you make if you are not going to see the other person for a long time, as if he was going away . . . oh!' he exclaimed and banged the side of his fist on the table, making the china teacups rattle and Liz jump. 'Now I know what it was!'

'What what was?' Liz let her open hands fall wide on the table in a gesture of despair, awaiting a new offering of news she instinctively knew would not in the long run bring joy to their immediate world.

'I know what I saw that was bothering me. On the back seat of Jim's car he had a big holdall with a civvies mac draped over it, as if he was leaving, going away, perhaps for some time.' He paused then quoted, ''Take care, you and Liz, look after each other.''

'That almost sounds like a man emigrating, or going away for good,' she said, then laughed at herself. 'But we know that can't be. We're reading too much into this.'

'I need an excuse to go to his home.'

She shook her head, unsure why she should try to help him on the path to interference Jim Maddern clearly did not want. 'He's a gardener of course,' she said. 'I suppose you could . . . '

'Ah!' He seized on the same idea before she could voice it. 'Bulbs!'

They had lifted all their daffodil bulbs from the edges of the pub garden in the autumn and had been amazed how they had multiplied.

'I'll sort some of the best out and take them over,' he said, 'tomorrow morning. I'll go early, be back well before lunchtime.'

She shook her head; it was a promise she had heard before.

★   ★   ★

He left immediately after the morning's cleaning and breakfast, reached the far side of Reed St Thomas shortly after nine. The

8

Madderns had moved to this village just over a year ago, and they had speculated Jim was beginning to think of his retirement; he had completed over twenty years in the force, and this cottage had an acre of land.

Cannon had timed his arrival for shortly after the departure of the bus which would have taken the two younger daughters to their high school, so if anyone was going to be at home it would be just Margaret, and possibly Jim if he was not on duty.

As he cruised to a stop and parked his jeep, he saw Margaret come from the side of the cottage and go to the recycling bins lined up against the far fence. She dropped a pile of newspapers into the appropriate box, then bent over and retrieved a double page. Clearly she had spotted an item of interest. He grinned — he had done that often enough himself. He called a greeting from the front gate, but the neat middle-aged woman — a slight five-four, he judged, to Jim's tall burly six-feet, her blonde hair cut in a short, practical style — was too engrossed to hear.

'Margaret,' he said gently as he approached. She started violently, her hand to her throat, her face stricken with extreme shock. 'What is it?' he asked.

She took a moment to focus on him. 'John? John Cannon? Oh, hello, what brings you here? I . . . well,' she seemed to be trying to bring a lot of emotions under control, 'if it's a joke its in bad taste.'

He frowned and took the sheet of newspaper from her.

'Jim,' she whispered, 'in the death column, where the black ink's come through the paper, that's what made me notice it.'

Cannon saw where a printed insertion had been made at the top of the column announcing deaths. In crude capitals it read, 'Maddern, Sergeant Jim. Only remaining member of his family.'

'Jim . . . ' she breathed, leaning, needing the support of the fence, and he saw on her face the same desperate concern he had felt for his partner when she had been in imminent danger.

'"The only remaining member of his family.'' He contained a surge of anger and said evenly, 'Well, we know that's not true.' He put a supporting hand under her elbow. 'Let's go inside. Where is Jim?'

'Had to go off on a course early yesterday,' she said.

'Oh, I . . . ' he wondered how tactful it would be to tell his wife her husband had been four miles away having a meal at The Trap late yesterday evening. She looked at him sharply as he hesitated. 'I'd brought him

10

some daffodil bulbs,' he said, thinking Maddern was getting on in his police career to be sent on courses. He supposed, as always, a lot of procedures were being changed, updated. It did explain the holdall in the back of the car, but why hadn't Maddern gone straight to his course, wherever it was?

'Who delivers your newspaper?' he asked.

'That's a point,' Margaret replied, a positive question bringing back some control. 'Yes, when was that written in, and who by?'

'Where do you get your newspapers from?' he asked.

'Local newsagent in the village. Well, he's everything really, grocer, greengrocery, the lot.'

'And you get it delivered?'

'Yes,' she said, 'he's a local lad — Jim said as soon as he saw him that he was from a local family. He always has a word or two if he happens to see him.'

'How does the boy take that word or two? I mean, is it all good-natured?'

Margaret frowned. 'When he first began delivering I know Jim had serious words with him because he was hurling the paper, American-style, from the front gate to the porch.' She shrugged. 'He seemed to take it in good part, the paper has always been through the letter-box since then, and I know Jim gave him a generous Christmas box, though he hadn't been delivering very long.'

'So he wouldn't bear a grudge, or write this in for a joke?'

'I wouldn't have thought so,' she said, shaking her head. 'He's quite cheerful when he sees Jim, shouts, 'Mornin', Sarge', and Jim calls back 'Mornin' young Jakes', which always makes the boy laugh, I don't know why.'

'This,' Cannon said, giving the newspaper a corrective straightening-out shake, 'has to have been done either at the shop, en route, or here.'

'Not here,' she stated emphatically. 'The girls rarely touch the paper and anyway they think too much of their dad, and why would they put 'the sole remaining member of the family'?' She paused then added, 'I'm not sure what to do.'

He was remembering Jim's remark that he did not want help and especially not from Cannon, as he said, 'I could take the paper and have a quiet word with your newsagent?'

'I'd like to find some answer to this, put my mind at rest, and . . . ' She stood, shaking her head a little. 'I wonder, should I tell Jim? He'll ring me every night.'

'He rang last night?'

'When he was there and settled in,' she confirmed, 'about eight.'

'Where has he been sent?' he asked, aware Jim Maddern must have been at The Trap when he rang his wife.

'Big place in Hampshire,' she said.

The only training college Cannon knew of in Hampshire he believed to be for international police students and senior officers.

He glanced at the date of the paper. 'This is three days ago. Have you got the others?'

'Jim took one with him, I saw him put it in his mac pocket.'

'And yesterday's?'

'Still in the house. I shall keep them for him to read when he gets back. Oh!' she exclaimed, 'do you think there's anything in that?'

'Let's go and see,' he suggested.

There were no words, but Cannon saw something Margaret did not, and as she drew a sigh of relief he closed the paper and refolded it, asking, 'How did Jim seem when he left?'

'He wasn't too pleased being sent on this course, said there was plenty to do here. I wasn't sure whether he meant at the police station or in the garden . . . '

'We haven't thought he looked too well

lately,' he ventured, still holding the folded paper.

'I've thought the same,' she agreed, 'but when you ask him he says he's all right — as he always does.'

'How long is this course?' Cannon asked.

'A week,' she said.

'I wouldn't mention anything to him when he phones tonight, let me have a discreet word with your newsagent first,' he said. 'I'll go now on my way back to the pub, then phone you?'

'Oh thanks, John, obviously Jim can't do anything about this while he's away, so I do appreciate it, and I know Jim will when he knows.'

I hope so, he thought, as he left, pausing only as he passed the bins and recycling boxes to lift the lid from the paper box and scoop up the top handful of newspapers. He took these and the newspaper from the house with him.

He drove out of sight of the house, then stopped. He went through all the other newspapers to see if there were any other added announcements. He concluded there had been, for in three of the papers the strip containing the death column had been torn out.

Then reopening the newspaper he had

purloined from Jim's house, he re-examined the tiny drawing Margaret had missed. It was of a tombstone in the space above the word 'Deaths' and on it was written 'No.1.'

2

Occupying a prominent position on the village green, the shop Cannon saw was also the post office. It was obviously like the village pump of yore, the meeting place for residents. A dozen or so had split into men with newspapers in their hands or under their arms, and women busy with handbags and carriers, talking on the pavement. They moved aside for him to enter.

He had never been in the shop before, but it seemed fairly obvious that the couple manning the post office section and the main counter were the husband and wife team named on the fascia, 'Reed St Thomas Stores. Props: Stuart and Joy Russell'. Listening as he lingered near the birthday card stand he realized the Russells were not local people. From the midlands he guessed, possibly captivated by the charm of the village when on holiday. They were probably now too busy to enjoy it. He waited until the shop was quiet then approached Mr Russell, who was behind the main counter.

He broached the subject carefully, pro-duced the newspaper and pointed out the insertion. The effect was immediate, the shopkeeper stopped in the middle of writing names on pre-ordered magazines and focused all his attention on Cannon.

'You be all right for a minute, Joy?' he called over, flourishing the paper and giving her a meaningful nod, then beckoned Cannon to follow him through a door to the back of the shop.

Here was part kitchen, part stockroom and part office. The price one paid for living on the job, Cannon thought.

'You're not on any of my delivery rounds, are you?' Stuart Russell asked.

'No, my name's John Cannon, I keep The Trap public house . . . '

'Ah! I know of you,' Russell said, 'former Met officer, and your partner the same.'

Cannon nodded the correctness of this, adding, 'and I'm a friend of Jim Maddern.'

'Police Sergeant Maddern?' Russell asked and gave him a questioning look.

'You obviously didn't read the insertion in the paper I gave you,' Cannon said.

'Well, no, I just saw the black printing,' the newsagent said, spreading the page out on his table. 'Hell!' he exclaimed, 'that's more serious. I've had another complaint . . . ' He picked up a folded sheet of newspaper from the windowsill and handed it to Cannon.

There was no name at the top of the death column in this paper, but in the same black print: 'The third member of the same family to die'.

'So this newspaper went to . . . '

'A pensioner who lives on her own.' Russell shook his head in vexation. 'I asked the delivery boy, but he swears he knows nothing about it, and never left his delivery bag anywhere unattended.' He looked thoughtful, indicated the two newspapers. 'The only thing is, the lady is on the same round as Sergeant Maddern's cottage.'

'Would the boy's name be Jakes?' Cannon asked.

'No,' Russell said, shaking his head, puzzled, 'I've no boy of that name, or anything like it. Not a name I have on my books at all. The lad who delivers that round is named Smithson, Danny Smithson, lives across the way, 24 Snyder Crescent.'

'A local family, or local connections?'

'Not as far as I know, in fact when they moved in on that estate just before Christmas,' he cast a derogatory thumb in the direction of a block of old council houses the area was not proud of, 'the talk was that they were one of these resettled families put into the house because it had stood empty so long.'

'So any idea why Sergeant Maddern should call your paperboy Jakes?'

Russell laughed. 'Probably after some character on telly,' he said, 'I wouldn't know.'

Cannon, remembering the newspapers retrieved from Maddern's bin, and his own two-year career as a delivery boy in London's East End, asked, 'You don't mark each newspaper with a house number or name?'

'Not on our local rag, most people take it. It's a good paper full of community news. I just write on the extras and the boys have to keep on eye on where these are for as they go along. Sometimes they slip up, and there'll be one left in the bag. I just give them a stern-faced reminder and put it in again for the next delivery.'

'How many houses between the lady who received this,' Cannon tapped the sheet from the windowsill, 'and Sergeant Maddern's?'

Russell looked at him with fresh interest. 'That's a point.' He leaned on the table and tapped the fingers of his right hand, thinking and counting. 'Five,' he said.

'And where does the round start and finish?'

Russell took up a pencil and a used envelope, explaining as he drew. 'Here's the shop, and the council house estate, then back the way you came from the Sergeant's house.

The round starts here on the main road, goes along towards the coast a bit, there are six cottages along Sea Lane, and Sergeant Maddern's is the last paper he would deliver — '

A sharp knocking on the door to the shop broke into his summary. 'Wife's getting busy, I'll have to go,' Russell said, 'but tell me what to do about this. You've come instead of — '

'Yes,' he said before the newsagent got to names.

'Can I leave it with you for now, and . . . ' Russell was on his way back into the shop as he spoke.

'Yes,' Cannon repeated, following and edging his way through half a dozen customers, 'I'll be in touch.'

When he arrived back at The Trap, Liz was anxious to hear everything. He spread all the newspapers over the kitchen table, those with the missing sections and the three with the printed inserts. 'So,' he said, 'four out of five of these newspapers went to the right person, Maddern, and probably the newspaper he took with him held another message.'

'Another threat,' Liz corrected, 'and Margaret thought he'd already left when he was here having a meal,' she said.

'Not only that, he rang to tell her he had arrived in Hampshire *when* he was here.'

'He may not even be on a course,' she speculated. 'Pity Helen's on maternity leave, otherwise we could just have asked.'

'Why not?' Cannon said, picking up the phone. Moments later, he was asking for Inspector Jones with Liz's scowling disapproval.

'Jones?' she mouthed.

'Ah, Inspector, John Cannon here — ' he was clearly interrupted from the other end, 'yes, that's the one,' he said and winked at Liz. 'I just need to speak to Sergeant Maddern . . . no, not a police matter, hope you don't mind me ringing the station.'

Liz could hear Jones's raised voice, though not his words.

'I thought engine-driver, rather than the oil can,' Cannon answered jovially, but Liz watched his face change as he listened, and after making an apology that sounded genuine enough, he put down the phone and sat solemnly absorbing what he had just been told.

'Well?' Liz queried.

Cannon looked directly at her, then said, 'Jim Maddern is on annual leave.'

Liz blinked, sat back in her chair. 'Leave? But . . . ' she began, then gestured to the despoiled newspaper columns, 'and to deceive his wife, it must be something really serious, deadly serious.'

'Something he dare not involve the police

21

in,' John paused, 'or his friends. Something, or someone, so threatening . . . '

'He's trying to run away from,' Liz suggested.

'No, something he's trying to deal with, and . . . ' then he added with complete certainty, 'he came here to ask for our help.'

'But, he didn't!'

'Not in the end, no,' John agreed, again reviewing the evening, but this time recalling other customers. There had been a lively group of young farmers and their girlfriends who had called in on the way to their annual Valentine Day's dance — animated young men, pretty, vivacious girls. He wondered if Jim had been reminded of his daughters, and anxiety had overcome the need to confide in him. Big, life-changing decisions often turned on simple unrelated events. Had it been this that had prompted the stinging remark, 'Not you of all people'? 'He decided I was too risky a friend to confide in,' Cannon murmured.

She stopped herself saying that she could well understand how a serving police sergeant might feel, asking instead, 'So what will you do?'

'Help him, whether he likes it or not.'

'But what can *you* do?' she interrupted, and knew immediately it was a mistake.

'Think first,' he said, giving her a withering

look, while wondering just what he might be getting into.

She wanted to make a smart-arse rejoinder like *that'd be a first*, but she knew that wasn't even true; what she was afraid of was that once more their lives were going to become pawns in someone else's game.

'For starters,' Cannon went on, 'we can be fairly sure the newsboy, Danny Smithson, knows nothing about the insertions . . . '

'Or he'd have made sure he delivered them all to the right address,' Liz finished for him.

'Right,' Cannon nodded. 'Good to have you aboard.' He went on before she could make any kind of retaliation. 'So Danny must have stopped somewhere, left his bag unattended at some point. We need to watch him deliver his papers — and we need to do it today, this afternoon.'

'This afternoon we have the brewery coming with the fortnightly delivery,' she reminded him.

'I don't want to waste any time,' he said. 'Maddern's reactions seem to say that whatever's going on can't wait. I think we can leave Alamat to deal with the brewery.' Not for the first time, he thought it had been an inspired piece of trust and guesswork that had made him go after the slightly built Croatian, living part on the streets, part in a hostel, in the nearby market town of Boston. They had found him work and lodgings in the new accommodation being finished in The Trap's old stable-block, where Alamat was now busy painting and decorating. Looking too feeble for fieldwork he had previously made a meagre living doing translations for his fellow countrymen. His cheerfulness and willingness more than made up for his size. He was quite simply an asset, a help they wondered how they had ever managed without.

He knew Liz was not overjoyed as they left for Reed St Thomas, timing their arrival some ten minutes before the school bus returned the children to the village. He had gone through the round as drawn by the newsagent. Once Danny Smithson had gone into the shop to collect his newspapers Cannon would leave Liz in the car and watch the boy until he left the main road, when Liz would sit in the car and watch him on the coast road towards the last five cottages.

'That'll be him,' John said some fifteen minutes later, after a whole gang of children had gone straight from the bus into the village shop — some were immediately sent out again, with Russell supervising numbers from his doorstep. Then a boy came out with a news-bag on one shoulder, satchel on the other. He also answered Russell's description of 'a well-put-together lad, good shoulders on him for a thirteen-year-old'. Cannon let the boy cross the green and make his way towards the estate before he got out of the car and Liz drove off to take up her station further along the newsround.

He followed the boy on to Snyder Crescent, using his old technique of setting himself an artificial goal: to walk aimlessly could draw attention. So now he walked, without haste, but as if making for the bus shelter at the far end of the street. He heard the noise of a vehicle turning into the estate behind him, and it seemed he was not the only one watching Danny Smithson, for a white Mercedes van drew up alongside the boy.

Cannon was near enough to see that the boy recognized whoever was driving. The passenger door was pushed open, and after a few words, Danny lifted the newspaper bag on his shoulder as if to show he had a job to do, but then he shrugged and got in anyway.

The van was immediately put into an acute three-point turn and driven out of the estate, making a left turn at the end of the road. Cannon had a brief glimpse of the driver as they passed — big, dark, grim-faced, hunched or rounded shoulders, he mentally recorded. As the van disappeared he saw he had reached number 24. He had a good look at

Danny Smithson's home as he passed, though there was nothing much to see, a half brick and half shabby white-concreted house, where neither the state of the nets nor the badly hung curtains upstairs looked inviting. One thing Danny's mother was not, was house-proud.

Once back on the green he took out his mobile and called Liz, told her what had happened and gave a description of the van and the number. 'He may be just helping the boy to deliver his papers — '

' — or taking the opportunity to write in them,' she said. 'What do you want me to do?'

'Stay where you are. I'll walk to you. I'd just like to check that the boy is OK and delivering his papers. I didn't much like the look of the van driver.'

It took Cannon ten minutes to reach Liz. 'Have you seen him?' he asked as he got in beside her.

'No, not a sign.'

'That feels a bit worrying,' he was saying when she interrupted.

'Wait a minute,' Liz looked with rapt attention in the rear-view mirror. 'There's a white van coming up behind us, and it's a Merc, don't look round, its coming past us now.'

They sat and watched the van turn into Sea Lane. Liz had only just reached forward to switch her engine on, when the vehicle came back. It slowed before it reached them and something was thrown from the driver's window, then it gathered speed, and they heard the screech of tyres as it negotiated the corner.

Cannon was out the car and running across to retrieve the object. He displayed the school satchel to Liz, then turned and ran on towards Sea Lane and the last five houses on Danny Smithson's round. Liz put the car in gear and followed.

As Cannon rounded the bend for a second he did not realize the balled-up shape on the grass verge was the boy. 'Shit!' he exclaimed, as the familiar surge of dread, concern, and adrenalin, swept over him. He thought for a moment the youngster was either dead or unconscious, but stooping close he could see the boy was breathing, and put a gentle hand on his shoulder.

'No, don't,' the boy moaned, balling himself tighter, 'I won't say anything.'

'You're all right, he's gone,' Cannon told him, then was startled as the boy's eyes shot open.

'Who're you? Leave me alone,' he said, shrugging off Cannon's hand. 'I fell down.

I'm all right. Leave me alone.' There was an edge of tears in his voice but the boy mastered it.

Cannon's heart went out to him, he'd seen plenty such city kids bullied by gangs. They learned early not to cry. There were no marks on the face, but as the boy uncurled experimentally Cannon would have liked to have seen the state of his torso, his stomach and kidneys; these were favourite punishment areas. He was becoming convinced the beating this boy had suffered was the work of an expert: swift, effective, frighteners applied, and no visible evidence. But why?

Liz was out of the car now and by their side.

'Leave me alone,' Danny Smithson repeated, trying to struggle to his feet, but the still-full newspaper bag, now over one shoulder and across his chest, made it difficult.

'Here,' Liz said, bent and deftly drew the strap up and over his head, removing the bag, before the boy could protest. 'Now try.'

'OK,' Cannon said, 'I think we should help you deliver this lot.'

'We'll be done in half the time,' Liz endorsed. 'You lean on the car here, or sit in it if you like, and tell us which houses to go to.'

'Then we can drop you back at the shop,'

Cannon urged and taking silence as agreement, he asked, 'Are the papers in any kind of order?'

The boy shook his head. 'It's the end cottage, then the one next to it, miss one then the next three,' he said.

'I'll do those,' Cannon told Liz. 'You turn the car round.'

Cannon walked up the path to Margaret Maddern's door and sheltered by the tiny porch, rang the bell long and hard, then made a great show, in case the boy could see, of carefully folding the paper as if to put it through the letterbox. Fortunately Margaret answered the door quickly, looked surprised but pleased to see him and stepped back, inviting him inside.

'No,' he said, 'but I need you to give Jim a message when he rings tonight. Can you tell him that the paperboy he calls Jakes has been beaten up and I need to speak to him about it.'

'What's happened, Mum?' Grace Maddern, her youngest daughter, who Cannon guessed must be about thirteen, came up behind her mother, and Louise, who would be fifteen, came rattling down the stairs and joined the group in the doorway, smiling, greeting Cannon.

'Not Dad is it?' Louise asked. 'He never

ought to be sent on courses at his age.'

'He's not that old,' her mother retorted.

'It's not, is it?' Grace looked from her mother to Cannon, her face now solemn. 'It's not Dad?'

Then all three looked at Cannon, two daughters and a wife, anxious faces all thinking of the most important man in their lives.

'No, no, the paperboy's had a fall in the lane, he's all right, but I'm just helping him finish his round.' He handed the paper to their mother and nodded to her, the nod incorporating a reminder about the message, hers acknowledging that she had not forgotten.

He said his goodbyes, turned away, still able to hear the girls questioning, and Louise repeating what they had all thought. 'I still don't think Dad's well.'

'He should take some of his annual leave and have a holiday,' Grace added.

Cannon walked away burdened with the thought that he already knew more than Maddern's wife and daughters. Given to the occasional fanciful idea, he also recognized he was leaving true family love behind him, and had fear sitting huddled in the back of Liz's car.

'I . . . ' he began again, then the rest came with a rush, 'could do with your help.'

Cannon wanted to shout, 'Hallelujah, at last', but knew Maddern could just ring off if he said the wrong thing, upset the precarious balance between need and pride. 'Tell me what you want me to do,' Cannon said quietly.

'I'm in Leicester,' he said. 'Katie's at university here.'

There was another silence while Cannon waited.

'It's a lot to explain on the phone,' Maddern said, 'but Katie was designated as the first to . . . to . . . go.'

Die, Cannon silently substituted as Maddern was unable to say the word, and he remembered that night's newspaper, which Maddern had not so far seen, the inserted drawing of a tombstone at the head of the deaths, with a No. 1 inscribed on it.

'Leicester,' Cannon said, calculating that he could be there in three hours or so. 'Want me to come?'

'Please,' he said, and now Maddern's voice did break.

'Where shall I meet you?'

'There's a big concert hall near the university called the De Montfort Hall, I'll be near the main gates.'

'I'll find it,' Cannon said to a dead line.

Three and a half hours later he was thanking technology for satnav as it directed him through a maze of one-way systems to a quieter street off a main thoroughfare. On one side were trees, the other a row of well-built three-storey houses: flats and offices Cannon thought. Then, wonder of wonder, as the upbeat voice announced he had reached his destination, he saw there was a car park immediately behind the trees, with no more than half a dozen cars parked there.

Locking the classic red MG — Liz had volunteered her car as quicker than his ancient jeep — he realized that, behind the car park, there was an extensive green area. Then by the look of the rather monumental gates and railings at the end of the trees, the Hall itself lay slightly downhill from the road. He walked in that direction and was soon raising respectful eyebrows to the pillared and domed De Montfort Hall, surrounded by well-maintained lawns and flower beds, a proud addition to any city.

The noise of the traffic on the main road was muted here, and it was dark except for the areas where Victorian lamp posts under-lit the still, leafless, spectral-looking, trees. He could neither see nor hear any other pedestrian. He checked his watch, 11.30 p.m.

He wondered if he was later than Maddern expected, perhaps he should have phoned when he was nearly here. It hadn't occurred to him, the meeting place was set, he had just been concentrating on arriving as soon as possible, but if Maddern did not show up in the next few minutes he would ring him.

As he strolled back the way he had come there was a sudden eruption of sound as two police cars sped along the main road, sirens blaring, blue lights flashing. They retreated into the distance and went around the far side of the parkland, as far as he could judge. He reached into his pocket for his phone, but as he approached the red MG he saw a familiar figure beneath one of the lamps. He hurried forward.

'Jim,' he greeted, but had hardly done so when two further police cars swept from the main road and into the car park, screeched to a halt next to them, all four doors of both vehicles opened, and they were surrounded by police.

'Just have a word,' a sergeant detailed one man, before leading the rest through a small gate at the far end of the car lot into the park, where they spread out and began to run.

'What's happened?' Maddern asked.

'Could I ask you gentlemen how long you've been here?' the constable, who

3

The first time the phone rang it was a wrong number. The second, as Cannon was about to go through to open The Trap for the evening's business, was a young woman who told him her name was Tina, she understood he had money worries, and she could consolidate all his debts so they were no longer a problem.

'My problem,' he told her, 'is you. Get off my line.'

'At least she's doing a job,' Liz said mildly.

The third time, Liz answered and immediately handed the phone over, 'Jim,' she said.

'Jim, glad you've rung. I . . . '

'What's happened?' Maddern interrupted, gruff, impatient. 'Margaret said — '

'The newspaper boy you call Jakes . . . ' He told the full story as briefly as he could, including the addition to the death column Margaret had seen, adding, 'And then there were those you had already torn out, and you took one with you to . . . wherever you are.'

The silence at the other end was leaden. Then Maddern cleared his throat, 'I'm . . . '

Cannon waited.

31

Maddern would have made four of, asked.

'We've not long arrived,' Cannon said, 'arranged to meet here, this is my car.'

'I've walked up from the town,' Maddern added. 'My daughter is at the university.'

'Did you arrange for your daughter to meet you here?' The question had a sharper edge.

'No,' Maddern said, 'but has something happened to a girl, a student?'

'There's been a disturbance at the other side of the park, that's all we know.'

'Four police cars?' Maddern questioned.

'I walked along by the hall and back,' Cannon raised his voice to interrupt as he felt Maddern might lose caution and control, 'and saw no one at all.'

'Thank you,' the constable nodded, and hurried after the other.

'Four police cars,' Maddern repeated.

'Come on,' Cannon said, unlocking the car, 'we'll drive to the other side of this park.'

Cannon drove back to the main road, turned right, then right again, and they were in sight of the other two police cars. He drove past them and stopped in a side street. No sooner had they left the car than they saw extra police vehicles arriving, the largest a white van.

'Is that Scene of Crime?' Maddern gasped. The question was rhetorical as he began to run, though Cannon could see the police were ready to prevent the public entering the park. There was also a concentration of police further into the green area, just under a group of trees, where hand-held lamps pointed downwards. The lights were motionless, the men in yellow jackets stationary, between the trunks of the dark, stark, trees, and in the centre two of their number knelt by something — someone — who was very still.

Maddern raised a dismissive hand at the police officer who confronted him. 'I have a daughter here at the university,' he said.

'Thousands have daughters and sons here, sir.' This constable was older, unperturbed. 'I will have to ask you not to go further,' and as he spoke men were bringing blue and white police tape, portable metal posts to hook it through, and rapidly segregating pavement from park.

Maddern seemed about to argue, force his way through. Cannon gripped his arm, steadied him, then drew him away.

'I need to know,' he said.

'You're not going to be able to force your way across there,' Cannon told him. 'Do you know where Katie's accommodation is?' he asked. 'Is it far away?'

'A few minutes in a car,' he said but was

looking fixedly at the increasing police activity, white-suited figures joining the group beneath the trees, taking over.

'Right, time to worry if she is not there,' Cannon said. 'Come on, I'll need you to direct me.'

The accommodation block looked new, huge, many storeys high.

'Six hundred rooms,' Maddern confirmed, 'private development, university runs it. Had a look around about yesterday, security is good.'

'You've not seen Katie so far?'

'Only from a distance, it's difficult,' Maddern admitted, 'and her mother will have . . . '

'Told her you're away on a course.'

'I hope to God I've not left it too late, wasted a day, and that Katie . . . '

Cannon refused to let him dwell on that prospect and led the way determinedly to the entrance to the tower block. 'What do you propose to say?' he asked, and when there was silence, 'How about, you find yourself unexpectedly in the city, here only a few hours and would love to have the chance to see your daughter? We don't need access to her room, just ask her if she would like to come down to have a word in the lobby.'

They rang the bell at the entrance, then

spoke into the slatted wall intercom; two minutes later two security men came out of the darkness and joined them outside.

'My name's Langton, I'm head of security. You've asked to see one of our students,' the taller of the two said. Cannon wondered if he was a senior ex-police officer, he exuded that kind of authority.

'My daughter. Katie Maddern,' and he repeated the story Cannon had just concocted, during which the other security man's phone burbled. He turned away but it was clear to Cannon he was talking to another uniformed security man walking towards the doors inside. The conversation over, the man came back to Langton and said, 'Dennis, the hall porter, suggests we ask the father what he does for a living.'

Maddern produced his warrant card, and the mood relaxed.

'Your daughter's talked about you to Dennis.' He nodded to the man in the lobby, who now pressed a button to open the doors.

'You'll be Police Sergeant Maddern, then,' he greeted, 'heard a lot about you.'

'All good, I hope,' Maddern gave the standard reply.

'Surprised there's no halo,' the porter said with a grin. 'Come on.' He led the way back to desk and switchboard.

Having relayed the message, he looked rather startled, said 'but' several times, then held the receiver out to Maddern. 'You'd better speak to her, convince her yourself. She seems to think it's a hoax, *another* hoax, she said.'

'Katie, it's your dad, I'm . . . '

All of the men in that quiet lobby heard her shout, 'No! No! I don't believe you!' and the slam of the receiver.

'Think we'd better go up there,' Langton said. 'There's something wrong.'

No one, Cannon thought, was referring to what might have happened in the park. Although these security men had arrived before he and Maddern had been admitted to the building he did not think they as yet knew much about the incident in the park, they had been too relaxed and affable, until Katie's outburst.

'She knows you, Dennis, you come,' Langton ordered, and turning to his junior said, 'You stay on the switchboard.'

Cannon moved with Maddern towards the lifts and when the senior officer paused to question this, Maddern said, 'He's ex-Met and my friend.'

'A lot of us ex's about,' he said and led the way into the lift.

'It's number 363,' Maddern supplied as

39

Dennis pressed the third-floor button.

'We'll keep this as quiet as possible,' Langton said as they walked along the rather stark corridor. 'We don't want to alarm anyone else if we can help it,' and as they arrived outside 363 he nodded to Dennis to take the lead.

The porter bent close to the door and knocked gently. 'It's Dennis, Miss Maddern, will you come to the door?'

Nothing. The very silence in the building seemed to intensify.

'Look through your spy-hole at us,' Dennis suggested.

Dennis moved back a step so he could be clearly seen through the tiny fisheye lens. Cannon was unsure whether he heard a movement near the door.

'Your father's here, Sergeant Jim Maddern,' Dennis said, and moved so that Maddern could take his place immediately in front of the lens.

'John Cannon's here with me, Katie,' Maddern said and Cannon raised a hand.

Then all eyes were on the door as the handle was depressed, then, slowly at first, the door opened, and Katie in pyjamas and dressing-gown stood open-mouthed, taking in the reality of who stood there.

She appeared like someone in extreme

shock, the shock Cannon had seen on the faces of those who had narrowly escaped violent death — and that thought gave him no comfort, as Katie, like someone walking in a nightmare, staggered into her father's open arms.

'Dad,' she said, tears thickening her voice now, 'I don't understand. What's happening?'

'Are you all right?'

They saw the fair head nod beneath Maddern's chin.

'Why are you here?'

'Tell me first why you're so upset.' Maddern stooped to kiss her cheek, but as the question was asked Cannon could see the answer.

On the narrow bed was a large square box, and, as if just tipped from it, a circle of laurel with spring flowers, daffodils and snowdrops — a funeral wreath — a wreath made for a young person.

'This came tonight,' she said as all the men filed in, filled the space between bed and desk.

'How did it come? Who delivered it?' Langton wanted to know.

'Not through me,' Dennis denied.

'A man gave it to my best friend here, Amy. He saw her outside, she said he was standing at the end of the roadway, and she saw him approach one or two people before he asked her.' She paused to pick up the box, turned it over so they could all read the words 'REED ST THOMAS' printed in capital letters in black marker pen. 'When Amy saw that she didn't hesitate to bring it up to my room. She knows that's where I live. I thought it was from home . . . '

'Where is Amy now?' Cannon asked and for the first time Katie really focussed on him.

'Mr Cannon?' she queried, 'Amy?'

'Yes, where is she now?'

'She went after the man, I told her not to, but she said she was *and* she was going to report him to security, find out what it was all about. Amy's like that.'

'I saw no one hanging about,' Dennis repeated, 'no one at all, and nothing's been reported about that.' He nodded towards the wreath.

Cannon was thinking of the figure prone between the trees. Maddern moved uneasily by his side and Langton's phone rang.

4

Langton turned from taking the call to nod his men towards the door, then said, 'We'll be back shortly, best if you all stay here.'

'I don't want to stay here,' Katie stated with surprising force as the door closed. 'Take me home, Dad, *please*.'

Cannon remembered she had referred to another hoax. 'What else has happened?' he asked.

'We just thought it was a mistake, but — ' she glanced at the wreath and shuddered. 'There was a crowd of us outside and we all thought it was terrible at first, then someone began to snigger, and then everyone laughed about it. Amy directed them to a nearby estate,' she paused to throw out a vague arm, 'said there must be someone with the same name there.'

'Who were they?' her father interrupted.

'It was a hearse,' she said and as Maddern's lips parted in shock she added, 'Dad, I just need to see Amy then we could go.'

Cannon prayed it would be that simple, but before Maddern could answer, his mobile jangled the beginning of a military march. He pulled it from his pocket, glanced at the screen, put it rapidly to his ear. 'Margaret?' he questioned.

'Mum?' Katie queried in a whisper. 'Don't tell her what's happened on the phone, she'll worry herself sick.'

'Wait. Hold on,' Maddern was saying, 'slow down and stop apologizing.'

As Maddern listened intently, Cannon heard someone approaching in the corridor, most likely the security men coming back. He caught Jim's eye and gave the slightest warning nod towards the door.

'Get dressed,' Cannon whispered the advice to Katie, who nodded, swept up clothes from a chair and went into her small shower room. Cannon saw her balancing her clothes on top of the toilet, not much room in these compact en suite facilities.

Maddern had gone to stand near the window, his back to the room, but he startled Cannon by suddenly spinning round, facing him, but certainly not seeing him, as he questioned, 'When was this? Is he still with you?'

Cannon moved closer as if to give support.

'Yes, I am coming as soon as I can. No, don't worry about Katie. I shall bring her home with me.'

There were more questions. Cannon could

hear the raised pitch of anxiety at the other end.

'I shall make a detour, and . . . ' Maddern seemed to swallow hard and finally looking at Cannon as if he actually saw him, added slowly, 'no, none of you go anywhere. No. No,' he interrupted another flow as there was a tap on the door. 'I'll explain everything when I see you.' He clicked off the phone and added, 'She found Danny Smithson hiding behind our rubbish bins and a white Mercedes van's been up and down the road several times.'

Cannon swore under his breath, remembered Danny Smithson lying terrified in Sea Lane, thrown from a white Mercedes van, and wondered what he had let the boy go back to. He and Liz had helped him finish his paper round then dropped him near the village green, as he had asked, assuring them he would be OK now, his mum would look after him.' Cannon's time to swallow hard now, then jerk his head towards the door as there was a second knock. Maddern made an urgent zipping motion across his mouth.

'Katie's getting dressed,' Cannon told Langton as he came in, alone this time, his face considerably more solemn than when he left.

'Let's talk outside,' Langton suggested.

'We'll be in the corridor, Katie,' Maddern called, 'give you a bit of space.'

'You won't go without me?' Katie called back.

'You know me better than that, young lady,' her father replied. Cannon admired his ability to keep his voice sounding so normal.

Langton led the way quickly to where access to the stairs faced the lifts and there were no bedrooms immediately near. 'The message,' he said, 'was from the police to all university security staff. They have a young female student dead in the park, the bag with her has the name Amy Congreve in it, and the room next to your daughter as her student residency.'

'Katie's friend,' Maddern stated. 'God Almighty!'

'Dennis has gone back with the police to help identify her. She's a striking, red-haired girl, the type once seen never forgotten . . . ' Langton added.

'So how . . . ?' Cannon began.

'No details yet, but I've told them about the wreath and Amy going after the man. They'll be here any moment . . . ' As if to confirm his words, the lift hummed into action as it was called back to the ground floor.

'I'd like to be the one to break this to my

daughter if it is her friend,' Maddern said.

'I can't see they will object to that,' Langton said as they all watched the indicator arrow change to up and half a minute later the doors opened at the third floor. Two men got out.

'Detective Inspector Hardy.' The older man, pale as a teenager dedicated to IT, introduced himself and DS Grove, who in contrast looked as if he spent his free time outdoors. Langton introduced Katie's father and Cannon.

'If it is my daughter's friend I would like to be the one to tell her,' Maddern said, adding 'and she wants to come home with me tonight.'

'Not surprised,' the DI said. 'Where's home?'

He listened carefully, watching both men from the fens. 'So you came just to see your daughter?' he asked, 'both of you?'

Cannon nodded.

'Not settled at university, has she?' he asked Maddern.

'Two younger sisters at home,' Maddern said. 'I think she misses them, but she was fine, until this . . . '

'But you didn't know about the delivery of the wreath until you arrived?' The DI left the remark hanging in the air like an accusation.

'No, but I'm on annual leave and it's only a three-hour drive,' Maddern said.

The DI turned to Cannon. 'So you came along for the ride?' the DI asked, adding, 'You came together in the same car?'

'No, I came in mine some time later,' Cannon said and stopped himself doing fanciful embroidery on the truth. Along the corridor Katie appeared out of her room, carrying a bag and a black and white tweed coat.

'Ah,' the DI breathed out, still looking at Cannon, 'so we might need to talk a little more about all this,' adding in muted tones, 'The porter has identified the girl as Amy Congreve.'

'I must just have a word with Amy,' Katie told them as they approached.

'She's not there, Katie.' Maddern reached his daughter and checked the hand she raised to knock on her friend's door, turned and propelled her gently back towards her own room. Cannon heard the father's quiet words and saw the violence of the daughter's reaction as she jerked to a stop, stricken, motionless for a long moment, then she dropped the bag she still carried and fell to her knees on top of it. Maddern crouched beside her, pulling her close in his arms, talking to her.

'I hope you're going to let her father take the girl home tonight,' Cannon muttered to the DI.

'I think we'll get a doctor to have a look at the young lady before we make any decisions on that,' the DI replied as Maddern lifted his daughter, who now seemed in a state of total collapse, and turned as if to put her on the bed.

'Wait a minute,' the DS warned, 'there's evidence on the bed.'

'Move it,' Maddern ordered.

The DS practically dived beneath Maddern's arms, pulling gloves from his pocket which he half put on, and lifted away the wreath and the box.

The DI produced clear plastic evidence bags from his pocket, but only after he had contacted the foyer to request a doctor be called.

Katie roused and would have sprung to her feet had Maddern not prevented it. 'No, Dad, no!' she exclaimed. 'I am going home. I'm not lying down, not here, I'm not staying here. Not now. Not now!'

'Sit in the chair for a bit then,' Maddern insisted.

When the doctor arrived, Dennis, the porter, had obviously filled him in with all the details. A square, grizzled-haired man, he brusquely turned everyone out of the room except Jim Maddern, and emerged some ten minutes later to say, 'She is a very determined young lady, with a mind that is definitely not for turning. She wants to go home with her father, and I think that is the best thing that can happen. She won't accept any help from *my* medical bag.'

Who does she take after, Cannon wondered ironically.

The DI frowned at the doctor and cleared his throat as if warning against interference in police matters.

'These people are victims not suspects I presume,' the doctor said unabashed as his phone bleeped again. 'There'll be many repercussions after this tragedy, so I won't be far away if you need me again. Students are highly strung creatures.'

As the doctor left, the DI's phone bleeped.

Going to be a busy night for everyone, Cannon thought.

His call over, the DI turned to Cannon and said the Lincolnshire police had vouched for him as the landlord of . . .

It had not been a question so much as a gap left for Cannon to fill. He did, with the name of his pub, its location and the name of his partner, 'Liz Makepeace, also a former Met officer, and whose red MG I have driven to Leicester.'

'Right,' the DI said, his lips pursing momentarily to stop any hint of amusement, 'you ticked all the right boxes, and I think if the young lady is up to it and can give a preliminary statement to my sergeant here, there is no reason why we should not let you take her home tonight, though we shall almost certainly need to contact her again.'

'If I drive Sergeant Maddern's car he can give all his attention to his daughter, but it will mean leaving the MG overnight, it's in a street nearby, is that OK?' Cannon asked, and explained where it was.

'No restrictions there,' the DI said. 'Tell me the registration number.'

Cannon obliged and the DS looked at the notebook he held, made a tick and nodded to the DI.

Katie was very shaky, but still controlled — almost alarmingly so, Cannon felt — as she made and signed her statement. Immediately afterwards, Jim left her with Cannon while he called a taxi to take him back to the hotel where he had left his Peugeot and bag. Cannon stayed very close to her, making her tea in her room, talking of being home in three hours or so. She was very quiet.

Once her father returned and they were loading the car, Katie seemed to go into overdrive, hurling her belongings into the boot, while Maddern stood meticulously repacking them.

'Dad, it doesn't matter, for God's sake!' she shouted at him. 'My friend's dead, murdered because of me! Do you understand that? Hey?'

Cannon saw the look he gave his daughter; he was a staunch churchgoer, and not a man who liked to hear the Lord's name taken in vain.

'No,' he said evenly, 'it is probably more to do with me.'

Cannon heard but Katie was too beside herself to listen, and stamped her feet like a child as her father finished the loading so that none of it could roll around as they travelled.

'Just get in,' he said mildly, opened the back door for her and got in beside her.

Taking the driving-seat Cannon wondered if there was a satnav in the car, probably shut away in the glove compartment, but decided it was not wise to delay a moment longer. He would not ask or stop until they were away from the immediate vicinity of the university and the park.

After a few minutes, he heard Katie apologize. Straining up in his seat he could see in his rear-view mirror that she was now huddled under her father's arm, but must have still been shaking because he heard Maddern ask if she was cold.

'A bit,' she said.

Maddern told him how to turn the car's heating up, adding, 'We've come the wrong way.'

Cannon had realized as much some moments ago as he found himself entangled in a system of one-way streets all heading in the opposite way to the one he felt they wanted. They were now on a multi-lane, one-way highway, well studded with a series of traffic lights, and it was obviously closing time for some popular clubs in the area. Young pedestrians were crowding the pavements and crossings, laughing, fooling about. He drove forward slowly as one set of lights changed, very aware of the youngsters, many of the boys, shirt-tails blowing, hardly looked old enough to have left primary school, while the scantily clad girls were enough to disturb men of any age. The old arguments about girls being allowed to be as undressed as they liked no matter what fires they lit in the minds of the opposite sex, flickered through his mind until one of the youths slipped off the kerb just in front of him, nearly falling. Several of his mates gave Cannon the finger as if it was his fault.

He passed this group and ahead could see

a large rugby stadium, that of the famous Leicester Tigers, he realized, while over to his right was a huge hospital and to his left what could only be the towering walls of Leicester Prison. Built by the Victorians, he imagined, to impress the power of the law on the local inhabitants, it had castellated towers and above its double doors a portcullis; the only thing missing, he thought, was the moat.

The road veered away from the prison, but not before he saw the wicket set in the huge double gates open and a broad-shouldered man turned sideways for ease of exit. Two men hurried to him, taking his bag. They were both big, broad-shouldered men but not as tall as the grey-haired man they greeted. A strange time for anyone to be released from prison, but that was certainly what was happening, although these matters were always at the discretion of the prison governor as far as he knew. There must be special circumstances.

The three converged into a kind of tight hug. Then one raised a beckoning arm; even from inside the car Cannon heard the piercing whistle he gave and saw a stretch limo draw to the end of the side wall of the prison. A man jumped out of the passenger side and ran to open the door rather as if it was royalty leaving the Savoy, London, than someone who had served their time in prison. Special circumstances indeed!

But something more was trickling into Cannon's consciousness — a Leicester connection? Russell, the newsagent, had described Danny Smithson, the boy Maddern called Jakes, as a well-put-together lad, good shoulders on him for a thirteen-year-old. The trio that had just climbed aboard the black stretch limousine could all have been heavyweight stars in the boxing world, from their build.

In normal circumstances he and Maddern would certainly have exchanged opinions about all this, but as it was the silence from the back of the car was absolute; far, far, too absolute.

5

As he drove, first light came as a thin grey strip over the flat Lincolnshire horizon — like a stage curtain lifting, Cannon thought, revealing the backdrop he had chosen for his life, and Liz's; and both he loved without reservations. 'Another hour,' he said quietly, then asked 'Is Katie asleep?'

Maddern whispered, 'Yes.'

'Those men?' Cannon questioned.

'Yes,' Maddern confirmed.

Cannon knew that was all he would hear until they were alone and could talk openly. He hoped it was not a bad sign as the line of light disappeared under a great lowering mass of black cloud.

It was barely light and raining hard when they pulled into Sea Lane and Maddern's drive. Margaret was at the door before they stopped, but Maddern was faster, out of the car and by her side as she saw Katie, and who the driver of her husband's car was.

'Jim,' she exclaimed. 'I don't understand. What is happening?'

Cannon's heart sank as he thought of the amount of explaining that was going to have to be done in this household, but Maddern had said to 'Sit tight, give me five minutes, then I'll drive you home, we can talk on the way. I'll unload Katie's things later.'

Cannon watched as Maddern — arm round the still sleep-and-shock stupefied Katie — included his wife in the embrace, stooped to kiss her and drew them both inside, closing the door behind them. Momentarily Cannon felt excluded. Then — as he was wont to do at such moments of enforced idleness — fell to dealing with the next item on life's agenda, this time composing a good verbal explanation for Liz, including why he had left her car behind, and how safe it was — he hoped. He also hoped that what Maddern was going to tell him on the short distance back to The Trap was going to make some sense of it all.

A light went on upstairs in the house, and a second, then the front door opened and Jim, closely followed by his wife, came out. Maddern shook his head at whatever she was requesting. Margaret lifted a hesitant per-functory hand in Cannon's direction then turned back inside. Maddern walked quickly to the car, got in the passenger's side. 'I must not be long,' he said.

'I'll drive and you talk.' Cannon heard his tone slip momentarily back into senior officer mode and when Maddern did not begin immediately added, 'According to Margaret, you seemed to have had a kind of special relationship with this newspaper boy, Danny Smithson.' Cannon flicked the wipers to fast speed as a great flurry of huge rain-spots thundered down onto the car.

'I felt sympathy for the lad.' Maddern raised his voice above the clamour. 'But as for the family, the last thing anyone would want is a relationship, or any kind of contact.'

Cannon reverted the wipers to normal as the brief onslaught subsided. 'The local newsagent tells me Danny and his mother are new to the area, but Margaret said you thought he was local, a local family, and you called him Jakes.'

'He's a Jakes all right,' Maddern confirmed darkly. 'That build and that square-jawed face are unmistakeable. Ask any other local family, and many of 'em will have suffered at the hands of a Jakes over the years. Ask Hoskins!'

Cannon thought wryly that his oldest and most loyal customer would certainly *not* have encountered the paperboy. Didn't he take the newspaper home with him from The Trap every single evening? Though when it came to local knowledge, Hoskins was probably one up even on the sergeant.

'Way back, my great-grandfather had

trouble with the family rustling and butchering his pigs. They were all pretty handy with knives and axes even then. My father used to say the police would clear up eighty per cent of all crime in the area if they could get rid of the Jakeses.' Maddern drew in a deep reflective breath. 'After the war, they graduated to blowing safes when a couple of the sons came out of the army with plenty of knowledge of explosives, but no wish to earn an honest living; that has never been what that family do, earn and live on a fixed wage.' Maddern paused to laugh at the very idea. 'They've moved higher up the criminal ladder with each generation, progressed in their chosen profession, you might say, and like a good many of these families they breed early, multiply fast.

'They were big-time,' Maddern went on, 'but they tried to move into too many fields — drugs, money-laundering, then gun-running, trod on the toes of a rival gang operating off the coast here, and there were several murders. The present grandfather, the one I'm sure we saw released today, was involved in revenge killings, but he had a good lawyer. The only charge they could make stick was accessory. I think he got about ten years. After that they moved away from our area. Some they said went north, some to

London, and I for one breathed a sigh of relief. Now I believe they're coming back to use the area they know to bring off some kind of coup.'

Maddern paused, shook his head sadly. 'The other thing that makes me sure, is that the Jakeses always like to cock a snoop at their victims, or the police. My great-grandfather to the day of his death kept the blackened shrivelled tails of five of his pigs they sent to him after they stole and slaughtered his herd. They're family heir-looms. I'm not keen to have them added to.'

'So hearses, wreaths, would be just their style,' Cannon said, 'as would meeting one of their own out of prison with a stretch limo, though if I hadn't got lost, we wouldn't have seen that.'

'And if I hadn't identified my paperboy as a Jakes, my family would not be receiving death threats and that innocent young girl, Katie's friend, would not have been murdered.'

'You must be standing in the way of something very big,' Cannon said. 'Big plans probably masterminded by the old man while he was in prison, geared to happen when he'd served his stretch?' Cannon made it a question, but his breathing became quicker. This all had hallmarks he recognized from many gangland plots: increased activity, family and gang members being regrouped, threats, or worse, to anyone who endangered their intentions. A big job was looming. 'Jim, you can't handle this alone.'

'What I can't handle is the thought of any of my family being harmed,' he replied, 'and you should understand that, the reason you left the Met had more to do with your heart than your head.'

A picture of Liz lying in hospital, face bandaged, ready to relinquish him if she was disfigured for life after an attack by a gangland heavy-man, flashed through his mind. He controlled his voice to remind the sergeant, 'But I was not within a hand's reach of my pension.'

'And what would my pension mean to me if I lost one of my family through telling what I suspect — and I have tried. Inspector Jones thinks I'm away with the fairies.'

A large, low-flying barn owl swooped across their path, pale as a ghost in the car headlights, and Cannon thought it was a dire situation when a man lost confidence in his senior officer.

They had reached and stopped at the front of The Trap before either of them spoke again.

'So what are we going to do?' Cannon asked.

'I'm going to take my family to my brother's place. He married a farmer's daughter in Cornwall. Whatever it costs me I shall move heaven and earth to keep my family safe, and my first move is to get them to Cornwall. I've told Margaret to be ready as soon as I get back. She will take turns with the driving and the roads'll be clear at this time in the morning, a good time to set out. I can be back Monday for duty after my week's leave, and no one the wiser.'

'Jim . . . ' Cannon began, shaking his head, 'it's only Wednesday tomorrow, you — '

'I know, I know,' he said, anger and resignation in his voice, 'that's what I'd like to do, but I know I've been a copper too long to be able to keep my mouth shut just because scum like the Jakeses threaten. I shall report all I know as soon as my family are away from here; that'll most likely be Thursday morning, and Jones can make of it what he will.'

As a civilian, Cannon felt he could not fault this man's judgment, or his bravery. His family safe, he would be the one man left in the firing line. 'What can I do?' he asked.

'Let me get my family away. Once I'm back I won't waste time going to Jones. Keep quiet until then,' the Sergeant asked, 'and, if you can, look out for young Danny. I don't know what can be done to help the lad, but . . . '

'I'll find out from Russell if he's turning up for his paper round,' Cannon said, then added, 'and you'll phone me when you can, let me know what's happening.'

'I will,' Maddern said, 'and thanks.'

Before Cannon relinquished the driving seat, the two men shook hands. Cannon stood looking after the blue estate as Jim Maddern set off — briefly — back to his home before setting off on a long drive to the South West.

Walking round to the back door of his pub he saw that the kitchen light was on. Liz had either left it on for him, or more likely not gone to bed. She, and the smell of metal polish cleaner, met him at the door. Nearly as tall as he was but as blonde as he was dark, she had on blackened rubber gloves and a black smudge on her cheek. Behind her, the table was covered in newspaper and the sparkling horse brasses and hunting horns that interspersed the display of traps that hung from the pub's beams. She must have been at it for hours.

'Not polished the traps yet, then?' he asked.

She pulled off her gloves. 'I'd thump you if I had the energy,' she said, and folded into his arms as he reached for her. 'Are you OK?' she asked, her hands going from his face to his shoulders as if checking him over. Then, finding him intact, she asked, 'Why didn't you bring the car round?'

He shook his head. 'Make me a cup of tea, love, and I'll try to explain.'

Experience had taught him that on the whole it was much better to put Liz completely in the picture from the word go, so it was three cups of tea later when Cannon reached the end of the story. 'So once the Madderns are safely away, I must find out if that boy's OK.'

She had listened intently, shaking her head in dismay and disbelief from time to time. 'Poor Jim,' she said quietly, then added, 'but there is something I have to tell you, and you'll find it fairly surprising. Inspector Jones came into the bar tonight — for a drink.'

Cannon laughed in disbelief. 'He doesn't drink here.'

'He did tonight. I told him you were visiting an old friend when he wanted to know where you were. Then he asked me if I knew where Sergeant Maddern had gone for his holidays, and when I said I had no idea . . . ' she paused for effect, 'he began to quiz Hoskins.'

'Hoskins?'

'Yes, about a local family called Jakes.'

6

'Alamat will come with me, then he can drive your jeep back.' Liz told him her plan to recover her MG. 'If we leave it any nearer the weekend we'll be too busy, then it'll stand there until next week. You know cars like that attract attention if they stay put long.'

'Does it have to be today?' Cannon had not been up long, half the day was already gone and his mind was on his promise to Jim Maddern.

Liz laid her hands on his shoulders as he sat over one of the pub's all-day breakfasts she had cooked for him. 'We should still be back before, say, midnight, and you've time to go and see Mr Russell about Danny before we go, *and* you'll also be able to talk to Hoskins when he's the first customer in tonight.'

She had, as always, worked out the pros and cons of her argument; he knew it made sense, daily life had to go on, but he would just rather Liz stayed put. There was always the wish to keep her out of any possible action, at home, safe, though driving to Leicester and back with Alamat could hardly be regarded as perilous. 'I'd rather you drove my jeep,' he said morosely. 'You understand it.'

'I understand *you*,' she said, kissed him on top of his head and sat next to him while he finished local bacon and sausages with all the trimmings. 'You know, all this business with Jim and the paperboy reminds me of a poem . . . '

'A poem!' He raised his eyebrows. 'Great.'

'No, seriously, it says just what this is all about, if only I could remember it. I think it's called 'Inheritance' or something like that. Definitely something about the 'family face'. I will remember, it'll come to me eventually.'

'Well, don't get carried away while you're driving,' he said as the kitchen door was knocked and Alamat came in. The slightly built Croatian had on his suit, the one he wore for worship on Sundays.

'Morning, Alamat, you're dressed up?' Cannon said.

'He looks very smart,' Liz said.

'We go joy-riding.' His grin was wide as, with a lift of a triumphant finger, he used another new phrase he had learned. He had begun basic translations into English some years ago for fellow countrymen and now took pleasure in learning the meanings of the more obscure sayings of the language. 'And when I see Mr Hoskins next, I shall tell him the true meaning of 'coming a cropper'. This he is always saying.'

'I'll be interested in that,' Cannon said, adding as Alamat drew breath, 'but not now. I've an errand to do in the jeep before you can leave.'

'Oh, I should change and do work.' Alamat was at once all remorse, his gratitude to them for giving him home, work and official residency was at times a little overwhelming.

'No,' Liz told him, 'sit down and I'll make you and me some lunch before we set off. There may be one or two in the bar, but nothing much, we can eat and keep an eye on things.'

Cannon left immediately, refraining from making a diversion to Sea Lane to see if Maddern was back, although he hardly thought that possible: the sergeant would have to crash out for a few hours before driving back from the South West.

When Cannon entered the newsagent's shop, Russell immediately raised a hand above the customers at the counter, and as soon as he was free took him through to the back room.

'Been hoping to see you,' he said. 'Have you found out anything?'

'It's not your paperboy who is making the

insertions in the death columns. Beyond that . . . ' he shrugged.

'Well, there's something very wrong with that boy,' Russell said, shaking his head, 'very wrong in his life, or at school, something bloody serious. Not the boy he was even a week ago. I was going to say something to the mother, but she's not been around. Then I thought of going to the house . . . '

'But?' Cannon prompted.

'I was warned off, actually,' Russell admitted, 'a neighbour said he would steer clear if he was me, so I've left it.'

'This neighbour . . . ' Cannon ventured, fishing for more.

'Thompson, loves a bit of gossip, always wants to know your business, not afraid to ask either. Talkative when anyone'll listen, lives alone, nosey old bugger really,' Russell paused to laugh, 'in both senses of the word. He must see a bit, though, his side door faces the Smithsons'.' He put his hand thoughtfully on a pile of news delivery bags. 'I think this lad needs some help. Thompson says there are some right roughnecks visit the house, but if you think it would help I'll . . . '

Cannon shook his head decisively. This shopkeeper would be well out of his depth. 'Sergeant Maddern knows more now. He's on the case,' Cannon said and Russell looked relieved.

'So I don't need to do anything?'

'No, I think you can say it's all being covered,' Cannon told him. He said he was in a rush and had to get back to the pub but he hoped Russell was still busy as, instead of going back to his jeep, he once more walked up Snyder Crescent.

There was no sign of life at the Smithsons', no hand moving a curtain as he turned in at the gate of the next house. He noted the difference in the state of the small front gardens. The path he walked along was edged with crocuses and snowdrops already blooming, backed by stout wallflower plants to follow with their fragrant flowers. The Smithsons' plot was no more than bare earth, looking as if a veritable army of feet had pounded across it, ignoring the path.

He tapped the shiny frosted glass and the door was opened with remarkable rapidity as if the occupier had seen him coming and was ready for him. 'Yes?' demanded a middle-sized pensioner with a nose that was large, red and pitted.

'I wondered if I could talk to you for a moment,' he said quietly, 'I am concerned about a neighbour of yours.' Cannon indicated the Smithsons' with a slight backwards movement of his head. The message went home.

Thompson stepped back for him to enter, closed the door and asked, 'You from social services?' then immediately contradicted himself. 'Nah! I've seen you afore, in the newsagent's, took you in the back he did. Asked old Russell who you were next time I went in. He said you were the landlord of The Trap public house out Reed St Clement way.'

'I can't say I recognize you,' Cannon said.

'You mean not even with a conk like mine,' Thompson said good-naturedly, and waved him to a kitchen chair, where the local newspaper was spread over the table. 'Read every word of it,' he said, adding, 'read a bit about your exploits in the past. Ex-London bobbie. Reckon you're the boy I need to talk to. Tea?' He lifted and waved the kettle, filling it even though Cannon said he had not much time.

'Reckon you're a god-send,' Thompson went on. 'I'm getting more and more worried about them two next door, need taking under somebody's wing a bit smartish, they do, and I'm not making a fool of myself at the police station again.'

'How come?' Cannon posed the question lightly.

'Went a few weeks back, said I was sure there was a lot going on that wanted looking into, spoke to an Inspector Jones, stout chap, sucks his teeth when he's talking to you; that didn't help.'

'And?'

'He said locals did tend to be suspicious of anyone new in an area, then his telephone rang, he said thanks for coming in and I was back out, thank you very much.'

So Jones had managed to lose the trust of the public as well as his own men, Cannon thought. 'Tell me what you know,' he said.

'It's more what I've seen,' he said, 'since they've been here, sort of adds up to . . . well no, let me just tell you from the beginning.'

Cannon suspected the story might be lengthy.

'When the lad and his mother first moved here, she didn't seem a bad gel — no one man around, no one the boy called 'Dad', but she spoke and I gave her quite a few bits out of the garden, carrots, peas.' He shook his head, then grinned. 'Don't think she was used to cooking fresh things, but she did when I took to handing them over ready for the pot. She's not a bad gel, just got involved with the wrong man, I reckon, with Danny the outcome.'

Cannon had known more than one case

where a girl had stuck to a criminal family to be near her child.

'Then suddenly she changed,' Thompson went on. 'Overnight, you might say. She didn't want to talk, gave me the cold shoulder.'

'Was there anything or anyone else you've actually seen?' Cannon asked, hoping to speed matters a little.

'Yes, I'm coming to that.' Thompson nodded enthusiastically. 'Not long after they'd been here, two of the men carted all kinds of stuff down and put it in the garden shed. Just after, we had a right windy night; the next morning the doors were wide, and there were wooden tripod things, planks and a red painted sign saying 'Road Closed'; didn't seem to me to be the sort of things ordinary folk had.'

Cannon pursed his lips, nodded, stored this piece of information for future reference.

'And I'll show you something else. Come up onto my landing.'

Thompson led the way up his worn stair-carpet to stand on the landing and look from his window directly towards next door's landing window — which as far as Cannon could see was blocked with cardboard.

'Someone did that about a fortnight ago. Until then at night when their light was on I could see along their landing into their box room, and boy was that room full of goods. Stacked high, it was, like a shop storeroom, but stuff in small boxes. I don't know, perhaps it could be phones or something small like that, but they were new boxes, sort of posh for expensive stuff — stolen stuff — I reckon.'

'Why do you think they blocked it up when they did?' Cannon asked.

'Someone new on the scene?' Thompson suggested. 'Only know there's been a lot more coming and going in the hours of darkness, usually during the early hours between three and four; more men carrying holdalls, more than I've seen before, but all about the same build, hefty blighters, some taller than others, but . . . you know.'

Cannon nodded. He believed he did know. Hadn't he seen a trio of them outside Leicester prison. 'Was there anything else?' Cannon asked. 'For instance, has Danny been going to school every day?'

Thompson nodded. 'Looking like death warmed up, mind.'

'And his mother, she been shopping, doing her usual things?'

'No, she's not. Not seen hide nor hair of her, and I tell you another strange thing. All of a sudden that posh shop — you know, top one for sales online thing — they've started delivering. Can't see what they bring, it's all in bags and plastic boxes. Man carries it in the front door, someone takes the bags from him, and off he goes. Plenty of bottles going in — I hear them rattling sometimes. What d'you make of that?'

Posh deliveries linked to the stretch limo? Thompson was probably right, someone new had probably arrived. Was Grandfather Jakes already next door incarcerated in a run-down ex-council house, but anxious to be resuming 'the high life' these big criminals enjoyed on the back of their ill-gotten gains? If that was so, events were likely to move pretty fast.

'I think you must be extra careful from now on,' Cannon said, suddenly very concerned for this all-seeing neighbour. 'Keep a low profile, stay away from your windows, don't let them suspect you are watching or listening.'

'I warned old Russell off,' Thompson said sanguinely, 'and I see them by the light of the street lamp, they don't see me. Now will you have that cup of tea with me?'

Cannon shook his head. 'I really haven't time. I'll come and have one with you another day,' he said, aware the old boy was disappointed. He pulled out one of the pub's cards. 'But if you're especially worried, ring me, and if that happens to be busy — ' he turned the card over and wrote his mobile number on the back, 'on that.'

'Thanks,' Thompson's face brightened. 'Wish The Trap was nearer.'

So did Cannon as he revved the jeep to its full speed — its deep agricultural note turning quite a few heads — and brought Liz to the kitchen door as he slewed it round ready for her to drive away.

She came to him as he was opening the door and he sat and waited, thinking she was dressed as if the two of them were going out together, which had become a bit rare with the pub to look after. He noted the designer jeans, sparkly embroidery down the front of each slim thigh, blonde hair spread loosely over the shoulders of a red military-style jacket. Smart and stylish. He wondered how he could bear to let her go even for a few hours. Alamat followed her out, still in his suit, jacket still buttoned, looking less than comfortable, and for a second Cannon really resented him; if there had been no second driver on hand Liz could not have gone anyway. 'No,' his lips framed the censure for the injustice.

'Everything all right?' she asked by his side, watching, reaching in to touch his shoulder.

He nodded. 'I'll tell you all the details later,

but Danny's going to school and delivering his papers.'

'We go now?' Alamat asked, coming up to the jeep.

'Yes,' Liz said, 'I'll just fetch my handbag, you get in, I'll drive.'

Cannon caught her hand as they returned to the kitchen. 'Sorry it took longer than I expected.'

'We're probably not going to be back until the early hours now,' she said, 'but I still think it's best to go, get it over with, and you'll have Hoskins here in less than an hour. He'll keep you company.'

'Hoskins? Thanks, not sure how good he'll be in bed.'

'John!' she exclaimed as she rounded up handbag and the keys for the MG from the kitchen table. 'The old one track . . . '

He silenced her with a kiss and a swift fierce embrace that made her gasp.

He wanted to say drive carefully, don't hurry, but did not want to earn the scathing look she was capable of if he overdid the nanny bit. Liz had already triumphantly survived more trauma than most women, or men. But before she left the kitchen it was she who turned and said quietly, 'Take care, my love.'

'And you.'

He did not go out, just listened to his jeep being driven away, then walked through to the bar. There were memories of other solitary times in this echoing place now she had gone.

He tried Maddern's number but there was no reply, and he was pleased when opening time came, pleased to slide back the bolts and step outside into the evening. Still fairly isolated, this road-house had its seventeenth-century roots in a coaching inn on a toll road leading from the Wash to the Humber. Nowadays it drew enough regular customers from nearby villages to support darts and table skittle teams during the winter, but came into its own when the holiday-makers arrived. Cannon loved it all, the hectic times and the peace, as now, and he smiled to himself as he saw his first customer approaching. Hoskins, right on time, cycling up to leave his bike inside the archway to the stable-block. Cannon walked out to meet him. He was thinking of having a special place reserved for Hoskins's bike when the conversions were finished.

'Not opening tonight then?' Hoskins greeted him as he emerged from the gateway carrying a sack weighted with something or other.

'No point till you got here,' Cannon

replied, 'you old poacher.'

'They're yours,' Hoskins said, 'as ordered by your better half.'

Cannon took the bloodied hessian sack cautiously.

'Vermin,' Hoskins said. As Cannon gave it a speculative shake, as if to make sure whatever was in there was well and truly dead, Hoskins added, 'Rabbits; everybody wants them since the telly chefs started cooking 'em.' He gave a derogatory snort. 'Kept my grandparents and most of the country going in the war. Hang 'em up in your back porch,' he instructed, 'I've told Liz I'll skin 'em if she wants me to.'

The rabbits disposed of, John pulled his first customer his first pint and Hoskins asked, 'So, what's going on?'

When John took time to answer, placing the brimming pint carefully on the counter, Hoskins added, 'Come on, you have that policeman's look about you. What was Jones doing here, leaning on the counter? Thought for one wild moment he was going to buy me a pint, but he wanted to talk about a family who left this area years ago,' and he added, 'thank God' with genuine reverence.

'What would you say if I told you they were back?'

'Never!' Hoskins stared intently at Cannon

as if it might make him deny such an outrageous statement, but as Cannon held his gaze he replied in a low, grim voice, 'Then I'd say there's a whole lot of trouble coming this way.'

'What were you able to tell Jones?'

'I could 'ave told him a lot, but why should I? He wrongly accused me of shooting someone — ' he said, shaking his head like an old dog trying to rid itself of a bad taste, 'and threatened to take my gun licence away.'

Cannon knew the story well, another incident of Jones not listening to local knowledge, but he did not want Hoskins to dwell on the past. 'Were they a big family, the Jakeses?' Cannon asked.

'Oh yes,' Hoskins said, 'enough Jakeses to go round, enough to terrorize anyone anywhere in the country I should think.'

Cannon recalled the glimpse of the men outside the prison. 'And are they alike?'

'Peas in a pod, though you'd not get many of those big buggers in a pod. There were seven brothers when I was a boy, seven and two girls and you never passed their cottage but one of 'em was getting a right thrashing. The father was built like a brick shit-house.' He paused and looked up. 'Liz not about is she?'

Cannon shook his head — Hoskins never

79

swore if Liz was behind the bar.

'The lads, in turn, took it out on everyone smaller than themselves, and most of us were,' Hoskins remembered. 'They terrorized everyone. Later on, it was their own wives and kids who suffered — the same thing all over again.'

And so poor Danny, Cannon thought.

'If something's brewing, don't get mixed up in it, John,' Hoskins said, and the use of his first name made Cannon realize how sincere the old chap was.

This, and a significant change in Hoskins's manner. The fact that he was quiet and thoughtful the whole evening made more impression on Cannon than Thompson's garrulous tour of 26 Snyder Crescent.

The evening trade was like Hoskins, quiet. It was without the usual sense of having had an enjoyable night with his customers that Cannon watched Hoskins, invariably first and last, leave just after ten o'clock. He stood on his front steps, closed his eyes and let the peace, the quiet and the chill of the night take him over. He shivered but stayed where he was.

The puzzle was Jones, of course. Jones enquiring after Maddern, then trying to pump Hoskins, of all people. Had Jones finally realized he was wrong to dismiss his sergeant's and Thompson's information? Should Cannon go to see Jones himself? Should he speak to Maddern first?

He decided he must keep faith with Maddern while knowing that time, the quick response, could be the difference between life and . . . He pulled himself up, he must not get too fanciful. Old Hoskins's dour mood was catching.

He went back inside, began putting everything to rights, dutifully wiped tables, washed the last glasses, went into his cellar to turn off taps on barrels and check the temperature. Then he activated the security lights, which would be useful when Liz and Alamat returned. Then, with no one to talk to, Cannon did not bother to make his usual night-time cup of tea and went straight to bed — to lie awake.

He supposed he dozed, but came to full wakefulness again sometime after 1 a.m., and saw the security lights were on. He listened for the sound of engines, his jeep and the MG, but could hear nothing, and the lights went out. Occasionally a fox triggered them. He presumed that was the case now but he was so fully awake — and Liz surely could not be much longer — that he decided to go down and make himself that cup of tea he had missed earlier.

His hand was on the kitchen light switch when the outside lights came on once more and the shadow of something much larger than a fox went swiftly past the kitchen blinds. He stood and listened. There was a definite thud against the porch door, and then something Cannon had not expected — a knock, quite an ordinary-sounding call to the door. Then knock, knock, like the game, and Cannon found even his heart was beating a little faster as he wondered who was there. Then harder and faster. Whoever was out there had truly decided to rouse someone, somehow.

Cannon took the keys to kitchen and porch doors from the dresser, pausing before he opened the second door, preparing himself to deal with whoever was so furious or so desperate to get in. He pulled it wide, at the same time stepping back so he was out of striking distance.

Danny Smithson fell onto the doormat at his feet. Cannon stooped to try to lift the boy. 'Danny, what is it, what's wrong?' he asked. Danny drew a great sobbing breath but no words came. 'Come on, let's get you inside,' Cannon said, struggling in the confined space to lift the bulky boy, but he managed to get him into the kitchen and onto a chair.

'I'm . . . I'm — ' the boy began.

'Get your breath, I'll make us some tea,' Cannon was saying as the boy suddenly sobbed convulsively. This tough boy, who could take a beating, now began to cry as if his heart was breaking.

'Hey, hey,' Cannon said, gently putting his arm around Danny's shoulders. This seemed to make matters worse and, in spite of all his knowledge and experience, Cannon nearly said, 'It can't be as bad as that.' Instead he asked, 'What can I do to help?'

7

'So we have to do what we can,' Cannon explained to Liz. She looked totally drained from six and a half hours' driving, only to find the drama of Danny in her kitchen when she arrived home and accepted the tea Cannon poured without question.

Danny shook his head at the cup Cannon offered him, still seeming shaken by the vehicles arriving at The Trap and being convinced it was men after him. Liz rose, waving a silencing hand at Cannon and fetched the boy a can of coke from the bar and opened it.

'Thank you,' Danny said, and sipped at it.

Liz had arrived in time to hear the trauma of his mother kept prisoner in her own home, or the home 'the family gang' had made them move to. Now she sat quietly across the table from Danny and asked why he thought they were not letting his mother go out.

'It's so I do as I'm told,' Danny had declared, 'go to school and stuff, so no one knows what's going on.'

'What is going on?' Cannon asked.

Danny shook his head. 'Me and my mum was all right until the *family* found us again.'

'Your father, he was a Jakes . . . ' Cannon began.

'I kept my mam's name,' he interrupted, scowling.

'Where is your dad?' Cannon asked.

'He got shot years ago, that's when me and Mam got away.'

'I believe one of the family came out of prison recently,' Cannon said.

'He's Dad's father,' Danny retaliated, 'nothing to do with me and Mam. I'm not like them,' then catching Cannon's swift glance added reluctantly, 'except in looks.'

'Is he at your house?'

'Yeah, and what he says goes, Mam says he thinks he's the big cheese.'

Cannon was glad Alamat had gone straight to his flat from the car park, taking his new interest in the English language with him.

'He's sleeping in our living-room where the telly is, and threatens to have my mam beat up, 'or worse', if *I* don't do what he says, keep quiet and stay upstairs, *and* they give her pills to keep her quiet.' Danny looked up defiantly. 'I put two in his brandy,' he said.

'Tonight?' Cannon asked sharply.

Danny nodded. 'The pills and his new bottle of brandy were in the kitchen. I wanted to be sure he wouldn't wake up while Mam's on her own.'

'So there's no one else in the house.'

'No, just him, and Mam chained to her bed.'

'Chained?' Liz was stirred to anger and to move to the chair next to the boy.

'One of them hit her across the mouth this morning, knocked her down, said she would be better out the way. Then I saw Mr Thompson at the papershop and he showed me the card you gave him, Mr Cannon, and you both helped me before and — '

'Right,' Cannon declared, 'OK, slow down.' He began striding around the kitchen, each pace a name, a question, a review of all he knew: Danny, his mother, Thompson, Maddern. The sergeant could not have been to the station yet. What was the right way to handle this? Find Maddern? Go to Jones? It was all going to take too long. He paused to glance at the clock, 2.30 a.m., and felt a pang of alarm. 'Mr Thompson said some of the men always come between three and four. Does anyone check on you?'

'They've stopped coming,' Danny said, 'I think that's all finished. I heard the old man say they had moved on to the last stage, and thank Christ because he didn't want to be in this dump long. They've stopped bringing things.' He stopped, informant suddenly turned back into a young boy, and added, 'That's when they stopped Mam going out when they started bringing things. His gaze dropped and he twirled the can of coke nervously as he went on, 'And they've been repacking what's there for days.'

Cannon got the impression the boy knew more than he was now saying, and pressed him. 'So what did you see?'

'They brought wooden packing cases . . . ' he stopped, shot Cannon a swift, frowning glance, making the ex-Met man realize that deeply engrained in this boy was mistrust of anything official, anyone connected with authority. It was the moment when Danny Smithson had to finally step from one camp into another, the same moment when so many battered wives, abused neighbours, victims of crime, stepped back from testifying. Cannon held his breath.

Danny swallowed hard. 'Everything that was in little boxes in the spare room was tipped out and put between layers of insulation they threw down from the roof. One of them said the stuff they had up there was too heavy to rattle. They laughed about that.'

'So did you see what they were repacking?'

'Yes, they didn't care,' he paused, looked

directly into Cannon's eyes and went on, 'said if I was a good boy I'd be able to live 'the life' one day. But the old man got mad with them, made them block up the landing window so no one could see in. There was only Mr Thompson, but they did as they were told.'

'So what were they . . . ?'

'Jewellery, all kinds, bracelets, necklaces, rings, and little bags, they tipped one out to show me; uncut diamonds they said they were.'

Cannon remembered there had recently been a violent raid on a renowned jeweller's in Birmingham, a specialist who cut his own stones. So had the gang been assembling the proceeds of raids over a time? The price of gold, the wisdom of putting spare cash into precious stones in the financial climate of the world, had seen the number of raids on jewellers soar.

'One of them tossed me a diamond ring, and said to put it in my pocket,' Danny was saying.

'And you did?' Cannon said more sharply than he intended.

'I gave it to Mam. She shoved it under her pillow.'

Cannon's instinct was to bawl the boy out. Didn't he know this was one of the ways criminals involved the innocent and the reluctant: planting evidence, instilling fear of discovery?

'I must get back to Mam,' Danny said, a new wave of concern making his voice higher, more boyish, as he asked, 'but what should I do, Mr Cannon? What can I do?'

In his mind Cannon was certain the safest thing to do was keep Danny there while he went along to try to get the mother out, but he would need Danny to keep his mother quiet and reassure her. He would also need bolt-cutters.

'We'll go and get your mother now, if you've drugged the old man it will be the perfect time.'

'John!' Liz exclaimed.

She limited her protest to his name as Danny turned to her and said, 'Please let him help me, Mrs Cannon.' The boy's appeal and assumption she was John's wife left her merely shaking her head at her partner.

'The sooner his mother is out of their clutches the better,' Cannon asserted. 'They'll assume Danny got her out somehow, they won't suspect, they won't think of looking here.'

'Here?' Liz repeated, aghast but too tired to argue with what she also thought of as John's overpowering need to inflict justice on everyone. 'Of course, where else?' she said.

Danny rose, mouth open, looking from one to the other first in disbelief and then in hope.

'Then I'll go and find Maddern, and if he's not already been to see Jones I'll go with him,' Cannon said. 'If we move quickly there's so much evidence.'

'You could just take the evidence to . . . ' Liz made one final effort to keep some kind of normality in their lives.

'I'm not risking it, timing is everything, these people are ruthless, they'll let no one — their own or anyone else — stand in their way.' Cannon also had a great curiosity about the 'heavy' stuff that they had in the roof-space of that rundown council house. 'It seems to me that the old man is accumulating all his assets and he, and those he favours, will be making a run for it . . . and to be assembling this near the coast means it will probably be abroad.'

'Are you up for this, Danny?' Cannon asked. 'Because we should go now.'

'My mother's chained to an iron bedstead,' he said.

'I have bolt-cutters, that won't be a problem,' Cannon told him.

'When I came home I saw a bike outside,' Liz said. 'Is that . . . ?'

'It belongs to Mr Russell, the newsagent, I borrowed it from his back yard.'

'Did you?' Liz said. 'Well, we'll have to have a word with him about his security. Go on, I'll put it out of sight for now,' she added, giving the boy a pat on the back, and receiving a cursory kiss on the cheek from Cannon.

'I'll take your car,' he said, 'it's quieter.'

'We're really going?' Danny asked as they left the kitchen.

'You can keep your nerve?' Cannon asked as they drove. 'And watch me closely once we're inside, do exactly as I say or indicate. We want to be quick, quiet — and no picking up extra things. We get your mother, and out, understand?' He glanced across and saw the boy nod. Cannon hoped he did, as some saying about not willingly putting your hand into a nest of vipers came into his mind.

The church clock ponderously rung out the quarters and then three o'clock as Cannon parked near Church Walk some distance beyond Russell's shop, and on the opposite side of the green to the old council estate. There was a wind, and clouds moved rapidly across a bright moon. The effect was a little like someone switching a light on and off. The solitary streetlamp looked like an old forty-watt bulb after every flash of the moon.

Cannon carried the bolt-cutters under his jacket in true burglar fashion.

They carefully negotiated the broken gate and the trodden front garden as Danny felt around his neck, pulled out a string and his front door key. Cannon wondered how long he had been a latch-key child, and also, glancing at the house next door, whether old Thompson was watching? He raised a gloved finger to his lips as Danny slipped the key into the lock.

The door hit and grated on a piece of grit as Cannon pushed it a little wider than Danny had done. They held their breaths and waited long seconds. Cannon could make out the stairs on his right and the door to the living-room where the grandfather held sway to his left. Cannon closed the door and gently propelled Danny ahead of him to the stairs, thinking he should have asked if any of the stairs had a particularly loud creak.

By the time they reached the top he had greater respect for the carpenter who had worked on this council house. Danny paused, and took charge, holding Cannon's sleeve to guide him into the first bedroom on the right, then clicked on the light in what was obviously his bedroom. Cannon, half in the doorway, immediately saw it was a wise move. The landing was a disaster area.

A loft ladder had been pulled down and left. Half-blocking the way between bedrooms and stairs were two small packing-cases, one nailed down and one half-full, a layer of insulation material in place ready to cushion the next deposit of goods, and beyond that a tide of tumbled empty boxes.

Cannon took a slim, flat torch from his pocket, gave it to Danny, took the bolt-cutters from beneath his coat, indicated they should get to work, and switched off the bedroom light.

They had negotiated ladder and boxes, Danny shining the beam carefully at Cannon's feet, and had reached the second bedroom door when there was a dull heavy thud from below, followed by a second which was equally heavy. Both froze, but there was no doubt about the next sound, as the grit under the front door again grated across the tiles. Whoever pushed the door this time, though, did not desist. The pushing and the grinding scrape went on until the door must certainly be wide open, from the draught that swept up the stairs.

Cannon took the torch and slipped it back into his pocket, stood holding the boy's arm as a man's low voice echoed from immediately below them and the hall light was put on. Whoever it was had been here before and was pretty confident.

'I'll take these upstairs, you get the rest,' a first, irritated-sounding man muttered.

'*We'll* get the rest,' a second voice decided, adding, 'I'll just check with the boss first.'

The sound now of a door being tapped, then opened, a low voice making an enquiry, and again a little louder, then the door quietly reclosing.

'He's well gone,' the man reported, 'empty brandy bottle on the table, and he does know we're coming with this extra lot.'

'Let's get on with it then,' his helper grumbled, 'back's killing me.'

'You're all moan,' the other warned in a low voice. 'I'd be careful it I were you, the boss likes quiet workers.' The door grit sounded again but the same voice ordered, 'No, leave it open.'

The second Cannon judged it was safe he whispered in Danny's ear, 'Get to bed, stay there, and remember you're not on your own now.' Danny gave a low, gasping sob, like a child drawing in air before tears. Cannon gripped his arm tighter. 'It'll be all right, I'll see to that,' he promised, took the torch, shone the light at Danny's feet, saw him into his bedroom and closed the door.

Outside there was the noise of a shoe scuffing on an uneven surface as Cannon scaled the loft ladder. He took one step into the blackness, stood perfectly still, thinking of the debris on the landing below. He allowed himself one shaded second of light from the torch, enough to locate the water supply tank near the middle, saw the pipes from the tank running along an inch from his left foot, and that the roof space was totally boarded in.

There were two contrasting smells in this place, sooty dust and new wood. He moved three steps in the direction of the tank, then stood recollecting what else he had seen in that brief second of illumination: fifty or more years of thick black cobwebs hanging like curtains from the roof timbers, while the whole of the floor area consisted of new planks of wood professionally laid. These were covered with bags — thick hessian bags, not large but well-made with wide, strengthening bands that ran all around and formed the handles. Sort of up-market, eco-friendly, super shopping-bags, but all the same square shape. Whatever filled them was of uniform size.

There was more movement below and the more authoritative man said, 'We'll get them all in and upstairs, then I can pass them up the ladder to you.'

'Me bending my back in the roof,' the other grumbled, 'great! Where is everybody?'

'Other duties, other fish to fry,' the first muttered.

Realizing they intended to leave the house again, Cannon waited, listened intently, heard them go back downstairs and out, then used his torch again, this time keeping it on long enough to make his way to the far side of the water tank, scanning the double line of regimented bags as he went. What came into his mind he did not accept, did not even let the fantastic idea develop.

He put his bolt-cutters carefully down at his feet, crouched and waited. He should get away with this, with luck. Up to now the bags were all stacked on the trap-side of the water tank — though if they were to take the trouble to bring this 'extra lot' to his end of the line he could well be in trouble. He let his hand rest over the handles of his only weapon, the bolt-cutters.

'What gets me is we've got to haul all this down again.'

'You won't be moaning when you get your share.'

'It better be spot on.'

'Your mouth'll be the death of you,' the other said matter-of-factly and from the noise and the echoing loudness of their voices, Cannon realized they were both just the other side of the cold water tank.

'It's these other hangers-on he wants to get rid of, this woman and her kid,' the man stated.

'You could be right about that.' The quietly spoken remarks of this man were far more chilling than the grumbling rants of the other. 'We just have to wait to be given the word.'

'It's the pay-out I'm waiting for. What d'you reckon this lot is worth?'

'It's more what he'll get — but the boss has good contacts in . . . '

Cannon felt the man stopped before he revealed more than he wanted the other man to know. The other seemed not to notice. 'Let's get out before he wakes up and finds us something else to lug about,' he said.

There was the sound of the goods they had carried up being put into place.

'He likes it tidy.'

'He likes to be able to count what he's got!'

The voices became more remote as the pair turned away and climbed down the steps. Then Cannon heard them push the ladder up and close the trap-door. He hoped it opened from the inside.

After a few moments he shone the torch onto his watch; from the time they had heard the church clock toll three o'clock, a mere fifty minutes had passed. It felt like several hours, but he would wait a little longer before he explored the intricacies of a loft ladder from a new direction. In the meantime there were the bags. He allowed the ridiculous notion that had tried to edge into his mind earlier to take a more definite hold. 'But . . .' he formed the word with his lips, 'surely not.'

He took the handles of the nearest bag, lifted it and tested the weight. It was *heavy*, seriously heavy, certainly heavy enough to cause a bad back. Carefully he lowered it back to the flooring laid specially to receive these bags — he had no doubt about that. He pulled the handles apart and shone his light directly in on the contents.

No one could be unimpressed by gold. It looks like what it is — a fortune in a solid block. It stirs possibilities in the mind of every man — if only — what if? Cannon blasphemed quietly, then ran his hand down inside the bag, counting, six, six ingots of gold — six in each bag . . .

'Brink's Mat' he mouthed, his fingers going to his lips. 'Come on,' he told himself, 'that was in 1983' — but this much gold? One day in November, six men had burst into the depot of the Brink's Mat security firm at Heathrow. They had disabled the security system, thrown petrol over the guards and threatened to set them alight unless they gave them the combinations of the safes, and while some of the thieves had been fairly quickly caught, since then there had been at least five gangland murders believed to be linked to the case . . . and the gold, the missing gold? Cannon seemed to remember reading a report by an eminent journalist that only eleven of the two thousand six hundred gold bars had so far been recovered.

Was he looking at a cache of some two hundred more?

The whole scenario of violence and ruthlessness linked to stolen gold in this quantity made him sure of one thing. He had to get Danny and his mother out of this place pretty damn quick.

He flashed his light all around the roof-space, the bags, the incongruous tower of shiny metal steps, a ladder to nowhere, and felt something like the curse of the Midas touch creep over him. Here he was, surrounded by the wealth some men would kill for, had killed for, but like the unfortunate Midas, having touched it, gold might well dominate his life for some time to come.

He walked back to the trap, bent over, then knelt down. The square was not only closed, it looked hermetically sealed. There was no catch on his side, not even the hinges were visible, but perhaps downwards pressure might do it? He applied it cautiously at first, then with more and more force. The thing never budged, but then as he pushed himself upright again, it opened and he not only nearly nose-dived through but saw the ladder above him sliding slickly down and likely to act as guillotine to whatever part of him was in the way. By sheer force of will and muscle-power he pulled himself back and out of the way.

Below him, Danny's mouth was wide with concern, the hooked pole that released the ladder still in his hand. Retrieving his bolt-cutters, Cannon made his way down, his knees slightly shaky, and it was certainly no time for such weaknesses.

'Heard you go up when the men came,' Danny explained.

'It's OK,' he said, putting his finger to his lips to remind the boy they must whisper. 'But we must hurry. You go to your mother first, reassure her.' He let the boy get inside the second bedroom, heard him speak, then followed, closed the door, flicked on the light switch and stood aghast.

He'd seen tidier violent murder scenes than this. It looked as if anything and everything the boss had not wanted in the lounge downstairs had been roughly thrown in here: a table lamp, its shade broken off; a coffee table, legs broken; a magazine rack and a strew of newspapers and magazines; a red and black pouffe, and a couple of wooden armchairs. Cared-for things had been thrown about, wilfully broken, but he forgot all this when he saw the woman on the bed. She too, he thought, was strewn on the bed as if carelessly thrown aside. She was forty perhaps, red-haired, a large woman, deeply unconscious and her facial skin sagged as if she had lost a lot of weight fast — and where the hell did the ankle-shackle and chain she wore come from?

They were monstrous, a broad anklet of iron attached to a long, thick, hand-forged chain which was woven around the foot of the bedstead. There were two padlocks: one on the chain, the other securing the clasp on the anklet. It was like something from an eighteenth century chain-gang.

'I hear that chain all the time,' Danny whispered, 'even at school.'

Cannon had to take a moment to let the red mist clear from his eyes, and to stop himself taking the hefty thirteen-year-old into his arms. It was definitely not the time for that.

He motioned the boy to his side, then picked a cushion from the floor, lifted the woman's foot and with the utmost care turned her foot gently sideways on it. 'Hold your mother's foot firmly like that,' he whispered, 'don't move at all, not a fraction. I am going to have to use real force to cut through that padlock.'

Danny knelt by the bed, held the foot but closed his eyes as Cannon stood over him and positioned the jaws of the cutters on the loop of the ankle padlock. He concentrated first on getting a steady grip with the cutters, sent a plea heavenwards for them not to slip and applied all the force he could. He felt the veins in his temples throbbing and his teeth hurt with clenching, but still the iron hoop did not give.

Danny opened his eyes as he felt Cannon relax. 'Can you do it?' he asked anxiously.

Cannon nodded and applied all his strength again. He felt his bottom jaw jutting, a primeval man with brutish determination, as Danny's words came back to him, 'I hear that chain all the time'. He thought he heard himself snarl and then the jaws of the cutter closed with a final swift snap. Cannon staggered.

'You've done it, Mr Cannon,' Danny said grinning but with tears streaming down his face, and before Cannon had recovered his balance he had opened the shackle and gently lifted his mother's foot free.

'We've a long way to go yet,' Cannon said. They still had to smuggle this unconscious woman from the house and to Liz's car. 'Put the loft ladder up out the way, then come back and stay with your mother,' he ordered gently. 'I'm going to check downstairs. We must be quick and quiet.' He glanced at the window, the fitful moon was being replaced by a general lightening of the sky.

Once down the stairs Cannon first stooped to sweep his hand several times across the floor tiles behind the front door until he found the offending piece of needle-sharp grit and placed it on the hall table. He listened outside the sitting-room, then very slowly opened the door. The man he had last seen getting into a stretch limo was lying in some style, covered by a fur rug on a wide, French-style chaise longue such as Cannon had only ever seen in films before, but he was just as unconscious as his victim had been upstairs. Cannon closed that door then opened the front door, wide, propping it open with a coat from the hall pegs, then hurried back to Danny.

'I'll carry your mother over my shoulder. Once I have lifted her I need you to go ahead, make sure there is nothing and no one in our way. Right!'

The whispered instructions were taken in

with repeated nods. 'Right! Ready!' Danny said and carefully prevented her arms from falling about as he helped Cannon lift his mother from the bed.

'Right,' Cannon said and Danny was immediately at the door, and with constant glances back did exactly what Cannon asked, three steps ahead, no faltering, no unnecessary pauses as they negotiated stairs, front door, front path, broken gate.

Once outside, Cannon had trouble keeping up with the boy. He struggled with the weight, glad of two things — that he was fit, and that all Reed St Thomas appeared to be sleeping, including Thompson, Cannon hoped.

8

'But why should you . . . ?'

It was well into the afternoon before Liz and Cannon could have a proper talk to Danny's mother and be sure she understood what had happened.

'Because you were being held against your will, and I feared for your safety,' Cannon replied. 'Someone had to move quickly.' If he had to, it would be the reason he would give to Inspector Jones later.

'And because he's like . . . ' For a moment, Danny sought for a description. 'Because he's like a gladiator,' and he imitated the force Cannon had used to sever the chain on his mother's ankle.

'Alamat said like a knight in shining armour,' Carol Smithson added.

'Yes,' Danny enthused.

Cannon scowled, almost squirmed. Liz let him suffer for a moment then helped him out of the spotlight by saying, 'He just can't mind his own business.'

'Until today, my boy's been the only one who cared,' Carol said.

'Mr Thompson's been kind,' Danny reminded her.

'Yes,' she nodded in agreement, 'in his way, he was, but . . .' she looked around the newly emulsioned apartment, 'letting us be here, I . . .' she paused again to look at Liz, 'I can see what a trouble it's been.'

Liz glanced at the sheets put up to curtain the windows, the blow-up mattress and the old camp-bed, bedding, electric heaters, a kettle and a few pots, all rapidly gathered together with Alamat's help while Cannon was at Reed St Thomas. She had wondered what Alamat's reaction would be as she had woken him from such a short sleep and asked for his help.

'Ah!' he exclaimed. 'Mr John Cannon is on another mission,' and rubbed his hands as if he could not wait to get started. 'This is a good place, people know I live in this block and now we hide these people away in the farthest corner, the one apartment all decorated.'

'It must be secret, very hush-hush,' she had impressed on him, feeling his enthusiasm could be dangerous.

He had made the now traditional zipping motion across his mouth, then grinned hugely.

'Hopefully we can make things a bit more

comfortable,' Liz said.

Carol shook her head. 'I'm just so grateful to be away from that old man . . . ' Her lips trembled but she turned the emotion into hate as she spat out, 'And his sons, *and* the other men.'

The policeman in Cannon knew this woman and her son had a lot of valuable information, much more probably than they realized, but for the time being he thought it best to let them talk, relax a little. Questioning would have to come, but not quite yet.

'I used to think my parents were boring,' Carol was saying. 'I thought my life was deadly dull, that's why I ran off with Danny's father, and that killed them, you know, my parents. Killed them.'

Liz shook her head, made a disbelieving noise but Danny's mother insisted,

'No, it is true, it did kill them. They just gave up . . . ' she nodded vigorously, confirming the truth of what she said. 'They never made a lot out of their small boarding-house in Skegness. For one thing, they never charged enough. After I ran off, my mam and dad gave up. I was their only child. Things went downhill. Our old neighbours told me at the funeral. Apparently they tried every way to find me,' her face hardened as she went on, 'those neighbours, they made a point of telling me that it made my father an old man. My parents sold out and just had enough to buy that house in Snyder Close. They saw the furniture van away from Skegness, and were driving there in our old Hillman Husky when they were both killed in an accident, an articulated lorry jack-knifed in front of them as they came round a corner. So they never lived in Snyder Close, and neither did I until the Jakes lot found me and Danny last year and made us come here. They've ruled our lives ever since.'

'I think you can say that time is over,' Cannon promised.

'I'm never going back,' Danny declared.

'No,' Cannon confirmed, 'but we must be careful. Danny obviously can't go to school or do his paper round. Neither of you must be seen. Alamat'll be working on the other apartments in the daytime and he sleeps in the small place just inside the entrance to the stable-block, so he will be a kind of sentry. This is the safest place I can think of until I have seen Sergeant Maddern,' Cannon said, and as Carol looked sharply up at him he added, 'you have nothing to fear from the police, you have done nothing wrong.'

Carol's stillness drew all their attention. She put a hand into the pocket of the cardigan she was wearing over an ancient pair of grey interlock pyjamas, then held out a clenched fist towards Cannon. He stretched out his hand and she dropped a solitaire diamond ring into it, the stone big enough to draw a gasp from Liz, and the question, 'Is it real?'

'Oh yes,' Cannon said, 'unfortunately.'

Danny told the story. 'I just wanted Mam to have something nice,' he said, 'but I should have thrown it back at him.'

'Yes,' Cannon confirmed, 'but I'll put it in the pub safe for the time being.'

'And we must go, it's very near opening time,' Liz said. 'Alamat will bring you supper later, and you can always send us a message by him if you need to.'

'And he'll entertain you,' Cannon said, wishing to lighten the woman's stricken expression. 'He'll tell you all kind of things about the sayings of the English language if you give him a chance. He's working on 'coming a cropper' at the moment. But he does know when to . . . hold his tongue.'

They shared a precious brief moment of laughter.

'I think he is a good man,' Carol said, 'and it would be nice to talk to someone in an ordinary way.'

Cannon wondered just how traumatic this

woman's life must have been to think of her present circumstances as anything near ordinary.

Once they had walked out under the archway, Cannon's phone was in his hand. 'Where is Jim Maddern? Why doesn't he answer his phone?'

'He could be driving, or just so exhausted he's not hearing it,' Liz said. 'Just do what I know you are itching to do, drive over there.'

'I really don't want any involvement with the police until I've seen him, and I'm particularly keen to avoid Jones.'

'Just go,' she said, 'I know you won't rest, or hear what anyone is saying to you in the bar or anywhere else until you've settled this.'

'I don't deserve you,' he said and left her shaking her head as he ran towards his jeep. He blew her a huge theatrical kiss before he opened the jeep door, feeling guilty because he already had the keys in his pocket.

When he reached Sea Lane he came to an abrupt stop, unsure whether to beat a tactical retreat or drive on. He did neither, he parked and walked towards the police car parked outside Maddern's house. He was just two properties away when he heard the sound of a door opening and men's voices. Instinctively he turned back, pulled up his collar and hunched his shoulders; one of those voices was that of Inspector Brian Jones.

'Damn,' he muttered. Jones would surely recognize him or his jeep. However, he then heard Jones splatter gravel as he turned the police car around and saw him go past at some speed. He glimpsed the inspector bent forward over the steering wheel, looking as if urging the car faster and totally absorbed in his own thoughts.

He spun on his heel again and walked quickly back to Maddern's front door where there was another surprise. The door was badly splintered near the lock.

He rang the bell twice before a pale and exhausted-looking Jim Maddern opened it. Maddern looked relieved when he saw who it was. 'I thought Jones had come back,' he said, stepping back for Cannon to enter.

'You've been broken into,' Cannon said. He was not prepared for the devastation as Maddern — with only the minimum of words — showed him from room to room. 'In here.' They went to the kitchen first. Every drawer and cupboard had been turned out onto the floor, pots, glasses, even the glass doors in the cooker and microwave had been smashed. Doors had been crow-barred from the washing-machine and the drier. The only glass he could see that was not broken was the window-glass. 'And here.' Maddern led him into the sitting-room where the television had been wrenched from the wall, a glass display cabinet pulled over and what looked like a comprehensive collection of charming Beatrix Potter figures decimated. 'Upstairs.'

This was worse, for not only had everything been tipped out, but obviously, as both men knew from experience and the smell, at least one of the intruders had found his excitement level so high that like a child he could not control his bladder and had emptied it in Maddern's bedroom.

But it was the red sprayed messages on every bedroom wall that were more alarming. 'This is just the start.' 'Got your address book.' 'We'll find them.' In the last bedroom, one of the girls', the message read 'Wreaths all round!'.

'Jones's reaction?' Cannon demanded.

'He said he'd tried to warn me off and if I'd done what he'd said and kept my knowledge to myself this would not have happened.'

'Why was he here — by himself?' Cannon asked, wondering about Scene of Crime and forensics.

'The surveillance teams were under instructions to just observe, not on any account to interfere with any member of the Jakes gang. Jones was just to be told when I was home. I'm only just back . . . ' His deep voice broke as he added, 'My bag's still in the car.'

'Surveillance teams?'

'He told me there's been a covert operation going on for some time between the Midland and East Anglian police forces. He said it's the biggest operation he's ever been involved in. They knew George Jakes — the old man we saw released — had been getting messages out of prison, organizing the regrouping of his gang, and his assets.'

'To leave the country,' Cannon guessed.

'Jones nearly drooled when he mentioned the assets,' Maddern said bitterly, looking at the damage done to the home he had bought for his retirement.

'Yes,' Cannon heard himself agree, 'but why didn't he tell you all this before? Doesn't he trust the longest serving man in his section?'

Maddern shrugged. 'He says it's all coming to a head fairly soon, and *nothing* must be done now to jeopardize what'll be the biggest police coup for years.'

'Did he say anything about our activities?' Cannon asked.

'Leicester?' Maddern asked, shook his head and leaned back on the wall as if he needed support, and added, 'I've been put on compassionate leave so I can re-join my family. Jones was surprised we had not all come home together.'

It had not been Leicester Cannon was thinking of. If the Jakeses were under surveillance . . .

'Jones asked me for a key, says he will ensure my home is put to rights,' Maddern said, then turned suddenly and drove his fist against the wall catching the door-frame with his knuckles.

Cannon could have joined him in the futile outburst as Maddern said, 'But he can't do that, can he? The bastards have destroyed twenty-six years of home-building, all the things Margaret's collected and loved . . . ' He looked like a man totally bereft. 'How can I tell her?' he asked.

Cannon wondered how many times a man could be knocked down and still get up. He hesitated to burden Maddern with the knowledge that Danny and his mother were hidden at The Trap, or that he had not only seen how vast the assets were, but that they were enough to make even an honest man drool. 'So you are going back to your brother's farm?'

'I am, if they've taken our address book I'm not risking anyone down there being at risk. I'll just drive to one of those travel inns, stay there the night, then go on tomorrow. As I say, my bag's still in the car.'

'Right,' Cannon agreed.

'The inspector said he would keep me fully informed,' Maddern interrupted, 'on everything. I don't think you should get involved any further.'

Cannon kept remarkably still, then offered his own advice, 'So just drive to the first overnight place you come to and rest, yes?'

Maddern nodded. 'I will, and thanks, you know, for everything you've done. Not sure how I would have coped in Leicester without you, but now Jones seems to have everything covered.'

'Right,' Cannon said again but hoping he kept the edge of doubt out of his voice this time.

* * *

The bar was already busy when he got back. He and Liz ran the gauntlet of uneasy half-messages all evening as they served in the bar — so much so that Hoskins had asked them if they had 'had a domestic'.

After they had closed, Liz had gone through to the kitchen and, by the time Cannon had seen Hoskins off into the mild damp February night and locked up, she was sitting at the table with cups of tea poured.

Cannon sat across the table from her, and felt a little like a man shown into the police station interview room. He pursed his lips to prevent the merest twist of a smile of pleasure as he looked at her, but he got away with nothing.

'This is serious, John,' she said, defying him to make any kind of jokey remark. 'I gather that we have blundered into a big police operation.'

'If what Jones has told Maddern is correct, yes.'

'If! You doubt it!' she exclaimed.

'With reason,' he said, sipping his tea, quizzing her through the steam.

'Tell me,' she said.

He put his cup down carefully. 'Jones,' he said, 'apparently didn't know about us having been to Leicester, of bringing Katie home, or of her friend being murdered merely because she went after, and saw, whoever delivered a box to the daughter of his police sergeant. A police sergeant who lives almost next door to where Grandpappie Jakes is holed up. So,' Cannon declared, 'not much liaison there between the Midland and East Anglian forces.'

'Perhaps Jones didn't have time to go into all that, I mean . . . '

'Jones thought the Madderns were *all* still on holiday. He was surprised when they didn't all come home together.' Cannon's voice had taken on the deeper, more serious note that Liz knew meant he was quite sure something was very wrong. 'Plus,' he went on, 'these *surveillance teams* let me walk across the village green with an unconscious woman on my shoulders and Danny by my side, then drive back here with no sign of any other vehicle anywhere in sight, no helicopter overhead, nothing!'

'On the other hand,' Liz intervened, 'if there was no liaison and no surveillance how could Jones know that Maddern was coming home? You said Jim's bag was still in the car.'

'Reason to doubt,' Cannon repeated, 'reason to question who is watching who.'

'What are you saying exactly?' she questioned.

'I'm asking if Jones is telling the truth.'

'I know you don't exactly like the man,' Liz said, 'but if you suspect him of lying, what can he be lying about?'

'Police involvement,' Cannon suggested.

'Why should he make that up?'

'Because he's a bent copper and needs to throw Maddern off the scent,' he suggested.

'Come on,' Liz appealed, 'you're making some Olympic-sized leaps in the dark.'

'Other things keep coming into my head. Jones came down here from the North, from a bigger force to a smaller one, but it didn't involve any promotion. In fact I would think his chances of advancement must be less here than where he was. He was here about four years, stagnating in his job, no home life, then suddenly, early last year, a woman appears. There's been no hint of any kind of relationship before, particularly not with the ulta-smart bit of stuff his partner's rumoured to be — and no one knows anything about her.

'She doesn't shop locally. I've heard that over that bar counter. Everything ordered online, weekly grocery deliveries, and clothes she goes to London for.

'And,' Cannon added, 'they hardly seemed together many weeks and they move into a rather splendid house overlooking the estuary. Did she have money?'

'Inspector Jones never gave any sign of being over-flush, so you're suggesting . . . '

'There are things that want looking into, questions to be asked.'

'So now I have a question,' she said pointedly, 'Danny and his mother?'

'I wouldn't put their lives at any great value if the family find out where they are. Knowing those two are on the loose must be driving old man Jakes spare,' he said, 'and, cornered, we both know these ruthless men will use extreme,' he twisted his lips into an expression of revulsion, 'even bizarre methods to stay out of the reach of the law.'

Liz moved uncomfortably; she had been at the wrong end of a vengeful gang member driving a 4x4. The memory had given her nightmares for years. 'Heaven help anyone who tries to stand in their way,' she said fervently, 'and you think they're going to try to move all the gold and stuff soon?'

'I know so,' he said with complete certainty.

'So we have to keep these two out of harm's way,' she said.

'Hopefully . . . ' he looked at her expectantly.

She took a deep breath and exhaled very slowly, accepting that they were inextricably involved and she might as well do her best. 'All right,' she said, 'so there's the question of Danny's school, and his paper round. Do we get Danny's mother to write a note to the school and we post it? Do we tell the newsagent?'

'Yes to both, I think. I'll see Russell — ' He stopped speaking when his mobile rang. 'Bit late,' he commented, 'though it may be Maddern.' He answered the call. 'Cannon.'

'Cannon,' a man's voice queried. There was a slight pause then, 'landlord of The Trap public house on the Reed St Thomas Road?'

'Who is this?' Cannon asked and the phone went dead. He tapped in 1471 and was told the caller had withheld their number. It left them both with a sense of unease. Everyone had plenty of such calls — but not usually this late. Perhaps they were just uneasy because, as Liz said, they did have something to hide.

Even so, Cannon felt the need to walk out and make a careful circuit of the whole place before he switched on his security lights and went to bed. He walked from the back door to the front of the pub, along by his front door, turned right past the arch into the stable-block — pausing to see that the only light was from Alamat's bedroom — then he paced the width of the beer garden to the hedge. As his eyes adjusted to the darkness he could make out and recognize every feature: benches, litterbin, children's slide and swings to the rear of the grassed area. Nothing, he thought, could look more orderly, be more normal. He walked on to the back boundary, to the fence which led out to the fields, marshes and eventually the beach, one of his favourite morning jogs.

He held the top rung and tipped his head back, looking upwards; there was quite a wind which felt cold but good — cleansing on his face. There were many miles of cloud cover to pass as there was no break in it, no glimpse of moon or stars.

He closed his eyes, valuing the moment, but then the hairs on the back of his neck rose as he sensed he was not alone. He remained motionless, every sense strained for proof. Was there a footfall? The faintest crack of a twig? Without any sign that he had been alerted he spun round, his back to the fence to provide leverage should he need it for escape — or attack.

For a second or two he still could not locate anything or anyone. It was not until he looked at the boundary hedge he had walked that he made out movement; a blacker shape moved against blackness. A man — a big man with big shoulders — was coming his way. A Jakes?

The figure came steadily on towards him and Cannon calculated that the back door of the pub was unlocked and there was no way he was leaving Liz vulnerable.

'That's close enough,' he said in a low hard voice.

'It's Maddern, John.'

'In the name of all the gods! Good thing

I'm not armed — I'd probably have shot you,' Cannon hissed.

'Listen,' Maddern said urgently, 'I reckon it was Jones who ordered my house trashed.'

Cannon caught his breath. 'Did you just phone me?'

'No.'

'I thought you were going to the nearest travel inn?'

'I did, but I'm going back *and* staying there until we've sorted this out.' Maddern was at his side now. 'I stopped some way along the road, wondering what to do as it was so late, then I saw you come walking round the pub.'

'What do you mean, Jones ordered your home trashed?' Cannon asked, but he felt like a hound with a fresh scent. He was not the only one who knew matters were not right.

'You think there's something not quite kosher,' Maddern said. 'I can hear it in your voice.' He leaned back with a great exhaled breath. That the man was totally weary, there was no doubt, but he was clear enough in what he had decided. 'That man showed me round my own home like someone displaying his handiwork,' he stated. 'I was so upset, so sick at heart, with everything, I couldn't think properly. It wasn't until I lay on the bed in that travel place that I knew what it was. Jones's manner was all wrong. Had he been the uncaring bastard he usually was I wouldn't have thought anything, but when he started saying things like, 'Look at your wife's beautiful collection of figures' and 'They've even broken . . . ' Whatever, we went around the whole house like that. Then he gives me leave from that moment . . . '

'To get you out of the way,' Cannon said.

'But he's not succeeded.'

'This is a dangerous game, and if we're wrong . . . '

'My cottage is paid for,' Maddern stated, 'and my family are as safe as me and my brother can make them. I spoke to him earlier.'

'You'd better come back to the kitchen with me. I've quite a lot to tell you before we decide what to do next.'

9

It struck Cannon that he had spent more time in the back of Russell's shop than in the shop itself.

'I managed to find an extra paperboy as it happens, but are Danny and his mother safe?' Russell asked, rubbing his hand backwards and forwards through his sparse grey hair, adding a halo of fluster to his look of concern.

'Safe?' Cannon quietly queried the word he would not have expected from the newsagent.

'It's just that old Thompson came in just before we closed last night, in quite a state. He'd come for bread and bacon, said he'd had nothing to eat all day, he was too 'churned up'. I brought him in here — he certainly needed to tell someone what he was worried about.'

Cannon hoped Smithson's neighbour had heeded his warning to stay out of sight. Russell's next statement did not reassure him.

'Well, what he'd seen, really,' the newsagent continued.

'Seen?' Cannon was becoming more concerned by the minute.

'I think he keeps an eye on most things on the estate, but yesterday he couldn't come out to do his shopping because of what was going on at Danny's house. He said he'd seen about everything and everybody except Danny and his mother . . . ' Russell paused and looked at Cannon for reassurance.

'They're safe,' he said. 'They're being looked after.'

'Thank God for that,' Russell said, and when Cannon was not forthcoming with any more detail, he added, 'You'll be in touch with Sergeant Maddern, so I don't want to pry into police business. As long as they're OK.'

Cannon nodded and encouraged him to go on, 'So Thompson saw . . . '

'Three men, he said, all in white overalls like removal men, but he said he'd seen at least two of 'em before. In particular, he mentioned a vicious, sour-faced-looking customer he'd seen coming and going in the small hours of the morning with another guy bringing things. But this time they were moving things out — bags and boxes — into a white Mercedes van, and in broad daylight. As soon as they had loaded the van, two men went with that, one man stayed behind. Thompson said he could hear him moving things, as if he was getting the next load ready.'

Not from inside his own house he couldn't, Cannon thought grimly.

'The van was back inside a couple of hours. It was reloaded the same as before and driven away. After this second lot had gone, the old boy came to do his shopping, wanting to know if young Danny had been to do his paper round. When I said he hadn't he was talking about having someone he could ring for help, and off he went.'

That would be me, Cannon thought, but no call had come, nothing until that late-night caller who had tried to check his name and address then rung off — and now he remembered the business card he had given Thompson, his mobile number written on the back. If that had fallen into the wrong hands . . .

Then both men jumped, lost in thoughts of other phone calls, as Cannon's mobile chimed faint Bow Bells in his pocket. 'Born a cockney,' he was explaining to Russell until he saw who was calling him.

'Liz?' he queried.

'Two men in a white Mercedes said they were selling building supplies cheap. According to Alamat they asked for you by name, but Danny spied them through the window and said one of them was his father's eldest brother, Uncle Sean. He says he only comes when it's serious and the godfather sends for him.'

'Are they still there?' he snapped.

'No, Alamat didn't believe they were selling anything, and stood out in the road to make sure they both drove off in the van. They did at some speed, but the message for you was that they'd be back. Sounded like a threat, he said, and he's staying on watch.'

'I'm on my way home now,' he said, then turned to Russell. 'I have to go,' he said. 'Problem at the pub.' He made a theatrical grimace of a minor problem being exaggerated. 'I'll be in touch.' He nodded reassurance to the newsagent, who thanked him.

As he left the shop, a white Mercedes van came at reckless speed around the far side of the village green and headed towards Snyder Crescent. The same men reporting back to the boss, Cannon wondered, or going to pick him up? Perhaps there was a last load, but to be taken where?

Had they been sure of Jones or if CI Helen Jefferson was not on maternity leave there would have been trust, a phone call would have brought help. The danger, though, was that if Jones was a bent copper, and this was the last time the gang were going to visit Snyder Crescent, all knowledge of where they had gone would be lost to the law.

If it was the same van, with the same men as had been to The Trap, then if he tailed it, they could not go back there without him knowing, and if it was taking a last load of stolen goods — and he followed it — then he *would* have the evidence the police needed to swoop, and time to find the man above Jones to give the information to. There had been changes but Maddern would know about those.

He trusted that these Jakeses did not know his Willy jeep as he drove around and into Snyder Crescent. The van was parked outside number 24, but as far as he could see there was no one in it and no sign of life at number 26. He drove to the far end, turned the jeep and parked on the right hand side just in sight of the back of the van, then he rang Liz back.

She answered immediately. He told her what he thought might be happening ending with a tense, 'We can't afford to lose them.'

'We?' she queried.

'Maddern, the police, me, you, Danny, Carol, the honest hardworking public.'

'So you are going to follow the van.' It was a statement made in a voice that conveyed no emotion whatsoever. There was neither anger, nor approval — nothing. It was as if she was saying on your head be it, John Cannon, on your head.

He heard himself say aloud, 'I know.' Then he broke off. 'The van's on the move.'

'John,' she said and this word contained all her anxiety.

'I love you,' he said. 'See you later.'

He heard the 'I hope so' but she did not say it.

*   *   *

Cannon kept the van in sight, just, until he reached a point where several articulated lorries came out of a side road in a kind of convoy and several cars in front of him 'obligingly' let them take preference, presumably so they could keep together. Cannon huffed and puffed in frustration as the artics, all loaded with early daffodils, would be making their way to the ports — most of them going to Scandinavia to lighten and brighten the hearts of those emerging from the almost constant dark nights and days of their winters.

When they had gone, so had the van, but he presumed that at the speed it was travelling the driver did not intend to turn off any time soon. He put his foot down and it pleased his heart that his old, lovingly renovated jeep seemed to revel in it.

He came to a long, straight stretch of road leading inland towards Boston and there was nothing ahead of him. He felt he should not be that far behind, slowed a little, took more care to look left and right at junctions — which mercifully were few on this stretch. He had gone by a smallish left turn when he registered he had seen something on the corner some way along the side turning. He drew in, waited until a following lorry had passed him then backed up and turned.

The van was parked to the left of one of those extended double gateways leading into a vast expanse of daffodils in green bud, just half a dozen flowers over the whole area showing pale yellow petals. Cannon parked just beyond the gateway and walked back. Next to it were fresh, crisp tyre-marks of a second vehicle. A vehicle switch?

The van did not appear to be damaged. He peered in the front windows, pulling gloves from his pocket. He felt the bonnet; it was still red hot and the doors he found were not locked. There was nothing in the front of the vehicle, under the seats, in the compartments, or behind the sun-visors. He calculated that there would not have been time to unload a great deal of stuff into another vehicle. He went to the rear and opened the doors; this too was empty, but there was a dark-red patch to one side. He did not have to climb in to know it was blood.

Somebody — or some *body* — had been in there until, he guessed, minutes earlier, and had been transferred to another vehicle. Why? He was reluctant to turn back, but there was no use trying to chase a vehicle he could not identify. His duty now was to get back to Liz as soon as possible.

10

Liz found Alamat some distance along the road, carrying a broom-handle and looking extremely anxious.

'You're still worried about that man?' she asked.

The little Croatian nodded urgently. 'He was evil man. I think he saw young boy, he went away too easy.' The shake of his head became a general shudder. 'He had found what he want. Is Mr Cannon coming back?'

'He should not be too long,' she answered guardedly.

'I think we should hide people other place, better place,' he said with certainty, 'and pretty damn quick.'

They found Danny and his mother even more disturbed by the visit. 'If it was my husband's eldest brother, he'll be back,' Carol Smithson said, her lips twisting with bitterness. 'He never lets go.'

'I don't want him to get us again.' Danny's voice was thick with tears and fear. 'It was 'im what found me and Mam and brought us here.'

Carol put an arm around her son.

'It won't happen if we can help it,' Liz said, her mind ranging from outbuildings to attics. She and John had meticulously cleared the attics when they first bought The Trap. The only things up there were boxes of Christmas decorations. 'There's the cellar,' she began, 'but it's — '

'Please, anywhere until we can get away,' Carol pleaded. 'He'll be back, he won't waste time.' She made the shape of a gun with her fingers but out of sight behind her son's head.

'Come on,' Liz said. She led the way from the stable-block to the back door of the pub, through to the passage leading to the bar. She told them to wait while she fetched the key Cannon kept on a hook next to the optics. The cellar door was always kept locked so no one could possibly open it by mistake and find themselves teetering on the edge of the steep brick steps.

Switching on the light just inside the door, she led the way down between the white-washed brick walls. There was no handrail and the steps and walls — part of the original 17th century coaching inn — were always slightly clammy but the installations were completely up-to-date. The metal barrels of beers with gauges and pressurized pumps lay on one side, on the other was a baffling array of pipes leading from several different lagers into a refrigeration unit, for while the beers must be at room temperature the lagers had to be colder — all pipes went up through the cellar ceiling to the pumps in the bar above.

'What's that?' Danny asked, having taken in the main part of the cellar. He pointed to where ribbons of broad plastic sheeting covered one end.

'I'll show you,' she said, holding back the plastic strips. 'Regulations to stop insects entering when the beer is delivered. The brewery lorry stops on the roadway, we make sure the double-hinged doors above your head are unbolted, the men pull them open from above, and use this kind of double chute with the steps in the middle to steady the barrels and slide our order down.'

'It's spooky though,' Danny said, peering up at the trapdoors, then all around. 'All dark in the corners.'

'Not as spooky as your Uncle Sean,' his mother reminded him, 'and I'm not chained up!'

'No,' he decided, 'we'll stay down here until Mr Cannon comes back.'

Liz sent Alamat for the torch kept behind the bar, and then left them sitting side by side on a piece of sacking at the far end of the stone thrall beyond the beer barrels.

'We're all right,' Carol reassured her,

putting her arm round Danny and pulling him close. Leaving them, Liz still felt like a jailer locking a dungeon, but she had no doubt whatsoever that John was right to try to help these two. No one could deny the mother and son bond was strong, strong enough to make them defy the savagery of the gang and try to leave 'the life' — that took real courage, extraordinary courage. Carol's gesture behind her son's head had made it very clear she knew she was playing with their lives, but was willing to take that chance to be free.

When it was less than half an hour before evening opening time, and even less, probably, before Hoskins arrived on his bike, she locked the back part of the premises and went upstairs to change — ready for the Saturday evening trade. Alamat would be along to help her later, but had gone back to the stable-block to finish tidying away any remaining evidence that anyone had been in the far corner apartment. She paused on the landing as she heard the sound of a vehicle approaching. It was certainly not the cross between car and tractor of Cannon's jeep.

Where was he? How long would he be? She applied her eyeliner and mascara, daydreaming that perhaps if they retired to a desert island he might keep out of trouble. 'No!' she

135

exclaimed aloud. 'He'd be diving off some cliff-face to save something or other.'

She remembered she had not replaced all the brassware she had removed and cleaned on her last marathon of keeping-busy-while-John's-away. She took a couple of hunting horns through to the bar — there would just be time to hang these before she opened.

She had put them back on their hooks above the fireplace, closed the bar curtains, put a match to the log fire and stood back to admire the effect when the clock struck six and she went to open the front doors. Alamat immediately burst through them; he was white-faced and clearly terrified. The propulsion had been supplied by one of the three men behind him. 'This is the man that called before,' he blurted out and received a violent push which sent him sprawling between the bar stools.

'You were told to keep your mouth shut!'

Liz presumed this was Uncle Sean. The older man of the same build — but even larger and wider of shoulder — must, she thought, be the godfather, the boss, Luke Jakes, recently released from Leicester prison. The other, a mean-faced individual, was obviously an underling but he carried a gun, a .32 automatic. Liz noticed that the old man also held a gun, a small new .22 revolver, which would have been expensive. It went with his clothes, she thought, suit and fur-collared overcoat.

'We haven't time to fuck about,' Sean said. 'I saw the boy, Danny, here when I called the first time. We just want him and his mother then we'll be away, and if you're wise you'll forget we've ever been. Where are they?'

Alamat had struggled to his feet. The godfather grunted and the underling strode over to him and pistol-whipped the butt of his revolver across the little Croatian's face. 'You tell us, or we take the place apart.'

'You search,' Alamat shouted back, hand to the side of his face and blood seeping through his fingers. 'I tell you no one here.'

'We don't believe foreign scum,' the underling sneered.

'You, darling,' Sean addressed Liz, 'you tell us, or perhaps Mr John Cannon is around now? We'd really like to meet him.'

'We're the only ones — ' she began then broke off as she thought she heard the scuff of a foot in the porch, and it was the time their first-in-and-last-out customer, Hoskins, usually arrived. 'I don't know who you're looking for,' Liz added, raising her voice, 'but get out! Go away!'

Sean laughed aloud. 'We've done the stables, darling, now we'll do the pub — and you if you don't behave.'

'Stop wasting time,' the godfather ordered. 'Go and lock the front doors again then get on with it. I want this woman and kid dealt with quick and I want away. Been hanging about in this dammed country too long now.'

Liz felt her heart give a great leap of alarm. Men like this did not make careless remarks in front of possible witnesses.

Jakes chose a wooden armchair near the fire and with his revolver gestured Liz and Alamat to the bench opposite.

The search was thorough, ruthless and fast, but still tested the patience of the old man. He sat gently bouncing the gun on his knee, barrel weaving between Liz and Alamat as they listened to the noise of the search accompanied by an almost unbroken drone of complaint from the underling and Sean's increasingly impatient orders as they ranged from room to room, attics, bedrooms, then the ground floor.

'Nothing, boss,' the underling reported as they came back, but behind him Sean called, 'There's a locked door in this passage.'

'A locked door,' the old man said. 'Dear, dear — so where's the bloody key?'

'It's the cellar,' Liz answered, 'and always kept locked; no one could get down there.'

'Not unless you put them down there,

darling, and locked the door afterwards,' Sean said, his acid pseudo-politeness more menacing than his father.

'Key!' the old man demanded again.

'The landlord keeps it always in his pocket,' Alamat shouted but shrank to the far end of the bench as the gun-butt was raised again.

'I've no time for bloody games. Force it open!' the old man ordered.

The two left at his bidding, and Liz's lips parted as she thought of anyone hurling themselves at that door and finding themselves teetering at the top of those steps. Looking up she saw satisfaction on the old man's face.

'Down there, are they?'

There was the sound of a door being shouldered, once, twice. 'You really shouldn't have delayed us like this, it'll be the worse for both of you.' But as he raised the gun in her direction there was the sound of another shoulder charge, a great splintering of wood followed by a man's scream. A few seconds of silence then what sounded like hysterical pleading, and Liz was no surer now whether the high-pitched voice was man, woman, or boy. It all went on long enough for Luke Jakes to rise from his seat, but the shot that rang out was not from his gun. Then there was silence.

Liz hung on to her nerves, waiting for more screams, more shots as Sean dealt with whoever was left, his sister-in-law or nephew who so resembled him — but there was no challenge, no sound, nothing. She couldn't endure this any longer.

'Somebody should go to see,' she said.

'Sit down.' The old man aimed the neat little revolver at her heart, and Liz knew he could shoot both of them before either she or Alamat could reach him. Old he might be but he looked fit — prison life had probably done that for him.

Then they heard one man coming back.

'They were down there,' Sean reported, 'but the trapdoors up to the outside are open, they must have heard us and gone. I've been up and out that way, but it's pitch-black, we'd need an army, they could be anywhere.'

'And?' The old man gave a casual nod back toward the cellar.

He broke his leg,' Sean reported, 'I shot him, he always was a bloody animal.'

'Too much mouth,' the old man agreed and finally rose.

'Right, ready?' Sean, who now had the other revolver, asked, and raised it in Liz's direction.

She had known this moment would come and prepared to do the only thing she could when Sean Jakes fired. She watched his hand, his trigger finger, and balanced herself.

The revolver was raised to the level with her heart, but again the gun that went off was not in that room. It was outside, at the rear of the pub somewhere, then a whole series of shots, a fusillade, moving in like an advancing army.

'Chri — ' Sean began.

Liz forced herself to take a deep, containing breath, moved a step to one side of Alamat as another burst of approaching shots sounded from the back of the pub — and their time ran out.

As Sean fired, his father was on his way to the front doors shouting something about not being taken, and Liz threw herself full force at Alamat, taking him to the floor. It was some seconds before she was able to drag air into her lungs again; the pain increased, reached a peak, then finally the spasm passed and she realized she was just winded — and the men had gone.

She pushed herself up off Alamat, unsure whether he was cursing or praying in his native language, but she shushed him urgently so they could listen and try to understand what was going on outside. She prayed it did not involve Danny or his mother. They heard the sound of a vehicle leaving at speed.

'The cellar . . . ' Liz began moving from hands and knees to her feet as she made for the passage, but stopped as she realized there was someone coming back into the pub. Had only one Jakes left? Was Sean coming back?

Alamat too had heard. She indicated he should get down behind the bench, and intended to get behind the counter-end, split the target, when a voice called, 'Liz, it's me, Hoskins, you all right?'

'Alan.' It was only in moments of extreme emotion that she felt allowed to use the old poacher's Christian name, and this was one of them.

'Those shots?' she questioned as he came in carrying one of his shotguns.

He nodded. 'I got your message, get out and keep away, and,' he said with far more significance in his voice, 'I recognised Luke Jakes's voice, the old bugger, what was he up to? Then I saw 'im and one of the sons take off like Old Nick himself was after 'em.'

'He will be,' she said grimly, though she silently and reluctantly admitted it was more likely to be Cannon.

'All those shots?' Alamat questioned.

'Just a few strategically placed old bird-scarers,' Hoskins grinned, 'surprising how you can herd things in the direction you want 'em to go.' He stepped forward to look at the smaller man more carefully. 'What's happened to you?'

Liz wanted to ask him about the gun and the bird-scarers — he had not had time to go home to fetch them — but that question could wait.

'A gun butt,' Liz explained, 'but I think we've got worse in the cellar,' she told him as she led the way to the top of the steps — the cloying smell of warm blood met them.

'No, I'll go first. Come on, lassie ... ' Hoskins said as she looked likely to protest. He brushed past her with surprising speed for his age and before either of the others reached the bottom the body was covered by his waterproof coat. 'No hope,' he said, 'shot straight through the heart.'

From the amount of blood the body lay in, Liz believed it. The heart was obviously Sean's chosen target; these gunmen had MOs even for casual murder.

'Who?'

'One of theirs,' Liz said.

'But not a Jakes,' Hoskins stated. 'I could see that.'

'No, but they were looking for one of their wives and her son hiding down here.' She heard Hoskins blaspheme under his breath as she stepped carefully around the blood still slowly seeping between the floor bricks, and went towards the plastic curtain. The sacking where Carol and Danny had sat was still in place, the heavy strips moved slightly in the draught from outside.

Pushing her way through she noted the black rectangle of sky above her head; surely if Danny and his mother were out there they would not have gone far. Then she noticed that a tarpaulin that had lain flat and discarded for months was now rucked up into a heap in the slight recess to the side of the barrel chute. What was it covering?

She reached over, took the top edge and pulled it away quickly.

The two figures huddled together as tight as a Japanese netsuke did not move and both had their eyes closed, screwed tight.

'Carol, Danny, they've gone, you're safe,' she said, and when they still did not move she bent to touch Danny's shoulder. He flinched as if it had been a blow, then he opened his eyes.

'Mrs Cannon,' he said. 'They've gone?'

'Yes, come on, let's get you up into the warmth.'

Before there could be any further discussion, Hoskins busied himself closing the overhead doors.

'Sean,' Carol said as she began to uncurl herself, 'he shot the moaner . . .'

'But they didn't find us,' Danny said gratefully as Liz led the way. 'It was Mam's idea to open those doors and then hide in that dark corner.'

'And it worked,' Liz said, 'thank all the gods.'

'You learn a lot of tricks to outwit your husband when he's a Jakes,' Carol said grimly and positioned herself so she walked the side of the body, sparing Danny as much as she was able from the sight of the form beneath the green waterproof coat.

'Will you phone Mr Cannon?' Danny found his voice again as they reached the bar. 'He'll know what to do.'

'You'll have to tell the police,' Carol said matter-of-factly.

'You could say it was a raid,' Danny suggested, 'not tell them about us.'

'What I must do is re-lock the front doors and put up a notice to say we cannot open tonight,' Liz said. 'I'll do that now or we'll have some of the regulars in here and that'll complicate matters even more.'

'We are nothing but trouble,' Carol said, 'we should just go.'

'Where though, Mam?' Danny asked.

'I'll think of something,' Carol said but there was no hope in her voice.

'*We'll* think of something,' Liz emphasized.

Alamat went to re-lock the doors. Liz led the others through to the kitchen and wrote the notice stating 'unforeseen circumstances' which Alamat went back to tape to one of the glass panels of the outer doors. Hoskins put the kettle on and Liz tried to reach Cannon, but his phone gave her the information that 'The person you are calling cannot take your call right now, please leave a message and I will get back to you as soon as possible.' You'd better, she thought, and resolved that she would make one more call before she had a proper look at Alamat's face.

Jim Maddern answered his phone almost immediately with a short sharp, 'Yes?'

'Jim, its Liz, I've another problem.' She walked back through to the bar area, lit only by the fire, to tell him exactly what it was.

'I'll come,' he said, 'don't contact the police, not yet, it could be even more dangerous for Danny and his mother if you do.'

'Where are you?' she asked.

'Near Jones's house,' he replied.

11

Whatever the circumstances of his homecoming Cannon always turned along the last straight stretch of road to The Trap with a sense of relief, looking for the glitter of a dyke, a swathe of bushes and then . . . and then he should see the lights of the pub.

The jeep hit the verge as he lost concentration. Where were the lights? What had happened? The phone call he had not taken a few minutes ago . . . 'Where are the bloody lights?' he shouted in the full, unrestrained cockney tones of his fruit-and-veg-stall father.

He stopped the jeep in a great splattering of gravel, threw himself out, left the engine running and door wide open, sprinted to the back door and burst in like a deranged marsh-devil. Then he stopped, taking in Carol, Danny, Liz bending over Alamat, and finally Alamat with a large dressing on his forehead and the beginnings of discolouration which would be a black eye of impressive proportions.

'So,' he said, addressing Liz, 'are you all right? What's happened?'

'We have a murdered member of the Jakes gang in the cellar,' she said.

Don't beat about the bush, he thought. When he immediately made for the cellar, Liz followed, telling him the story as they went. He took in the smashed door, switched on the light and went down, lifted Hoskins's coat, aware they both stood reviewing the body keeping the old professional emotional distance in order to deal.

'Broke his leg and had too much to say,' Liz said.

'So Sean Jakes executed him.' Cannon lowered the coat gently and wondered if this was the one who'd had too much to say at the Smithsons' house. 'And,' he added, 'I think it's not the only man they've killed today.' He told of his find in the back of the dumped Mercedes van.

'I think we have to wait for Maddern to arrive before we do anything . . . ' Liz began.

'If he was at Jones's home he shouldn't be long,' he said.

'So you knew where he was,' she said.

'We decided someone should keep an eye on his movements,' he answered. As they reached the bar he caught her hand. 'You really all right?' he asked.

She nodded. 'You?' she asked and received an answering nod. 'But I think we're in this well over our heads.'

'Talking of heads, should we ask the doctor to see Alamat?'

'He says not . . . ' she broke off as they heard the sound of another car pulling on to the gravel.

By the time they reached the kitchen, Maddern was there, and he had a different air about him. He extended his hand towards Cannon, who automatically held out his. The sergeant dropped the jeep keys into his palm. Cannon half expected to be charged with leaving a vehicle running while unattended. Maddern was no longer a victim, this was a man of the law with all his old authority — and there was no doubting the comfort Danny got from his presence.

'You going to help us, Sarge?' he asked.

'This your mam?' Maddern asked.

Danny nodded enthusiastically and told his mother, 'We'll be all right, now Mr Cannon *and* Sarge are here.'

'Yes, I've booked a room for the two of you at the travel inn where I'm staying,' he said, 'and I'm going to take you there as soon as I've sorted a minor problem. Could you come and have a look at my car?' he asked Cannon.

'There's — ' Danny began, ' — in the cellar, Sarge.'

'Yes, I know what's happened,' he said,

then nodded to Hoskins and added, 'glad you're here.'

'Are you?' Hoskins asked cautiously.

'We all are,' Cannon said as he picked up the torch from the table and followed Maddern. It was not the time to say more.

'It's not a mechanical problem,' Maddern told him as Cannon swept the beam of light over the Peugeot, 'it's on the back seat.'

Cannon went to the back and shone the light in onto a large dog, a large full-grown greyhound, long legs concertinaed beneath bony frame, dark eyes wary and blinking in the light.

'Where have you picked that up from? It's hardly the time to be dealing with stray dogs,' Cannon said.

'It belongs to Jones.'

'Jones?'

'I found the perfect place to keep watch on him. At the end of his garden there's a purpose-built bird-watching hut someone had built years ago, the whole place is more like the pad you'd expect a chief constable to have than an inspector,' Maddern said. Cannon wondered not for the first time if the keys to the place had not been dropped into Jones's palm as a sweetener and a lasting obligation to the Jakeses. He remembered the diamond ring tossed to Danny.

'I didn't realize Jones wasn't there for a start, his car was in the drive,' Maddern was saying, 'then he came back on his own in a police patrol car — which surprised me a bit — and in a right mood, as far as I could judge. The place is isolated and they don't bother drawing curtains. I could keep my binoculars trained on Jones and his missus most of the time. He went upstairs and she's following, backwards and forwards arguing with him, but whatever she's saying he's not having any of it. He hurls suitcases on to a bed and begins packing.'

'He could be going on holiday,' Cannon suggested.

'Hold on,' Maddern said.

'Not long after, he comes out with his dog on a lead, goes off along a sandy path in the dunes. Just walking the dog, I thought, but he'd no intention the dog should enjoy it. He marched along and if it tried to stop he yanked it on hard, much more like the man I know. I didn't try to follow him, but I watched him go into a clump of pines beyond a little row of old beach-huts. While he's gone, his wife spends much of the time on her phone, and she's still walking up and down, up and down past the windows while she's talking.'

'Go on,' Cannon said grimly.

151

'Then he comes back without the dog, goes in, and they're arguing in earnest now. She throws her mobile at him but he ducks and just goes on packing. I thought they were leaving there and then, but she goes into the kitchen, looks as if she's preparing a meal and he comes down in lounging pyjamas.' he paused. 'I knew because the girls bought me the same pair for Christmas. Anyway, he begins to go through a desk. They look settled for a bit so I walk over to the trees and find the dog strung up.'

'What d'you mean strung up?'

'Hanging,' Maddern said. 'The bastard had put a rope round its neck, thrown it over a branch, pulled the dog up and left it to strangle itself. It'd only lasted as long as it had because it was managing to scrabble its back legs up the trunk of the tree and take some of the weight off its neck. It was getting very weak,' Maddern leaned down to look in at the animal, 'but I'm pretty sure it's going to be all right.'

'The bastard,' Cannon repeated. 'I heard that's how some of 'em dispatch their greyhounds up where he comes from, if they stop winning.' He thought of Jones's lack of advancement since he came to the area and wondered if he was hanging up his career for something more immediate from the Jakeses, and more substantial if gold, anything like the Brink's Mat robbery, was involved.

'I wondered if old Hoskins would take the dog on for a bit, keep it out of sight?' Maddern said.

'We'll ask, but the woman and the boy, do you think the travel inn is a good place?' Cannon wondered as they hovered outside.

'It's out of the immediate area,' Maddern said, 'no better place to lose people than in a crowd, and there everyone is busy about their own affairs and their own journeys.'

'Right, so that's your next move,' Cannon said.

'Then back to the Jones's pad, we keep each other informed all the time and — '

'We consider our next move,' Cannon said, 'who we can go to . . . who you trust.'

Maddern did not reply.

'We have evidence enough about the Jakes family — '

' — but not about Jones,' Maddern said grimly, 'and prising out a bent copper would mean more to me. I love my job, been proud to be part of it all . . . ' He tailed off; emotional outpourings were not part of his make-up.

'So once you've gone,' Cannon said, 'I shall ring the police, say we've had a raid, three men broke in, injured Alamat, smashed the

153

cellar door perhaps thinking it might be a spirits and cigarette store, one fell and broke his leg and the other shot him to shut him up, then the other two made off empty-handed.'

'All almost true as far as it goes,' Maddern commented, 'good thing you're on the side of the righteous, and . . . ' he paused, 'it's going to be very interesting who turns up after you ring the station.'

12

It was Jones. His face was its normal pale mask with small watchful eyes, but tonight there was something else. Tonight he looked as if he'd drawn in his lips and cheeks prior to giving the derogatory-sounding suck of his teeth — but had forgotten to complete the trick.

Cannon had hardly let him into the kitchen when two further cars pulled in. Jones seemed agitated by their arrival. Cannon wondered if he had wanted time on his own to view the body. Outside under the lights he saw two uniformed constables being detailed to deal with other cars and customers. Two men in plain clothes came towards Cannon. He recognized one, Detective Inspector Betterson of the regional crime squad, and he knew the other man by sight as his detective sergeant.

'In the line of fire again,' Betterson greeted him as Cannon led the way into the kitchen.

'Well, my partner was,' he said. 'I didn't arrive until it was all over.'

The first thing Betterson did was send for the doctor to look at Alamat, view the body, its position and its surroundings, then he began to listen in more detail to what had taken place. To keep Jones in ignorance and as hastily agreed with Hoskins and Alamat, the presence of Carol Smithson, Danny, Sergeant Maddern and Jones's dog (dropped off in Hoskins's kitchen and left with water and biscuits as instructed by the old man) was omitted from all their stories. It worked well, Cannon thought, with Hoskins in particular receiving some admiration from the detectives for picking up Liz's warning not to enter the pub and then managing to frighten them off, 'with bird scarers'. Betterson was both incredulous and impressed.

'And you were where?' Betterson asked Cannon.

'Coming back from the village.'

'The village?'

'The newsagent's.'

'Right, and when did you realize something was wrong?'

'As I came down the road, the outside lights were not on,' Cannon said. He was hopeful of being quickly left to one side as the routine of questioning, statements and forensics began to take over the untidy business of sudden violent death and make it into a manageable format. At his most cynical Cannon had always seen the process as a kind of street-cleansing exercise. Put up the screens, shield the public from the worst with the ubiquitous blue and white tape. Even now he could hear a loud, intense murmur of voices from the front of The Trap as his customers were turned away. Speculation would be rife, but none of it, he imagined, would be anywhere near the truth.

But Betterson had not finished with him. 'So do you think they were looking for your safe, Mr Cannon?'

The question sent a slight pang of concern through Cannon's system as he thought of the diamond ring dropped into the small drawer below the cash takings and documents he kept in the safe. He shook his head. 'It was never mentioned,' he answered.

'The class of criminals who make such a daring entry to premises just at opening time, and with firearms, usually have a specific objective,' Betterson said, watching Cannon closely. 'When do you bank, Mr Cannon?' the detective persisted.

'Monday, first thing after the weekend.'

'So Saturday before the evening opening hour is not a good time to raid for money?'

'No.'

'The cash would not be a large amount?'

Cannon shook his head. 'Not at this time of year anyway.'

Whether this was leading to being asked to display the safe, which was in fact no more than a strong box inside an old gun cabinet bolted to the wall of the pantry, Cannon did not find out, for Jones's mobile burbled. His private phone, Cannon noted as Jones turned away to answer it.

'June?' he queried. 'What! When?'

Betterson had turned to Liz and indicated they might go through to the bar where his sergeant had finished interviewing Hoskins, when Jones interrupted. 'It's my wife, she's been out looking for our dog and she's found a body, a man's body. It could be just an old man died out walking, but I feel I should go back to her.'

'Of course,' Betterson responded immediately, 'my sergeant will go with you. The Scene of Crime people are on their way here so they'll want us out of the way.'

Liz glanced at Cannon as both registered the fact that Jones's wife had found a body while looking for a dog her husband had left to die — and Cannon had a very bad feeling about the 'old man'.

When Jones and the detective sergeant had gone it left only Hoskins, Liz and Cannon with Betterson. Alamat had told his story, been taken to his room and the doctor was with him. Hoskins, who had also made his statement, was asked whether he was planning to leave the area.

'Born here, not planning to move,' he answered, deadpan. He was told he could go but his coat would be needed by forensics.

'Right,' Hoskins said and, nodding his goodnights, left.

Cannon touched a metaphorical cap to him; he had played his part to perfection.

When he had gone, Betterson stretched himself to his full height, exhaled heartily and pronounced, 'Well,' as if now he could start the job in hand properly, 'you seem to be having traumatic times.' He looked from one to the other, then focusing on Cannon added, 'Traumatic trips . . . ' When this drew no response, he added, 'to Leicester.'

'It had a few unpleasant surprises,' Cannon answered, quickly adding his own question, 'I understand you and the Leicester Police are liaising?'

'Leicester?' Betterson frowned, then said, 'I'd hardly call it liaising, we certainly had a call to check your identity. In a murder case we don't want to let anyone go until we're sure we can contact them again, as you will know. They were satisfied about Sergeant Maddern but unsure why you were there.'

'I felt he needed company, I consider

myself a friend of Jim Maddern,' Cannon said.

'Bit of family trouble, I understand.' Betterson nodded. 'Jones told me he's put him on leave to sort it out.'

'Did he?' Cannon began, images of Maddern's ruined home in his mind, and he too wondered if Jones had arranged to have it done to keep Maddern — the man with too much local knowledge — out of the way.

There was another flurry of activity in the doorway and four plain-clothed officers piled in. There were Scene of Crime officers, officers with cases, cameras, tripods and white suits. Betterson greeted their manager as they all proceeded to pull on their protective pristine coveralls while the Detective Inspector gave a résumé of events.

'We have a lounge upstairs, we could go there out of the way,' Cannon volunteered.

Betterson nodded. 'I'll come and see you up there when I've shown these officers everything.'

Cannon and Liz retreated to their spacious lounge, which in daylight commanded a broad view of marsh, sea and sky, with Cannon's bird-watching telescope in the central window.

'So what's this about looking for the dog and finding a body?' Liz asked.

'Is this body a plant they want found?' Cannon wondered.

'But why?' Liz asked.

'A decoy of some kind,' Cannon suggested, 'to divert attention from somewhere else, but it's *who* it is that worries me.'

'What worries me is at what point do we — ' Liz hesitated and her voice fell, 'tell all?'

'I want Maddern by my side, in all senses of the word, when we do,' Cannon said. 'I don't think Betterson has any doubts about Jones at all. We mustn't wrong-foot Maddern. He may think he doesn't care about losing his job and his pension now while his family are threatened, but he would later.'

'It would be the loss of local respect that would hit him hardest,' Liz was saying as there was a knock at the door, and Betterson came in.

Cannon gestured towards an armchair, but Betterson shook his head. 'I must get over to Inspector Jones, but I have a message for you,' he said, 'from an old colleague. Detective Chief Inspector Robert Austin.'

'*Chief* Inspector!' Cannon exclaimed. 'Well done, Robert. He was my sergeant when I was in the Met,' he told Betterson. 'So when did you see Austin?'

'It's the Met we're liaising with, not

Leicester, they believe we have a couple of vicious criminal gangs about to clash here. Chief Inspector Austin thinks the London lot are already moving in to settle old scores.'

'With a local gang?' Cannon asked.

Betterson nodded. 'We've been doubtful, particularly when the Met said they were talking of a king's ransom in gold bars, but the man shot in your cellar . . . ' he paused, 'is one of our local villains. Not only that but Inspector Jones, through his local contacts, believes this body found on the estuary is also connected. Good man, Jones, built up local knowledge, and does his paperwork on time, not many are good at both.'

Betterson, already on his way to the door, added 'You'll be closed until the forensic people have finished, of course, but we'll do it all as soon as we can. The only mystery is why these people chose to break into your premises. They must have thought you had *something* they wanted.'

'Well, Jones was here drinking the other night,' Liz said. 'Perhaps they thought they might waylay him.'

'And pick up a bit of loot on the side,' Cannon added.

The propositions were way out, but they certainly seemed to give Betterson another straw to chew on.

When he had gone, Cannon looked at Liz with raised eyebrows, but Liz tossed her head defiantly. 'Jones is using everyone for his own ends, why shouldn't we use him. I don't want you in lock-up for abducting vital witnesses and withholding evidence, and,' she added with extreme sarcasm, 'what's this about Jones, the perfect copper, with his *local knowledge*?'

'It's probably one of these classic cases where Jones is giving the police — '

'His colleagues,' Liz added bitterly.

Cannon nodded, his face grim. ' — a few valid bits of information they could work on to make him look good to his superiors, while diverting attention from the true activities of the Jakes clan — leaving them free to gather up the loot and make a run for it before the opposition get organized.'

'So what is *our* plan of action?' Liz asked, 'Now, at this moment.'

'We wait until the police have finished here and until we hear from Maddern that Danny and his mother are safe.'

'And why are we doing these things?' Liz added relentlessly.

Cannon lifted his hand and counted the reasons. 'First, because the gold has been moved and we don't know where to. Second, because we suspect Jones may be trying to send the police in the wrong direction. Third, we don't want to reveal where Carol Smithson and Danny are because, if Jones is a traitor, that could lead to their deaths. Fourth, Maddern is the key person the Jakeses and Jones are trying to shut up and they've done everything now except carry out their threats to murder either him or one of his family.' Having counted along all his fingers, he hovered above his thumb.

'You needn't go on,' Liz said. 'I just hope we hear from Maddern quickly.'

There was a police presence at The Trap all that night, the next day and night and until lunchtime on the Monday, during which Cannon and Liz learned that the body found on the coast was that of William Thompson, who had apparently drowned. Cannon had been incredulous.

'Drowned!' he exclaimed in private to Liz. 'They are not trying to say he went especially, all the way from Snyder Crescent to the sea, to drown himself? Never!'

He watched the police tape being gathered up and the last of their vehicles move away, but he grumbled his way around the public house as they spent the rest of the day putting things to rights, removing the last traces of forensic activity, replacing chairs and tables to usual positions. They had decided to give themselves the whole of Tuesday to, as Liz said, 'get their minds in gear again for business' and not to reopen until the Wednesday morning. Cannon had contacted a local carpenter who could repair the cellar door on the Tuesday and put handrails down both sides of the steps. Both wondered why they had not had this done before. Cannon wondered how long it would take for him to stop noticing the over-clean area of brickwork at the bottom of the steps.

Both were on high alert for the call from Jim Maddern. Every time the phone rang, nerves tingled — but it was never Maddern.

13

By midday Tuesday, Cannon was looking for things to do, things to distract himself from endless calculations of how long it had been since Maddern had left with Danny and his mother. The big question was: why wasn't he answering his phone? He got out the road map and Liz used the internet to confirm the nearest motorway service-station hotel, then suggested, 'Why not go for a jog, help you relax.'

'How will that help?'

'If we've heard nothing by the time you come back we'll both go to the service station and make discreet enquiries,' she said. 'Alamat looks a mess but says he's fine, he can take any calls and phone us if he hears anything.'

It was a relief to slip on joggers and trainers, to launch himself into steady, muscle-stretching exercise. The air was mild, still, not how he liked it, as he padded along narrow lanes, in the opposite direction to his usual routes. The wide, flat countryside, views of meadows interspersed with wide drainage dykes and the great expanse of sky were all part of everything he would have enjoyed about a normal run. This wasn't a normal run, not a normal day. If he were still in the Met it would be normal, his mind full of regrets about victims, concerns about those threatened, but most of all concern for a man he still felt to be a colleague. 'Once a policeman, always a policeman,' he muttered.

He wanted to be doing something, pushing things forward to a conclusion, to fair play, to justice. The only useful thing he had decided he could do on this run was go and see Hoskins and the dog.

It was with a sense of some irritation that he realized someone was coming towards him. He did like his runs solitary, but this was midday not early morning. Then he realized that the man approaching was Hoskins, on his bike, with the dog on a long piece of garden twine running by his side.

'Kept hearing this noise,' Hoskins shouted as they neared each other, and he slowed to a halt. Cannon caught the bike and then held on to the twine as Hoskins made an excited and clumsy dismount.

'Noise?' he queried as Hoskins, both hands free, now rummaged in his capacious coat-pockets. With a grunt of satisfaction he located something with his right hand.

'Think I heard it last night when I took the

dog out at bedtime, very faint, then it stopped. Then this morning I heard it again, several times and realized it was coming from the same place all the time.'

He finally extricated a mobile phone from a tangle of more twine. 'It's Jim Maddern's,' he said. 'It's got his name inside the cover.'

Cannon felt the bottom of his stomach chill. 'Where did you find it?' he asked.

Hoskins pointed back the way he had come. 'Opposite my place, the lane that leads to the main road.'

'Show me,' Cannon said.

Hoskins took the bike and Cannon held on to the dog, which seemed placidly to accept what was meted out to it, and walked with all the quiet elegance these lanky dogs have.

'Its name's Charlie,' Hoskins said, 'it's on his collar. He doesn't know much about kindness; if I put my hand out to him he cowers, but he'll improve.'

'You'll keep him?'

Hoskins nodded and it was left at that as they reached the T-junction with its signpost indicating it led on to the town of Boston.

'It were here, near the edge of the road.' He indicated a spot about six metres into the lane. 'Can't understand it. I mean, he would have been driving his car, wouldn't he, why should he get out and drop his phone?' His

168

tone went from anxiety to grumbling as he added, 'Too many bloody queer things going on around here.'

'Such as?' Cannon asked as he scanned the verges both sides and then the road ahead. There was a tyre mark as if a vehicle had swung sharply into the lane, gone to the right then corrected sharply to the left — or had it pulled over in front of another vehicle? Maddern's vehicle?

'I don't know what's going on, but knew it would be serious from the second you mentioned the name Jakes. Not too sure I want to know, but I tell you one thing — while most of us round here just make ends meet there are some who have ready money to pay out huge sums for things.'

'Such as?' Cannon repeated.

'I know one chap, and heard from him of three others, *three others*, who've been paid over the odds *in cash* for their motor cruisers.'

'Motor cruisers?' Cannon questioned, not sure how relevant this would be or where this fitted into the equation.

'I know the holiday season's coming, but at this time of year . . . ' Hoskins turned his lips down in disbelief and doubt, 'nobody's that desperate for a boat.'

'No,' Cannon said, the possibility of it

being someone money-laundering flipping in and out of his mind as he found there were eight missed calls on Maddern's phone.

'You'll let him have it back?' Hoskins asked.

Cannon was aware Hoskins watched him carefully as if to gauge how worried he was about the sergeant. 'I'll drive over to where I think he is as soon as I get back,' he said, 'but I can't tell you more than that.'

'When do you open again?' Hoskins asked.

'Tomorrow,' Cannon replied.

'I'll see you then,' he said as they reached his cottage. Hoskins leaned his bike on the fence, took over the dog and Cannon began a sprint back to The Trap fast enough to make it feel like there was a breeze.

He burst into the back door, ready to hurry Liz on the way to the service station, but she was on the phone and waved his haste down. 'He's just come back, I'll pass you over.'

'Yes!' he said sharply.

'Dear, dear,' an educated voice said mildly.

'Austin!' he immediately recognized the voice that could command attention without volume and in its lower register revealed his mother's French origins. 'Just who I need!' Cannon exclaimed.

Chief Inspector Austin laughed, briefly, then went on. 'The man shot in your cellar,' he stated the premise for his call, then his concern, 'a lackey of your local villains, the Jakeses.'

'Known to the police here for generations, and . . .'

'I've not much time . . .' Austin interrupted, but there was respect in his voice for his old superior as he went on, 'Godfather Jakes just out of prison, regrouping his family and his assets in a dash to renew 'the life-style' in a new venue. Unfortunately we've no clue where this might be.'

Cannon listened intently, realized Austin was walking as he talked, walking quickly.

'This new life will be funded by assets hijacked from a London gang. The story in gangland is both gangs decided to do the same heist. The Faima . . .'

'The what?' Cannon muttered. 'Never heard of them.'

'Fay-ma,' Austin pronounced, 'anagram of Mafia. They've grown up from urchins to villains since your time. The Faima got there first, did the job, took the risks, then the Jakeses came in and took the loot from them with minimum trouble and only a few hundred metres from the security firm's gates. There's been sniping ever since, several murders but, like the Brink's Mat job, the majority of the gold is still out there. We're sure of that, because every one of the Faima is now either in your area, or on the motorways keeping watch for the Jakeses.'

'The motorways,' Cannon repeated, then added, 'I know some of this.'

'Why am I not surprised?' Austin said.

'Are you in the area? I need to see you, talk face to face.'

'Tomorrow,' he said briefly, 'early.'

'Right,' Cannon answered.

'Keep a low profile,' Austin said, 'and be warned: these villains have made a study of all the Mafia's arts.'

'I know their ideas about family,' Cannon muttered as he closed the line and, turning to Liz, added, 'You drive and I'll talk.'

'The service station?' she queried. 'And you're going like that?'

'Yes and yes. I'll tell you about this,' he brandished the phone, 'Maddern's, found at the side of the road.'

★　★　★

In under an hour, and after the telling about Austin and Hoskins, they reached the service station in a dour mood. They located the square accommodation block behind the restaurants, protected from traffic noise by a bank and a screen of evergreen laurels and rhododendrons. They walked into reception and, as planned, Liz did the talking.

The girl behind the desk seemed entranced by her own silver-flecked black nail-polish, turning her fingers this way and that to see them glint under the lights. Her young features were wiped out by a pallid mask of make-up, her eyes as black and exaggerated as any ancient Egyptian queen. She looked up reluctantly only after the usual throat-clearing and Liz had knocked on the counter almost beneath her nose. Cannon wondered how she'd got the job — a young, susceptible, male manager?

'I've arranged to meet an old friend and her thirteen-year-old son here,' Liz said, 'I wonder if you could tell me if they've arrived.'

'A man booked for his sister and her son, but they didn't come,' the girl answered, her mouth almost a sneer.

'Her brother would be staying here,' Liz said, 'a big man, six foot, well built, may have been here a day or two.'

The girl finally looked at the registration book. 'Yeah, know him, he's booked till the end of next week,' she conceded.

'So he's not here now?' Cannon asked.

She shrugged.

'Could you ring his room? Tell him Liz and John are here.'

Another shrug. 'I suppose.'

There was no answer. They thanked the girl and turned to leave, but both glanced back as they reached the entrance. The girl was entranced by her nails once more and as one they turned left along the corridor towards the accommodation.

'Room 76,' Cannon whispered.

'I know, I saw,' she said. 'Come on.'

Room 76 was left, just beyond the first corner. They knocked and waited, there was a trolley laden with towels and cleaning materials further along. A middle-aged woman in maid's uniform and apron came out of a room a few doors away.

'Good morning,' she said, 'I've just done that room, there's no one in. In fact the gentleman hasn't slept in the bed for a night or two, but he's been back and brought more of his things.'

'Thanks for telling us,' Liz said.

'We're also looking for a woman in her thirties with her son, a thirteen-year-old . . . ' Cannon said and the woman's attitude changed.

She merely shook her head. 'You can get out by that door there,' she said, 'saves going all the way back to reception, but you can't get back in that way.'

They nodded their thanks and left. 'A

question too far,' Liz said, 'she'll be worrying now she's said too much.'

'She thinks we're police,' Cannon guessed, 'but I think we can take it none of them are here.'

'So where, and what do we do next?'

'We should check the car parks for Maddern's car before we leave.'

After they had walked every rank of cars and found one blue Peugeot but not Maddern's, Liz said, 'I could do with a cup of tea and a bun.'

Cannon blew out his lips in despair. 'Feel I should neither eat nor drink till we've found them.'

'You don't function well without regular food,' she said with certainty, 'and there's Austin coming crack of dawn.'

'Yes,' he agreed, 'I should make a few notes before he arrives, don't want to dither about.'

'And tell all?' she asked.

'Yes, it's time, gone time, for some proper action this end,' he said and, picking up a tray, banged it decisively on the end of the counter rails. A middle-aged woman, smartly dressed, complete with brown tweed trilby-type hat, turned and glared at him, looked his jogging outfit up and down, tipped her head up and away in some distaste and tried to hurry her husband along.

To add to their mutual discomfort a table for four emptied as they approached the crowded restaurant area and they found themselves sharing the same table.

Liz was too grateful for the tea and intake of sugar in the shape of an iced bun to care. Cannon sat where he could see the length of the concourse and stared resolutely out of the window. He held his mug of hot chocolate to his lips, sipping slowly, resisting the impulse to do so as noisily as possible.

It was the approach of four men, two from each end of the walkway — each pair having seemingly consulted with a third, better-dressed colleague — that drew his attention. The better-dressed went their ways, the four met at the doorway of the restaurant and conferred, their presence holding the automatic doors open as they stood gazing all around. The woman with the tweed hat turned round sharply as the draught caught her, but as she opened her mouth to reprimand the men, obviously having had enough of this place and its dodgy customers, Cannon touched her foot with his muddy trainer. When she swung sharply back towards him he shook his head minimally. She opened her mouth to reprimand him, but Liz pushed the assortment of sugars and sweetener packets over to her and said,

176

'Please, have sugar.'

The woman's mouth opened, but something in the manner of the two who shared their table made her do as she was told. Cannon went on looking over the top of his mug and Liz engaged the woman and her husband in conversation.

Cannon had seen men like this almost every other day when he worked in London, either when he was investigating gangland territory, as they were hauled in and on their way to the cells, or later in smarter gear as they attended the courts. However old they were, they never lost that teenage swagger.

Even from the doorway they made their presence felt and, for a moment, conversation levels dropped as they split and went different ways right through the restaurant, this time examining every individual.

As with many who had spent hours under the tattooists' needles, their arms were bare, looked more blue than flesh-coloured and the one who passed nearest to their table had 'FAIMA' tattooed down his right cheek.

14

Cannon did not mince his words. 'I think you have a corrupt officer at this end.'

Austin had arrived at 7 a.m. looking every inch a Metropolitan Chief Inspector. A powerfully built man, he was an imposing figure in full uniform. 'Meeting at nine,' he explained the full dress after the initial greetings. They were all so pleased to see each other again, the grins had been wide, the hugs fierce and getting down to the pressing business in hand had needed willpower.

'Lounge or kitchen?' Austin asked.

'Lounge,' Cannon replied, 'I've made a few notes.'

'In the usual format, I hope,' Austin said.

'Clear and in full colour, you'll see.' Cannon led the way, carrying the breakfast tray Liz had prepared for them all.

'Ah!' Austin exclaimed as he walked into the lounge. 'The old logic bubbles. I miss them and I still miss you, old boy.' With all the disarming charm of his French mother and tact of his barrister father, he added, 'I miss you both, of course.'

He went to stand in front of the series of

cards Cannon had laid out on the table, looking like the spread of a family tree.

'Red bubbles for certainties,' Austin said as he approached the table and then fell silent. 'So what's this about Jones's dog and Sergeant Maddern's phone found in a lane, and he with ... ' Austin looked up incredulously, 'the wife and son of one of the Jakeses missing together?'

'Coffee?' Liz asked and poured without waiting for an answer.

'And,' Austin exclaimed, 'a policeman's house trashed? There's a lot of certainties here I've heard nothing about. Why Maddern? He seems to be being targeted.'

The smell of hot, strong, filter coffee pervaded the room and Cannon breathed a sigh of relief. At last someone had grasped the nub of the case, the centre of his concern.

'Because,' Liz said, 'he recognized a local family face in the features of his newspaper delivery boy. His name is Danny Smithson, but his father was a Jakes.' She straightened from pouring her own coffee. 'Oh!' she said turning to Cannon, 'I remember, I think,' and began to quote:

"'I am the family face;
Flesh perishes, I live on,
Projecting trait and trace

179

Through time to times anon . . . ''

As she stalled Austin took up the poem:

"'And leaping from place to place
Over oblivion.

The years-heired feature that can
In curve and voice and eye
Despise the human span
Of durance — that is I;
The eternal thing in man,
That heeds no call to die.''

'Thomas Hardy, of course!' Liz exclaimed, 'I remember now.'

'Heredity,' Austin added the title, putting his cap on the table and unbuttoning his jacket.

'And that was the beginning of the Maddern family's troubles,' Cannon said, pointing along the line of interlinked red circles detailing the newspaper cuttings, the photographing of the sergeant's younger daughters, the threats to the eldest, the hearse, the wreath, the murder in the Leicester park. Keeping his finger on the word Leicester he added, 'Where Jim Maddern and I witnessed the old man Jakes met out of prison by a stretch limo.'

'You'd better tell me all,' Austin said, taking his jacket off and hanging it on the back of a chair before helping himself to croissants, jam and butter.

The coffee was gone and the mood of the room sombre when Cannon had told all he knew for certain — all he had done — and handed over the ring surrendered to him by Carol Smithson. When he rose and went back to the table, Austin followed. 'Now,' Cannon said, pointing to the cards with the green-circled information, 'we come to the suppositions.'

Austin touched the name featured in several of these cards. 'Hoskins,' he said. 'I remember him well, he's still pretty sharp, judging by how you say he reacted to your trauma and body in your cellar.'

'Yes,' Cannon agreed, 'and like Maddern and the neighbour, Thompson, whose body was found on the Wash,' Cannon stabbed back to a red circle, 'all have tried to tell Jones that the Jakeses were back and that it meant *big* trouble.'

'So,' Austin said, watching his old boss steadily for reaction as he went on, 'your assumption that Jones is a wrong-un is mainly the dog left tied up, and his wife then searching for it, and finding the neighbour's body. In which case the body was deliberately taken there to throw us off the scent. The other thing of course is that now the stolen goods have been moved, Jones — if he is implicated — will know where they are, and be very anxious to keep them on his own radar. But — '

' — If you move too quickly you could lose the lot — the loot, possibly the lives of Maddern, Carol Smithson and her son . . . ' Cannon said.

'I want to avoid the possibility of local mayhem when the two gangs finally clash,' Austin said, 'which they will. It was perhaps a blessing that Maddern and his charges were not there at that service station.'

'But where are they?' Cannon asked. 'Maddern's not a man to lose his phone. I think he managed to drop it from his pocket as he was hustled from his own car to another — so where is *his* car?'

'I'll put out a general call, observation only if it's on the move,' Austin stated, then looked down again at the green circled information. 'The suppositions about motor cruisers? Is this a separate money-laundering affair do you think?'

'It could be, but I could find out more about the men who sold their cruisers from Hoskins,' Cannon suggested. 'There's something about the neighbour's body on the coast, the Faima watching the motorways, and men buying boats for cash that makes me uneasy. The Jakeses are local. The old man in particular would have grown up here — he'd know the waterways.'

'I must go,' Austin said, 'but I guess you'll see Hoskins today.'

Cannon nodded and Austin left with the promise to try to be back, or in touch, later in the day.

He was in touch within the half hour. Maddern's car had not been found but there were reports of a similar vehicle being seen not far from where Thompson's body had lain at the edge of the tide.

'So are they expecting to find evidence that Thompson's body was . . . ' Liz said, abruptly aware that whatever she said at that moment her partner would not hear. He was standing as if turned to stone, eyes open but not seeing, and she knew an idea, probably an outrageous idea, was circling his brain. 'John?' she queried, but gently, recognizing what she had come to know as one of his moments of epiphany, when he seemed to see more than was obvious.

'No, not Maddern's, that's a red herring,' he murmured, unable to drag himself from the image of that decent old man lying on a cold, desolate beach. Death would have drained his great red nose of colour.

He remembered the blood in the back of the abandoned white van, then the police car going the opposite way — and Maddern saying Jones had arrived home in a police car. Had the inspector 'rectified' a mistake being made by the Jakeses? Had they been going to dump the body at a place which might have given a clue to where they and the loot were being reassembled for a final getaway? If so, that would mean Jones had used a police vehicle to move a murder victim.

'Hmm,' he said again but this time he looked at her.

'What have you decided to do?' she asked with some trepidation.

'Go with Hoskins to see these people who have sold boats for cash.'

He and Hoskins left in the jeep after the morning pub opening hours. 'We shouldn't be too long,' he said.

★ ★ ★

'I was a bit worried about it, have to say, but . . . ' the man who had sold his two-berth cabin cruiser for cash, said, 'I'd had it for sale for a couple of years and my wife was getting worse. Now I can get extra help without filling in any more forms or answering more questions,' he added with distaste. 'We've always been independent and I'm going to see that the rest of my Viv's life is a bit more comfortable from now on.'

Hoskins had said he knew their cherished motor cruiser had been up for sale for ten thousand pounds. There would have been questions asked by any bank or building society if he'd arrived with that much cash. Cannon wondered where the pensioner had stashed the money. He didn't ask. The approach had been careful, through Hoskins, an old acquaintance, and based on the man's assumption that Cannon had a similar boat for sale. When they were leaving he said he'd noticed the local boatyard had several empty spaces where motor cruisers had stood for some time. 'So it seems boats are suddenly selling — you might be lucky.'

'Next stop the boatyard, then,' Cannon said as they climbed back into the jeep. 'You know it?'

'Aye, and the owner. Now there's a chap who wouldn't turn a hair at any amount of cash as long as he was doing a deal.'

'So how do we approach this one?'

'As a customer,' Hoskins said immediately. 'You'll get nothing out of Mr Slingsby unless he thinks he's going to get something out of you.'

★　★　★

The bungalow on the small neat estate was a world away from the boatyard complex, which must have covered quite a few acres, consisted of many sheds, many boats in all stages of dismantling or repair, and even in one corner of complete dereliction.

A young man in navy overalls came striding over to them. 'Hello, Mr Hoskins, how are y'doing? Not come to buy a boat, 'ave you?'

Hoskins chuckled, greeted the young man with enthusiasm. 'Not on the profits you lot pay for my rabbits, young Callum.' By a suggestive nod, he implied that Cannon might be in the market.

'Another customer; old Slingsby'll be beside himself, three cruisers gone out recently,' Callum told them, dropping his voice as a burly man in very clean overalls walked towards them. He held his shoulders back and his arms slightly out to his sides as if he was about to star in a wrestling match. His hair was silver, his complexion ruddy and his eyes small and sharp. Cannon thought his overalls looked as if *he* handled nothing dirtier than money.

'Mr Slingsby,' Callum introduced.

'Looking for me?' the man questioned and while he obviously knew Alan Hoskins he

186

neither looked at him nor spoke to him.

'You deal in motor-cruisers . . . ' Cannon began.

'I do. You interested?'

'Very,' he answered just as shortly, 'but I'm in a hurry.'

Slingsby glanced at him more sharply. 'To purchase?'

'Price and condition important. What've you got?' Two, he thought, can play at this monosyllabic conversation game.

'How many berths?' Slingsby asked, turning to lead the way further into the yard.

'See you, Mr Hoskins,' Callum said, touched his baseball cap and turned away, grinning.

'Three, possibly four,' Cannon said. 'What have you got?'

'Not as many as you had when I was last by,' Hoskins said.

'Spring coming, sales always pick up,' he replied brusquely, leading the way to where two partly restored and repainted cruisers rested on wooden cradles next to the water.

'Do you deliver by road as well as on the water?' Cannon asked.

'Hardly ever, most customers take delivery from the yard in the water,' Slingsby said, mellowing now the talk was of delivery. 'One of our boys goes with them for half an hour or so; every boat is a little bit different.'

'That's good, so when will work be finished on these?' he asked as they walked around the cradled cruisers.

'If you're interested and don't want a lot of internal extras, pay a deposit and I'll have either of these in the water within a week.'

Cannon walked to the edge of the creek, which formed an extension to the River Witham. 'I'm curious,' he said. 'Just how far can you get on these waterways?'

Slingsby led him to a map on the wall. 'The Inland Waterways of England,' he said. 'Broad canals in red — they're over seven feet wide. Narrow canals — approximately seven feet wide, in purple, navigable rivers in blue.'

'So, looking at the possibilities from here, it is possible to go to the midlands, Rugby, Banbury, Oxford, London even.'

'And north, some good wide canals up around Liverpool and Leeds,' Slingsby added. 'Never been that far myself, but some spend their lives on the canals and rivers.'

Hoskins had wandered over to where his young friend was rigging a mast for a sailing boat and they looked deep in conversation. Cannon forced himself to go back to examine the cruisers again to give them more time.

'I'll have to consult my partner,' he said after Slingsby had talked about possible extras and prices, 'but if you had a copy of that waterways map . . . '

Slingsby walked over to his office and took a map from a rack of brochures, shook Cannon's hand and said he hoped to hear from him. Outside, Hoskins moved not towards the jeep but towards the small marina belonging to the yard.

'What did you find out?' he asked.

'Walk along a bit,' Hoskins said, leading the way past the moored boats and on towards the old towpath. 'Young Callum's going to meet us around the first bend. I want you to hear what he has to say.'

They walked in silence, their footsteps muffled by the growth of grasses either side of this ancient track. In no time it felt as if they had left the world far behind. Cold February desolation cloaked them and the landscape. He looked along the river. On the opposite bank, the black, bare branches of overhanging trees trailed in the water, which ran slowly, almost secretively, between them. The first cold mists of the evening were gathering on the surface of the water and seemed to be rolling slowly but irrevocably towards them. Thinking of Jim Maddern, Carol Smithson and young Danny — taken God knows where — he felt a first shiver become a full-blown shudder.

It was a relief to round a bend and see the young man, leaning back on a stile, cigarette in hand, blowing the smoke up above his head and watching it twirl in the air. He greeted them both heartily. 'I thought you'd like to know I don't think old Slingsby'll be in the market for any low offers. He's just sold three in quick time for ready money, and one of the boys in the yard said the same big bloke had been back and bought an old two-berth for cash, though what he wanted that old tub for no one knows. It was only just sound.'

'You're sure it was all ready cash?' Cannon asked.

'Oh I'm quite sure, I saw it. I'd heard of folks buying for cash and bringing it in carrier-bags but never thought *I'd* see it! The men and the boats had gone but I was up on a crane in the yard and could see over the frosted glass at the bottom of the office window. There were three bags on Mr Slingsby's desk, and he sat counting notes out of one and putting them into piles.'

'And these boats were taken away on the river by the new owners?' Cannon asked.

'Yes, Callum told me about the men.' It was Hoskins who replied. 'Tell us again what they were like.'

'There were two ordinary-looking guys,

well, everyday sort of villains, shaven heads, but the one with the money, certainly the boss, he was a *big* man,' Callum said, pursing his lips and shaking his head. 'Shoulders on him like a prize-fighter. Can't imagine anyone tackling him.'

He went on to tell them that the names of the boats sold were *Merrybell, Bluebell* and *Jollybell*, all bought from the same small hire company some time ago. The little one, he said, 'was called something *Boy*, ought to have been *Rotten Boy*.'

When the amiable young man had departed back to the boatyard, Hoskins added two vital bits of information. 'Callum said he overheard one of the men mention the Stump, Boston Stump, and his description of that man . . . '

'At a guess, Sean Jakes,' Cannon said. Why would Sean Jakes come back for yet another cruiser, a two-berth and one that was barely water-worthy?

15

'Jones has made an arrest,' Austin told Cannon as they once more went up to the lounge — this time leaving Liz in charge of the bar. 'His DNA is on record linking him to at least one gang killing.'

Cannon held up a gin bottle from the sideboard, but Austin shook his head regretfully.

'Wouldn't mind some of your great coffee.'

'The tray's here, ready.' He went to a corner table and switched on a kettle.

Jacket abandoned once more, Austin pulled his shirt sleeves away from his armpits. 'Whatever the time of day or night when I finally get home, I shall be glad to get in the shower and have a large g and t.'

Cannon smiled, knowing Austin's fastidious habits and his love of his end-of-day drink in a fine crystal tumbler.

'So, Jones?' he questioned.

'His reputation is riding high,' Austin said. 'He picked this man up after a chase on the motorway.'

'This man is one of your London lot?'

Austin shook his head. 'No, bit of a maverick, but we believe he worked for old

Jakes at one time.'

'Expendable,' Cannon suggested.

Austin regarded him solemnly. 'You think the Jakeses have made a sacrificial lamb of him?'

'Yes,' he said without hesitation. 'It keeps Jones in a good light and firmly in place so he can make sure the police and the Jakeses never clash. In return, Jones has already received a lady partner, a small mansion and has a promise of a share in the ultimate loot when they run — and I think Jones intends to go with them.'

'He's adamant that the Jakeses will be heading south any hour, that there'll be a confrontation with the London gang, so he's advising the detailing of all our men on the exits from the motorways.'

'Meanwhile the Jakeses depart by water,' Cannon said, and told Austin all he and Hoskins had learned at the boatyard that afternoon.

Austin listened intently, his eyes on Cannon's face all the time. 'We have to keep Jones in ignorance of all this, but . . . ' Austin paused, then made his decision, 'I need to . . . ' Once more he broke off, then asked, 'What do you think of Betterson?'

'Regional Detective Inspector Betterson? Sound,' Cannon said.

'Do you know where he lives?'

'I do, as it happens. Liz and I catered for his silver wedding party here,' he answered and went to the desk for his address book of customers.

'I know Jones is still involved with this arrest,' Austin said, rising and putting his jacket back on. 'There are times when phone calls are not the thing. Face to face is the best policy. I shall go to Betterson's home now and hope he is there.'

Cannon nodded. What Austin needed was a group, a network of astute senior officers to manage what could become messy in all senses of the word. 'Meanwhile there's Maddern and . . . ' The kettle clicked off; both men ignored it.

'I'll keep you informed,' Austin said, adding, 'resources are stretched and going to be more so, but I can honestly say we've every man we've got on the lookout for any sign, clue, the slightest thing.'

When he had gone, Cannon found Liz moderately busy in the bar, but she nodded him towards the kitchen. 'Hoskins, he's obviously got something he needs to tell you in private.'

'Listen,' Hoskins said without preamble, 'one of my mates has seen that rotten old tub Callum was telling us about — *Sailor Boy* it's called — heading out toward Boston. I asked him about the other three, but he's confident they haven't gone that way.'

'Boston, but isn't Boston . . . '

'The wrong way if you're thinking of cruising anywhere on inland waters,' Hoskins confirmed.

But the right way, he thought, if one wanted to take attention from the real centre of action. Hadn't Thompson's body been taken to the coast? Now an old boat 'hardly water-worthy' was being taken that way. Why? What was its cargo? 'So the Jakes buy a second-rate boat and take it . . . ' Cannon began.

'Up waterways that go nowhere,' Hoskins finished the sentence.

'Except out to sea,' Cannon added, and remembered Austin saying that they had a three-hostage situation and resources were stretched.

'This old boy,' Hoskins said, 'has a boat I know he'd lend us, good outboard engine and a spotlight.'

Cannon raised his eyebrows; activities that needed a fast boat and a bright light usually meant some kind of illegal activities, poaching, probably, if he was a friend of Hoskins. 'So, could we borrow this boat now, tonight?' he asked.

'Can I leave . . . ' he opened the door to the back porch and Jones's greyhound rose from a blanket and came to stand meekly by Hoskins' side. Cannon saw it had water and a saucer of broken rich tea biscuits — Liz had seen it was comfortable.

'Well, I don't think there's any chance of Jones turning up here tonight.'

As the greyhound was resettled in the porch, Cannon's mobile rang. To his surprise it was Austin again. 'A local motor patrol has reported three cruisers travelling late on the waterways going towards Lincoln. The boats answered the descriptions you gave, but all had their names painted out — and I've seen Betterson.'

'Lincoln,' Cannon repeated, then told Austin that someone has seen the small, older boat bought by the same man, going the opposite way.

'Noted,' Austin said, 'I'll get someone on to that as soon as I can.'

The quick update left Cannon with no doubt in his mind what he must do. Three good cabin cruisers going inland, he could guess what they were destined to carry: gold was heavy and water was the perfect way to transport it, particularly if you think all your enemies are watching the motorways. The possible cargo of the old tub being taken the other way, without its name painted out, was of far more concern to him. 'Let's go,' he said.

He made a quick assessment of the number of customers in his bar. Liz would manage and Alamat was in attendance. 'Just taking Hoskins to see a man about another boat,' he told Liz. 'Leaving his bike and the dog here.'

He saw her mouth open, though whether in surprise or protest he was not sure, then she pursed her lips in wry acceptance, shook her head a fraction before nodding.

'But our lives are never dull, love, are they?' he said.

'Don't push your luck, John Cannon, and don't be long,' she told him.

Hoskins directed and they covered the few miles to the edges of Boston in good time.

'Turn here,' Cannon was ordered as they came to the edge of marsh and meadowland. 'It's the first cottage on the right. I'll go in on my own.'

Even ex-cops not welcome, he thought, as he watched an outside light come on and Hoskins disappear around the back of the cottage. He knew Hoskins would not waste time and had sensed that he too had the same fear — that the old boat was a perfect way of neatly disposing of unwanted hostages. They both knew old Jakes would have little time or mercy for either his eldest son's widow or his grandson since their escape from Snyder Crescent — and Maddern? The local bobby must have been a thorn in the family's side ever since Danny innocently revealed that the sergeant had called him 'Jakes' — and it seemed the family were again taking pains to leave evidence well away from their real centre of activity.

He was relieved to see Hoskins reappear but instead of coming back to the jeep he raised an arm and waved a bunch of keys. Cannon was out of the jeep and behind him as he led the way through the back garden and a wicket-gate and along a path to a small boathouse. He opened the door with a key from the bunch and flicked a light switch. Cannon saw a smart little boat with a sleek outboard motor fitted to the stern and a spotlight in the bow, moored alongside a tidy landing-stage.

Hoskins wasted no time in going to the end of the wooden staging and pulling a rope which hung from the rafters — double wooden doors opened like theatre curtains out onto the river. The light from the boat house streaked out across the immediate waters, and where the light reached the far bank the long grasses showed green in the dark sepia, peaty-smelling gloom.

Hoskins got into the boat and switched on the spotlight, angling it low to the water, then moved back to the outboard motor. 'Can you put the . . . ' he indicated the bulb above their heads, 'out, and untie her?'

Cannon obliged.

'You take the spotlight and I'll steer,' Hoskins said as he pushed the boat clear of the staging before dropping the outboard motor into its working position. Once clear he had the motor started and turned down to no more than a purr in seconds. Cannon recognized a well-practised skill when he encountered it.

If he had thought the sound of the engine might intrude on the late February evening, he was wrong. Instead, the noise seemed subdued, dissipated by the surrounding expanse of fenland, and the earthy smell of that was in turn blown away by a wind from the east, bringing ozone from the omnipresent sea. To Cannon, it seemed a sharp reminder to man to know his place. Generations back, the Dutch had brought their expertise to help wrest this land from the sea, but it would need vigilance to make it a permanent arrangement. He turned to look at Hoskins, a man born of this land, and inadvertently raised the spotlight a little.

'Keep that well down when we get to the

town,' Hoskins ordered. 'It's about ten miles, mid-tide and rising.'

'We should keep a look out all the time but as they took Thompson all the way to the coast, I doubt they'll abandon anything or anybody this side of the town,' Cannon said, adding, 'if you watch the right-hand bank I'll concentrate on the left, a pale coloured boat should show up well in the darkness.'

'There are plenty of reed-beds they could run her into,' Hoskins said grimly.

They came to the town, to the old wharf area. There were apartments, a museum and the looming presence of St Botolph's. This parish church, with its huge tower, had been the tallest structure in the world in the nineteenth century. Known as Boston Stump and topped by a lantern-like structure, it had acted as a religious and secular lighthouse ever since it was erected in the fifteenth century.

Beyond the town the river was visibly widening with the rising tide. Hoskins cut the speed of the engine.

'Perhaps we should scan one bank then come back along the other,' Cannon suggested.

'Take us a while,' Hoskins said, 'but guess it'll be the only way as we get nearer the sea.'

'We might of course encounter the boat

coming back,' Cannon said.

'You mean having dumped . . . '

'Yes,' Cannon said grimly, then asked, 'how far could they go, ditch the boat and then be able to walk back to where they had left a vehicle?'

'There's a place with a notice-board about the Pilgrim Fathers that's coming up,' Hoskins said. He slowed to a mere walking pace and continued. 'Beyond that there's thickets of bushes and reeds. The path is less easy, so before that would be a good place for someone who had to walk back.'

The notice-board came into view and as they laboured by, something pale, something with a smooth line in the tangle of natural disorderly growth caught their attention. Hoskins stopped the engine in the same moment as Cannon swung the light back in that direction.

'I'll have to come round,' Hoskins said, revving the engine to begin the difficult task of turning the boat against the incoming press of water. He tried to judge how far to go before beginning his circle to come back anywhere near the streak of pale, smooth wood — which could be just a post or a piece of random driftwood. Cannon tried to keep the light turned to their target as the boat was swept much too fast by the current and they came in a dozen or so metres away, but close enough for them both to see it was certainly more than a piece of driftwood.

'I think it's a boat,' Cannon said.

'I'll have to go well past it and come round again,' Hoskins said.

He doggedly repeated the manoeuvre and came in short, but this time Cannon was able to read the name across the flat stern of the little cruiser. '*Sailor Boy*,' he cried, 'and she's sinking bow first,' he added, and remembered how old man Jakes had chained Carol Smithson to her bed.

Slowly, Hoskins edged the boat closer, until they were more or less alongside. 'Her bow's stuck on the mud, the tide'll swamp her,' he shouted above the waters now rushing and swirling around the bigger obstruction the two boats had formed. 'There's not much time . . .'

'Stay alongside if you can, I'll jump . . .' Cannon said, then as a sudden extra surge of water took their boat into the other he did so without much preparation or caution, landing with an ankle- and knee-jerking bang in the tiny well of the cruiser.

With no spotlight focused on the steeply angled cruiser, it was a matter of feeling and trying to keep his feet. He found and clung to the steering wheel on the port side, and having pushed with his free hand at the cabin doors with no result, he clung to the wheel with both hands and kicked them in. He anticipated the usual steps down, three, then a small galley and beyond that a two-berth cabin.

'Anyone there?' he called, though he hardly expected an answer — for there had been no sound, no one shouting for assistance — but then his heart jumped with sudden hope as from deeper in the downward sloping darkness there was a thump, as if someone had managed to move a foot or hand to bang on the woodwork to answer his question.

He felt his way along the galley work-surfaces and beyond found the raised wooden side of the bunk on his right. He ran his hand along and then in across the narrow bed — started as he encountered a bare foot, a woman's, a foot that reacted to his touch.

'Carol!' he exclaimed instinctively and found her ankles bound with ropes this time. Anger sped his hands to try to release her, but he found more rope was stretched across her body, laced, maliciously and meticulously, it seemed, in and out of the decorative woodwork both sides of the bunk. Then he had to grab for the side again as the boat lurched downward and he slid with it to the far end of the sleeping compartment. The water was over his shoe-tops and there was a new sound, water coming over the lip of some obstruction and falling down to a new level.

He threw out a hand to the other side of the cabin and as he did so the boat moved again, the noise of the falling water increased and he was up to his thighs. On the opposite bunk he felt the broad shoulders of young Danny — but here there was no reaction to his touch — and with this latest downward plunge of the boat the boy and his mother were both in danger of drowning.

Hoskins!' he yelled. 'Your knife, quick, ropes! Heads under water.'

He tried to find some way of raising Carol's face above the water level, but there was no chance. The boat lurched again as Hoskins came aboard. Cannon caught and steadied him in the steeply sloping cabin, guided his hand to the ropes and held him firm. The old man was breathing heavily but he handled his knife with precision and in seconds he was through the ropes. Cannon heaved the women's head above the water level, ripping the tape from her mouth.

'Danny,' she gasped, 'Danny . . . '

The extra weight and movement was badly affecting the boat. It settled lower and Hoskins slipped. Cannon grabbed his arm and took the knife from his hand as he tried to recover his feet. 'Hold on to Carol,' he ordered. 'Keep her head above water while I get the boy.'

Danny was trussed up in the same way and the water was up to Cannon's elbows as he cut through the ropes restraining the boy's head and shoulders. He thanked God Hoskins's knife was sharp as a razor. Once through, he heaved the boy's head out of the water, got his shoulder behind the boy's body and ripped the tape from his mouth.

At first there was nothing, Cannon bent his body further over and the boy belched water, sucked air, choked. 'Hold on to my arm while I . . . ' and he cut the rope binding the wrists, then began frantically pulling the rope from the woodwork, like a giant, manic, unlacing exercise, then he cut the rope from the feet. 'Hold on, Danny, while we free your mother.'

The boy was in a poor way — barely conscious as he retched and choked — and the boat began to sink in earnest, sliding down at an acute angle, the gurgling, bubbling noises of the water getting louder, more sinister.

'The tide's swamping 'er, she'll go down quick,' Hoskins shouted.

Cannon began to push Danny up towards the galley, but the boy suddenly resisted as his mother called his name. 'Mam?' he questioned, then seemed to realize what was happening. 'No,' he protested, 'Mam first.'

There was not going to be time to argue and as Hoskins gasped, 'Your mother's free,' Cannon realized that the only way any of them was going to get out of this was if he, the strongest, was in the cockpit and able to pull the others up after him.

'Move up as far as you can and hold on,' Cannon ordered.

'Mam,' Danny cried out.

'I'm coming, Danny.'

Cannon felt the two of them reach each other, and unceremoniously pushed them out of the cabin space. 'Go on, climb! Climb!'

He urged them on, found hand-holds on cupboards and towel rails, then went ahead, climbing his way into the cockpit which after the complete darkness inside seemed quite light.

He pulled Carol up alongside himself first, then Danny — recovering fast — followed without much help.

'Get over into the boat alongside,' he ordered, aware that Hoskins had not followed. Danny stepped over to join his mother and as he left it, the cruiser made a serious downward movement. In one movement Cannon slipped the rope and pushed mother and son clear. 'Hold her off, if you can,' he said before forcing his way back into the galley, against the water boiling in to finally claim the boat for its own.

He located Hoskins half-way along the galley, head just above water, just.

'Foot caught,' he gasped as Cannon gripped his hand. Cannon took a deep breath before going underwater, to find Hoskins's foot was trapped by a cupboard door that had twisted on one hinge and clamped the old man's foot as tight as any trap.

He felt the boot, well laced. He could fiddle about with that for ages, drown them both. He rose to the surface, took a great gulp of air then went down again. He concentrated on the door, used brute force tactics once more, braced his feet either side of the skewed door and Hoskins's trapped foot, pulled and twisted against the remaining hinge, with the desperation of a man who would drown himself rather than leave Hoskins trapped.

At the third attempt — his lungs bursting, his brain questioning how strong a screw you needed to keep a cupboard door in place, for God's sake — it gave. There was one more obstacle, the doorway out into the air. He was beneath Hoskins and aimed him for the lighter square like a missile, swimming against the final pull as the little cruiser found its resting place, to be resurrected every low tide, but not with its intended victims.

He realized that young Danny had the engine going on the borrowed boat and was laying-off some metres away, but as soon as he saw them rise to the surface he edged the boat back their way. They swam to meet it. Cannon held on to one side while Danny helped Hoskins aboard over the other, then both balanced the boat while Cannon climbed in.

'I owe you,' Hoskins said to Cannon, who in return nodded towards the other two. 'We're even,' he said, then bending close asked, 'Maddern?'

'Not on that boat.' Hoskins shook his head.

'No.' Cannon confirmed what he had thought — it would not have been possible to hide a man of that size.

Hoskins moved to sit next to Danny, but when the boy went to relinquish his post Hoskins said, 'Carry on for now, you're doing OK. Near slack water now.'

The sea finally reached its peak, had obliterated all the river's mud-banks with several feet of water and now paused before the waters began their return trip to the ocean.

It was a moment of relief even though they

were all wet through and shivering, but some things could not wait.

'Sergeant Maddern?' Cannon questioned. 'He was with you in the car.'

'He struggled and fought,' Danny said, 'he wouldn't stop . . . fell out the car once.'

To drop his mobile phone, Cannon thought.

'He was trying to take attention from you and me, Danny,' Carol said, 'making a nuisance of himself . . . so Sean would leave me alone.'

'Sean knocked him out with his gun,' Danny burst in. 'They left him in the car when they took us on that boat.'

Cannon pulled his phone from his pocket only to confirm what he feared, that it *had* drowned. 'We must get back.'

'Will he be all right?' Danny asked, then in the same breath, 'What will they do to him?'

No one answered.

16

As they pushed the boat to maximum speed back towards the bungalow, Cannon knew he had to contact Austin to put him in the picture, but by the time Hoskins hung the keys on a hook in the boathouse there was no sign of life anywhere, and the urgency to get warmth for his passengers became paramount. He packed everyone in the jeep, found a car-rug for Carol and Danny, put the heater on full and drove back to The Trap at speed.

Left early in the evening to cope, Liz was on the doorstep the moment she heard the jeep. She took in the state of Cannon's passengers and seemed to step straight into her mother's role as a nurse in Accident and Emergency, as Cannon went through to use the bar's mobile.

Austin listened without interruption, until Cannon said, 'I have a theory about Jones.'

'In a nutshell then,' Austin demanded, 'we have a development just outside Bristol, one of the Faima motorbike sections arriving in force.'

'I think Jones used a police patrol car to

take Thompson's body from the lay-by to the coast,' Cannon told him, 'where Jones's wife then conveniently 'found' it in time to divert attention from their activities inland.'

'Right,' Austin said briskly, 'I'll arrange for the car Jones had use of to be picked up for servicing, then get forensics secretly on to it. In the meantime, Maddern . . . ?'

'No, nothing. I'm going to see if either Carol Smithson or Danny can remember anything else, otherwise it's finding his car that might give us a lead.'

'Quite.' Austin's voice took on the clipped note of his barrister father, but then he was interrupted at his end. 'Right,' he said and as the call ended Cannon was unsure who the 'right' was for.

Cannon started as Liz spread a fleecy throw over his shoulders. 'Didn't see you coming,' he said, adding, 'that was Austin.'

'I heard,' she said. 'Would Margaret and their daughters know about any of this?'

'No, nothing.' He shook his head.

'Poor woman,' she breathed, 'poor girls.'

'I must talk to Carol and Danny . . . '

'They're upstairs, putting on dry clothes,' she said. 'What is going to happen to them?'

'Austin's arranging for them to be picked up and taken to a safe house well out of the area.'

'Pity they can't just stay here,' Liz said, 'at least they know us.'

'Too near Jones's home.'

'There's the dog?' she remembered.

'Didn't mention it, I've watched Hoskins with it, I think he'd like to keep it.' He paused as he heard Carol and Danny coming downstairs and would have led the way back to the kitchen, but Liz stopped him.

'No,' she said, pushing her arm under the fleece and around his waist to feel his clothes, 'it'll take you five minutes to get out of these. Go on!'

'What about Hoskins?'

'He knows how to look after himself — he stripped off in the porch straightaway. He's in your jogging clothes and he's in charge of preparing food and drink — not sure what.' Then both instinctively lifted their heads to take in the homely smell of grilling bacon — Hoskins's staple food.

'Hope you've not let him free with my bottle of brandy,' Cannon said as he climbed the stairs, prior to throwing his clothes into a heap on the bedroom floor, pulling on dry underwear, a tracksuit and sheepskin slippers. For a second, he revelled in the boon of dry warm clothes before running back downstairs.

In the kitchen Liz had taken over the

grill-pan. Hoskins sat down and Cannon poured him a generous brandy and said, 'I'll run you and the dog home later.'

'And my bike,' Hoskins added.

'And your bike,' Cannon confirmed, sitting next to him and across the table from Carol and her son. 'I am desperately worried about Sergeant Maddern,' he said, 'I wondered if you could go through exactly what happened when you were stopped and taken by the Jakeses. There might just be some tiny clue about what they intended to do with the sergeant, or where they might have taken him.'

Danny instinctively moved closer to his mother as they thought back and Carol took his hand, holding it tight between her own.

'Mr Hoskins found the sergeant's mobile just past a sharp bend,' he told them.

'Ooh!' Danny exclaimed. 'I wondered what he was doing. He suddenly started fighting like a mad thing when they pulled him out of the driving seat, knocked two of them flying.'

'I thought he was doing it because Sean was hurting me as much as he could when he dragged me out,' Carol said, 'spiteful sod.'

'Like his great-grandfather, then,' Hoskins said, 'he was always thrashing somebody.'

'Maddern would be doing both,' Cannon

said, 'giving us a clue and . . . '

'The other one smashed him over the head with a gun for his pains,' Carol said, shuddering, 'knocked him out cold.'

'So you were all dragged out of Maddern's car?'

'Yes, but not Sarge, he was lying on the ground.'

'What I need you to try to remember is if anything was said, anything at all, about what they intended to do with him or where they were going? Anything at all you can remember. It might not seem important, but it could give us a clue, could save the sergeant's life.' He felt he had indulged in a little moral blackmail as he saw Danny straighten up in his chair and scowl in an effort of remembering.

'I can't . . . ' Carol began, 'they were on edge, angry, but not about us. It sounded as if someone had torn them off a strip for taking somebody and leaving them in the wrong place. Sean said he wouldn't put up with 'that smarmy bastard' telling him what to do for much longer.'

'And the other one said, it wouldn't *be* for much longer,' Danny added, 'and they both made noises like yeah, they'd both see to *that*.'

'I think they must have put Sergeant

Maddern back into his own car,' Carol said, 'and the third man drove that.'

'You're doing really well,' Cannon encouraged. 'Just keep thinking back. What happened next?'

'It seemed like . . . ' Carol struggled on, 'kind of, all prearranged what they were going to do with us. They put tape over our mouths and hands, made us lie down in the back of their car . . . '

'Covered us with a blanket, then they drove,' Danny said, 'and when we stopped it was like nowhere. There was nothing, no lights, only water and bog, and — '

'The boat, they put us on . . . '

'And left us to . . . ' Danny said. His young voice wavered but he gritted his teeth, fought back tears and added, 'and left us to drown, wanted us to die. They mustn't kill Sarge! I don't want him to die. I — '

Cannon felt the boy was about to say he loved him. With so few people beyond his mother who had cared for and about him in his life, it was quite possible that he had — in his mind — formed that kind of relationship with the police sergeant whose newspaper he delivered and who'd taken time to talk to the boy.

'We'll do everything in our power to stop that happening,' Cannon assured him, 'and remembering everything as you are doing could really help.'

'Sean muttered something when the other car drove off, but they were tying us up and the only word I thought I heard . . . ' She paused as if the word was too stupid to repeat but when she looked up, she found all eyes on her and added, 'was 'rabbits', then the other laughed.'

'Rabbits?' It was Hoskins who took up this word.

'What are you thinking?' It was Liz who asked, but the old man did not reply, or did not say exactly what he was thinking.

Hoskins was evasive as he said, 'I know where there are plenty of rabbit warrens, but . . . ' he scowled like a child hiding the truth, 'only in my own area.'

★ ★ ★

It was only as Cannon drove Hoskins, the dog and his bike home that he admitted that what he was thinking was that rabbits lived underground and rabbit warrens usually made easy digging.

'Glad you didn't say that in front of the boy,' Cannon said, but the strange word still kept popping in and out of his mind as morning came and, true to his word, Austin rang to say two plain-clothes policewomen would be calling to pick up Carol and Danny in the next hour.

'Where are we going?' Danny wanted to know.

'Somewhere safe,' Liz said, going over to him. Putting an arm around his shoulders, she gave him a hug and a kiss on his cheek. 'We won't lose sight of you. When this is over we'll get in touch.' Danny looked up at her, and she asked, 'You believe me?'

'Yes,' he said, trying to frown away the emotion that an unexpected tenderness brought, and nearly managing it.

'Where they're taking us, will we hear what happens?' Carol asked.

'You will,' Cannon said with certainty, and his mind ran the gamut of evidence and court cases. They both had a way to go yet.

Danny was somewhat mollified when the car that arrived to pick them up could not have looked less like anything official. As it pulled in close to the back door, they could see it was a bright-green, soft-topped sports-car, with rugs and pillows in the back. No time was lost. The women were kind but correct — and the pub, the kitchen, was suddenly empty and quiet.

'Another kind of closing time,' Cannon said.

'Yes, and you know what,' Liz said, 'Alamat has slept through all of it. He put the glasses through the sterilizer last thing and went to bed,'

'Perhaps he needn't know,' he said, 'the fewer people who do the better.'

'And we should go to bed. There's no more you can do. You can hardly call Austin and say Carol Smithson thought she heard the word rabbits.'

'No, but . . . '

'Don't, John, you're whacked, I'm whacked, we'll think clearer after a few hours' sleep, and the police will have been looking for Maddern ever since you first spoke to Austin. What more can you do, and actually . . . ' she came behind him as he sat at the table and put her nose deep into his neck, 'you smell a bit duck-pondy. A shower and a sleep and you'll be a new man.'

He had both, but woke at first light shouting, 'Rabbits!'

'For goodness sake,' Liz exclaimed, 'you frightened me to death.'

Cannon lay, his own heart pounding.

'No one else can shout rabbits and make it sound like — well — *torpedo*, or something fatal,' she said, flopping back onto her pillow.

'Yes, well.' He sounded and felt morose.

She turned towards him and he lifted an

arm so she might snuggle under it and lay her head on his chest. He lay very still, but as she heard his heart slowing, she asked, 'What are you going to do?'

'I'm not too sure. It's just . . . 'rabbits' . . . rabbits!' She felt his arm tighten round her. 'Oh my God! Rabbits. Rabbits!' he exclaimed.

'It's what they say when they want to pretend to be talking, isn't it?' she said. 'Or is that rhubarb?' She proceeded to say the word over and over at different pitches and different speeds.

'No, Liz,' he stopped her, 'Maddern had a collection of Beatrix Potter figures, all smashed — there were a lot of rabbits. Why didn't I think of that before? Come on!'

'Come on?' she questioned as he pulled his arm free.

'He could be lying there, they could have just abandoned him in his own home.' He flung out a violent arm towards the window, the outside world, and exclaimed bitterly, 'Isn't that just the sort of perverted humour these people have, certainly Sean Jakes has. We've time to go now. It'll be quiet, here and there. I'll tell Alamat we have to go over to Maddern's bungalow for a look-see. We can explain later.'

'My car, then,' she said, her reluctance to

lose the comfort of his presence and leave the warmth of their bed dispelled by his vehemence — and she knew he was right. Many criminals did seem to have a high opinion of their own perverted cleverness and humour. Their cruel tricks could have an MO as distinctive as the way they committed murder.

★   ★   ★

Maddern came to consciousness aware of a searing hot pain across the side of his skull, a feeling of extreme nausea and the knowledge that he was bound, his eyes and mouth taped.

He forced himself to swallow, not to think of choking to death on his own vomit, and took stock. His wrists were taped behind his back and his arms roped tight above the elbows. His ankles were taped, his legs roped together just above his knees. Someone had done a very thorough job.

He felt sure he was in the back of his own estate car. He slowly pushed out his feet and felt the netted compartment in the side where he kept his car-cleaning kit. Then there was a smell, cologne or perfume, he had noticed it when loading Katie's bags, as strong as if she had broken a bottle in a bag as she threw them into the back. Katie's friend had been murdered because she had recognized and gone after one of the Jakeses, so what were they now doing to young Danny and his mother? Why was he trussed up so securely? Where were they taking him? Why hadn't they just . . . ?

The next moment he was flung hard up against the back seats, then over toward the door as the car slewed. He heard the driver muttering as he fought the wheel for control and did all the wrong things to control a skid. Maddern drew in great angry breaths — they'd scattered his family, trashed his house and now it was the turn of his car. Somehow, in spite of turning a full circle, they hit nothing and stayed on the road.

They travelled a little slower after this, though disregarding any great need for safety along the winding route. Then there was another alarming veer to the left and the car stopped abruptly. He heard the driver get out, the back door of the estate was lifted up, and cool air rushed in. He braced himself but the man walked away. So was he being abandoned, or was there worse to follow? Was it the end? Would the man fire the vehicle? He sniffed the air, only the smell of the sea was stronger.

Then he heard the unmistakeable sound of a door being forced, shouldered open by sheer brute force. There were more faint noises and then footsteps coming back. The rope around his knees was grabbed and he was half dragged, half lifted to the edge of the boot. Then the rope around his arms was pulled and he fell to the ground. There was no pause in the punishment. The man must be big, strong like all the Jakeses, there was no doubt about that, but there was also something bumbling and clumsy in his movements. Progress was a series of great jerks and lifts as his body came into contact with corners and steps, just as if his captor did not realize they would be a problem until he was stopped in his tracks. Maddern felt he must be being taken into a house of some kind because in the first room there was a lingering smell of homemade bread; a kitchen, then. Margaret often made bread.

He was dragged further, through into another room, for his side hit the doorframe. A few more steps and his ankles were released. It sounded as if the task was done as the man straightened and drew in a few breaths. Then, as he walked away, something crunched under his foot and whatever it was was kicked aside.

The man must have got back to the kitchen when he was confronted by someone else, another man. Maddern concentrated, held his breath to listen. One thing was certain — there was not just anger, but fury in *this* man's voice. He seemed to be shouting in spite of his own intentions not to.

'What's that car doing here? What're you doing here?'

The explanation was a low mumble.

'What? You have to get him out!'

A rumble of complaint, mention of a name, 'Sean.'

'I might have known! A bloody clown and a punch-drunk idiot, what more . . . ' He broke off, then said, 'Well, you've got half an hour to get him out and the car well out towards the coast somewhere, I don't care where, just off the face of the earth, you, him and the car.'

'Sean said — '

'Sean said! Do you always do what your Uncle Sean says? You're a big boy now!'

The sneering, mocking voice left Maddern in no doubt who this man was, and he expected to hear Jones suck his teeth at any moment.

'He told me — ' the voice became a thick nasal whine.

'Told you! You've about twenty minutes before the police get here. Just thank your lucky stars, lad, that I'm early.'

Maddern had heard many a police recruit cowed by this man and at the back of his mind was a story he'd been told of another young Jakes who had tried to slip the family, but he was too busy trying to catch every word to think of worrying about it.

'Why are the police coming?' the sulky voice asked.

'They're going to decide what they'll do to put this house right, now forensics have finished. Now get him, his car and yourself out of here!'

It hit Maddern like another blow, a kick in the guts — he was in his own house! The way from kitchen to lounge, the broken china underfoot. He was still coming to terms with this knowledge as the two of them began man-handling him out again.

The reverse journey was quicker, fiercer. Jones helped, but bullied the younger man all the time. Even as he was being dragged and bruised on doorways and down steps, if he could have recoiled from the touch of the traitor he would have, *and* taken the side of this member of the Jakes family, probably another Danny in his time. If there was such a thing as surviving against the odds, he resolved he was going to do it and see this turncoat, this bad apple, publicly ousted from the police barrel.

* * *

Liz drove and her passenger could not grumble at the speed or her skill. She was fast but aware, though there were few about this early. They saw only one or two early land-workers, a milkman and a solitary post-van, until they reached the outskirts of Reed St Thomas and turned into Sea Lane.

'Pull in,' Cannon ordered, as ahead — parked at Maddern's bungalow — was a police car and the black chauffeured car of a more senior officer, which had obviously just arrived. The driver was opening one door for his uniformed passenger, a man in plain clothes getting out, the other.

'It's Jones in the police car,' Cannon said in a low voice as they stopped, 'he's come to meet a superintendent, a chief super if I'm not mistaken, and there's another official looking geezer in plain clothes.'

Then both of them jumped as someone tapped the side window of the car. They were so busy looking ahead they had not seen this man coming from one of the other homes.

'Mr Russell!' Cannon exclaimed, opening the window. 'What are you doing here at this hour?'

'What d'ya think,' he snorted, 'delivering

my own papers. Had two boys leave, parents have hold of something terrible having happened to young Danny, so now we're the cursed newsagents.

'What you doing here?' Russell asked in return. 'Not more trouble I hope, but . . . '

'But?' Liz queried.

'Unless I'm mistaken, as my wife dropped me off on the main road, the sergeant's car came out of Sea Lane as if all the hounds of hell were after him.'

'He was driving?' Cannon asked.

'Oh couldn't say that, couldn't even be sure it was his car, it was pretty muddied up, never seen the sergeant's in that state come to think of it,' he said, then nodded towards the end of the lane, 'but looks like there's plenty going on at his house.'

'Yes,' Cannon said, wanting to get in there, to know exactly what was going on.

'Everybody knows what happened to his home,' Russell said, 'you can't keep that sort of thing quiet in a place like this. Everyone's on his side.' He patted his bag of newspapers. 'Must get on.'

'But what good is it doing?' Cannon asked as they watched him go. 'Everybody being on his side, caring? I bloody care but what good am I doing?'

'They're all going into the house,' Liz said,

ignoring the sudden pessimism, then reminding him, 'you and Hoskins have saved two
lives in the last few hours.'

'But not Jim Maddern.'

'If he's in there we'll soon know,' Liz
answered.

They watched and waited. About twenty
minutes later they all emerged, the plain-
clothes man with a notebook making notes as
the chief superintendent jabbed a finger
towards the notepad as if emphasizing a final
point.

'Seems I was wrong,' Cannon said.

'But should you let Austin know about the
car Russell saw?' she said.

'Tell me why it should be Maddern's car,'
he muttered. 'What did they do, bring him
home for a change of clothes?'

17

'Hello,' the woman's voice said, 'it's Margaret Maddern here, I . . . '

Cannon's concern for Jim Maddern switched to Maddern's family as he answered the phone behind the pub's counter. The voice at the other end wavered and broke. 'Are you all all right?' he demanded. 'Has something happened down there?'

'I know I shouldn't be phoning, Jim told me not to, so I'm sorry for bothering you,' Margaret gabbled her apologies.

'You're not bothering me. What's the trouble? Not you or the girls, or Jim's brother?'

'No, it's . . . ' she hesitated then rushed into her concern. 'It's just that yesterday I was so uneasy all day thinking about Jim, and this morning I woke with such a sense of dread . . . '

There was a silence as if she was waiting for news, for details he could not give her.

'Have you heard anything?' she ventured.

'I have just spoken to the London officer in charge,' he began cautiously, 'it sounds as if it is very much a watch and wait operation.'

'With Jim involved?' she asked.

'Oh yes,' he said gently.

'And Jim's all right?' she persisted.

'I haven't seen him.'

'So you can't tell me anything?'

'No, but he'll be pleased to know everything is all right with you all when I do see him . . . '

'Yes,' she said flatly, 'we're OK.'

He rang off and went to the kitchen. 'Now I really know what being divisive is,' he said, but Liz shushed him and indicated the twenty-four-hour news programme she was watching. He went to stand by her side. On screen a reporter was talking in front of a service station on a motorway; in the background, while the car park area was full of cars the motorway behind was completely empty.

'In the early hours of this morning,' the grim-faced reporter was saying, 'a scene was repeated here that many had previously only seen on gangster movies. Ten or more men on motorbikes roared into this service sta-tion . . . ' he half turned and the camera scanned the area behind him, focusing on a white tent and a blue and white taped-off area at the far end of the lorry park ' . . . and, using a sub machine-gun, *shot* — at point-blank range — two men, who witnesses thought came from that direction.' The reporter extended a hand towards the taped off area. 'After parking a vehicle like a large furniture van, the two men were walking from the van towards . . . ' his voice fell dramatically as now he indicated a further taped-off area and a powerful-looking black car ' . . . that car, when they were gunned down. The driver of the Mercedes was also killed.'

The camera panned in, followed a line of bullet holes running up from the back wing and finishing in a hole through the driver's side-window and a blood-splattered front windscreen. The focus now came back to the reporter.

'While this was happening, we understand that men leapt from the pillion-seats of two of the motorbikes, hi-jacked the lorry the dead men had parked and drove away before, as one witness told me . . . ' he paused to refer to a piece of paper, 'anyone had time to recover their breath.' He looked back at the camera. 'So far, none of the dead have been named, but people here have talked about 'an atmosphere' before it all happened and some even seem to believe there was a police presence *before* the motorcyclists arrived, but we have no confirmation of this.'

'Have the police given out any information?' the woman newsreader asked from the studio.

'Merely that their investigations are ongoing, but . . . ' the outside reporter turned in the other direction and the camera moved to show the restaurant area — where many people were standing close to the windows staring out. A gel-haired youth pulled a comical face and one or two waved as they realized they might be seen on television. The reporter continued. 'There are many travellers held up here, many on their way to workplaces in the Bristol area and neighbouring docks, mothers with young children taking them to nurseries and play-schools before going on to their own work.'

'So are the police keeping people there?' the studio presenter asked.

'Yes, that's right. It seems to be a question of proving identities and destinations. This reinforces the feeling that the police were already around, looking for people known to them, but that, you understand, is not from any official sources.'

The news moved on.

'You think this is connected?' Liz asked. 'This is the London gang?'

'Faima,' he supplied, 'yes, Austin said they were spawned back in the sixties, apparently an offshoot of the first UK chapter of the Hell's Angels.'

'Live fast, die young,' she said, repeating the tag the bikers had earned, 'and closing in for the kill, *if* they can find the Jakeses.'

'They seem to have found three,' Cannon said. 'Seeing what we know about them buying boats this van'll be a plant to put the London boys off the real scent. The driver and his mate were going to be picked up by the driver of the black car and they should have been away before the information was leaked to the Faima. But the Faima were obviously already in the know, and that of course,' he paused, lifted his eyebrows at her, 'could have been deliberate.'

'Making the final share-out larger for the remainder of the Jakes gang,' Liz finished. 'Well we've seen that happen a few times while we were in the Met.'

The phone rang again; it was Austin. 'Have you seen the news?'

'From the service station, yes,' he answered.

'The van's already been found abandoned near London; it was carrying crates packed with house-bricks.' Austin paused then added, 'The van had false number plates.'

'No surprise there,' Cannon commented.

'No, but the plates came from a car stolen from Reed St Thomas months ago. It's never been traced. The owner lives in Snyder Crescent.'

Cannon swore under his breath as Austin asked, 'The Smithsons, they'll be well away by now?'

'Left early hours of this morning,' he said, then asked, 'Would the Faima know about the plates?'

'They have a skilled computer hacker — we know that — but what I wanted to tell you is that we've a helicopter up tracking two separate groups of motorcyclists with gangland-type logos on their bikers' leathers and helmets heading your way, and another reported assembling north of London.'

'So it's possible they could be . . . ' He stopped short of naming Reed St Thomas. It seemed ludicrous when he thought of that sleepy village green, of Stuart and Joy Russell's shop, ludicrous and outrageous. There was nothing and no one there now as far as he knew. Meanwhile the bikers were swooping in for revenge, bloody retribution, and heaven help anyone who got in their way.

' . . . And having hi-jacked a load of bricks . . . ' he continued.

'Their tempers may be a little frayed,' Austin added, with that mastery of supreme understatement he was noted for in times of crisis.

'Jim Maddern's wife has just rung me,' he said. 'She suspects Jim is in real trouble, but knows nothing.'

'I've a countrywide watch for his car,' Austin said.

Cannon registered the edge of anguish and frustration in his friend's voice as he said, 'He's not forgotten,' then Austin added, 'and I've a twenty-four hour watch on Jones.'

★　★　★

Reloaded into the car, Maddern had been pushed in head first, face down, and the tape at one side of his mouth had been rolled into a tight band. He realized if he kept repeating the same action with his head, he might be able to free his mouth, perhaps even make himself heard, call for help. He knew the estate's horizontal blind to cover objects left in the boot had been pulled out and secured — no one would *see* him.

Like a dog cleaning its mouth on a carpet he pressed the side of his face to the harshness of the mat. At first the tape made the constriction of his mouth and jaw greater, felt like a steel band, but he persisted, and as the car lurched down into a bad pothole, his face rasped across the matting and the tape was pushed the rest of the way. Once off one side, using his tongue and repeatedly stretching up his chin did the rest; for a second or two it felt like a great victory. Then common sense set in.

What had he gained? At best perhaps the possibility of talking to the man given the job of disposing of him and his car — wherever in the middle of the North Sea Jones had suggested. However, the driver did have to make his way back from whatever deserted spot he chose.

Maddern tried to figure out where they were heading. He knew they had turned left from Sea Lane, a few miles of winding lanes, then another left turn had brought them on to this straighter, faster, stretch of road. They might well be travelling along the south side of the Wash.

There was one other thing he could do. He could try to recall all that had been said, and all he could remember about this driver.

He had called Sean his uncle, or Jones had, so assuming he was a Jakes — and his strength seemed to confirm that — he was the son of another of the brothers. Another Danny, who had not managed to escape. He recalled that, when the family had removed themselves from the area, a story had come back that a young Jakes was doing well in the boxing world. 'Jockey Jakes' he had been called because he had the skill of riding hard punches, then coming back with a sharp retaliation. He had won quite a few good fights, had been making his way up to the big time. Maddern recalled his own father saying, the boy made one big mistake, and that was keeping his own name. The story went that the family had moved in on him, hoping to make big money. Jockey Jakes had been used and exploited — the family rigged fights and Jockey had finished up being banned from the sport. He had become a back-street illegal bare-knuckle fighter — a money spinner for the family, for a time. Finally, punch-drunk, he became dogsbody for and totally dependent on his family. He was obviously still dependent and still being used.

There was a change to the driving pattern now, stopping, pausing, travelling on but not far before another stop. They were clearly in an area where there were traffic lights. He wondered if he could possibly get onto his back and pushed his feet up under the obscuring blind above him, but at that moment the car turned sharply left again and he was rolled onto his face. They travelled some distance quite slowly and then stopped. He prepared himself for what might be the biggest, and the last, gamble of his life.

'Jockey!' he called as loud as he could.

'Jockey Jakes. Jockey Jakes, is that you?'

He heard the front door of the car being opened, and, once it was, he could hear the distant noise of a fairground ride. From the pattern of the drive and the distance, he felt he knew where he might be. He had been brought to the car park at the extreme end of Skegness fairground, but he was under no illusions, he could perish here just as easily as on some distant deserted beach. Visitors were sparse at this seaside town at this time of the year and cars could be parked much nearer the attractions that *were* open.

He wanted to shout and keep shouting, but knew he could panic the man into hasty action if he did. What he needed was a calm contact, the chance to distract this man from his purpose, to make ordinary conversation with this ex-boxer, and because he had been driven to this place, full of childish delights, Maddern was confident it was the punch-stupefied Jockey Jakes.

'Do you like Skegness, Jockey?' he called. 'Did the family bring you here as a child?'

The back door of his hatchback was lifted.

18

'It's coming to a head, and the pus, our own bloody pus, will soon be all over us,' Regional Detective Inspector Betterson said without preamble, adding, 'Mind if I sit down.' He did so on one of the benches outside The Trap's front door.

Liz had insisted that normal life must go on, that Cannon might as well help her do something useful, and anyway gardening was therapeutic. She had him wheel out sacks of compost from the garage and they had shovelled out the old compost from all the tubs into the barrow and were replacing it with the new when the DI arrived.

She had not felt pleased when this tall, gangling detective inspector had arrived looking gaunt and grim, or by the way Cannon had so readily abandoned his spade.

'Your friend from the Met was anxious you should know that Jones has found out the police patrol car he had use of had gone to forensics, and we believe he and his wife have gone missing. I've just been to their house — to the mansion,' he corrected, 'and the size of that place says it all.'

'I thought he was being watched?'

'No sign of my man either,' Betterson said, 'I'm hoping he's just in a situation where it's too difficult to make contact.'

'So Jones is officially on the run,' Cannon said and wished he could tell Maddern, wished to God he knew where the sergeant was.

Betterson nodded, then immediately shook his head at the betrayal. 'Some of the shit, most of it, will come the way of the police; you know that.'

Cannon could imagine the headlines. 'We must make sure they know the full story, not half of it,' he said, then asked, 'Any news of the bikers?'

'Some are in the county,' he said, 'and we're having to pull back men from Operation Jakes to stand by for trouble. There's to be a press conference this evening asking for any further information about the service station incident, and advising people not to take on any of the unknown bikers.'

By the time Betterson had risen wearily and said he hoped none of the trouble came their way, Cannon had already decided on a face-to-face warning to Stuart and Joy Russell. He left immediately after Betterson, handing his spade to Alamat, who had wandered out from the stable-block in paint-stained overalls for a break.

Reed St Clement seemed an oasis of peace, taking a siesta, pausing before the children arrived back on the school bus and early-shift workers began to call at the local shops on their way home, but even as Cannon parked his jeep and walked purposefully towards the newsagent's he could hear motorbike engines in the distance. He could also hear the wail of police sirens. It sounded like a pursuit. He got back into his jeep, drove right up to the newsagent's shop then backed it into Russell's private parking space at the side of the shop, making it more difficult for anyone to approach the shop from the rear, or for any bikers to park there.

Inside the shop, Russell stood — mug of tea in hand — watching open-mouthed as he completed the operation and walked in. Man and wife had obviously been enjoying a cup of tea before the rush of school-children and delivery boys: the full news-bags were all waiting for them in a line by the birthday card stands.

'I presume there's a good reason?' Russell said, nodding his head towards the jeep.

'Yes,' he said, and he pointed to the head-line on the newspapers lying on the counter and the graphic pictures of the service station shooting, 'there's a gang of London bikers heading for the village. I mean now, at this moment . . . ' He raised a hand, went to the shop door and re-opened it, 'and it sounds like the police are in hot pursuit.'

'Let's close,' Joy Russell said. 'We don't want them in here.'

'The school bus'll be here any moment,' Russell said. 'At least the children can come in here out of harm's way. We can't close.'

Not for the first time, Cannon thought that Russell had too rosy a picture of life today, a man who thought of trouble as shouted abuse and fist-fights, a man who could blunder into trouble at any time. He hoped it wasn't to be now.

All three of them moved to stand looking out of the shop window. Russell nodded to where a solitary biker cruised around the village green. He stopped alongside a mother with a child.

'She's waiting to meet her elder boy off the school bus,' Russell said.

In answer to a question the woman pointed towards Snyder Crescent.

The computer hacker had done his stuff, the Faima were following a trail.

'This is to do with Danny Smithson and his mother, isn't it?' Russell guessed. 'With Sergeant Maddern and . . . God knows what else.'

'It's not unconnected, but there's no one in Snyder Crescent now as far as I know,' Cannon answered.

'No, not even poor old Thompson,' the newsagent answered grimly. 'He warned me off, then got finished off himself. Well, they'd better not come in here asking questions.'

'I hope they don't, but if they do don't give them any aggravation. You, your shop and perhaps your wife may come off the worst.' He turned to look directly at Stuart Russell. 'Believe me,' he emphasized.

The newsagent grunted.

'The last biker incident I was involved in in London involved the use of an axe, knives, metal bars and baseball bats — and we know there has been a triple shooting on the motorway today,' Cannon said quietly.

'Stuart,' his wife appealed, 'listen to Mr Cannon or you'll be . . . '

Whatever she was going to say went unfinished as the village green was suddenly full of bikes, most of them huge expensive Harley-Davidsons. They roared round the green and over it. Some parked in the middle of it, revving up their machines. By his side, Russell seethed.

'Go in the back,' Cannon advised, 'I'll stay here with your wife until they've gone.'

'Some hopes,' Russell said and lifting a

hand indicated the school bus arriving, 'but I'll keep myself in check.'

The driver of the bus must have been completely nonplussed by the sight of the sea of bikers as he pulled up in the usual place not far from the shop. The sound of the enormous revving machines, and the sight of the leather-clad riders, faces hidden behind scarves and visors, made the children uncertain as they left the bus.

Before he could stop him, Russell had gone to his shop door and opened it wide. 'No restrictions on numbers today,' he called, and as if finding a refuge in a storm most of the boys and girls headed for the shop. As soon as they had alighted, Russell waved an energetic arm urging the bus-driver to move off, taking his remaining passengers out of the village, which he did.

'Who are they?'

'Darth Vader!'

'What they want?'

'I can hear police cars.'

'Is there going to be a gunfight?'

The children packed into the shop, asking questions. One or two braver, or more foolhardy, boys stayed outside. Then there was only one, who suddenly flung up his arms and shouted, 'It's the Hairy Bikers!'

Cannon thought the duo of cooking TV

bikers would need a lot more leather and aggression to make them anything like this lot, and as one of them swung his leg over the back of his bike and dismounted, the boy turned, fled into the shop, ran behind Stuart Russell and clung to the back of his shop-overall.

The man in black leather trousers and boots, black T-shirt with the words 'Fully Patched' gold sprayed across the front and FAIMA down one side, filled the doorway.

Perhaps only Cannon knew the meaning of the message. This 'fully-patched' biker would have received a hundred per cent vote of confidence from his chapter. What he had done to achieve such support would most certainly include violence. It was a trick such groups used to ensure no undercover policeman, who would not be authorized to break the law, could penetrate their world.

'We're looking for the Smithsons,' the biker said without removing his helmet.

'They've left,' Cannon said, taking the initiative before Russell could speak.

'From where?' The man took a step inside and the children all took a step back, as did Joy Russell.

'From 24 Snyder Crescent,' Cannon told him.

'That's right,' the biker said softly, 'but

we'll check. Know where they've gone?'

Cannon thought everyone in the shop shook their heads but as the man came forward more aggressively he said calmly, 'The police took them away to a safe house.'

The boy behind Russell's apron leaned out to add, 'Yeah, Danny told me his uncle threatened to kill him.'

The boy's voice was drowned out by a blare of motorbike horns, and they all looked up to see that several police cars had come up behind the bikes in the square and several of the bikers were waving at their spokesman to get a move on. He turned and walked, almost tiptoeing towards the door. Cannon waited for the intention behind the act. At the last moment the leathered giant turned and shouted, 'Boo!' at the children, laughing maniacally as all jumped and several of the girls started to cry. Russell clenched his fists but Cannon stepped in front of him.

'How did you keep your hands off 'em when you were a copper?' he breathed as the man strode with an exaggerated swagger back to his bike.

'With difficulty,' Cannon admitted, watching as the three police cars were brought to a halt by a line of engine-revving but unmoving motor-bikes. The police in the cars sat and watched, waiting for back-up. The biker who had been into the shop revved his machine harder, wove his way between the others and roared off in the direction of Snyder Crescent. The rest, with the exception of those blocking the way of the police cars, followed.

'What are they up to?' Russell asked.

'They'll be checking an empty house, nothing is taken on trust, and the police hopefully will arrive in force in the meantime.'

Russell nodded back towards the line of bikes in front of the police cars; several of them were now driving right up to the front of the cars, touching them, backing up and then coming back faster, braking hard. Taunting by motorbike, Cannon thought, but then the police cars, as one, suddenly backed up and opened their ranks as two police vans came on to the scene, the back doors opened and armed police got out. The situation altered in seconds, the bikers made arm-wide gestures of innocence but as the police advanced, short automatic rifles balanced on their forearms, fingers on triggers, they retreated little by little. The police shepherded them to one side and the police cars drove through and on towards Snyder Crescent. The armed police split into two, one lot remaining, supervising the bikers on the green, the others getting back into one of the vans and following the police cars.

Cannon could see one of the bikers had taken out what looked like a very modern phone and was busy touching the screen, texting — but to whom? Was he sending news of the arrival of armed police to someone in the other group?

One of the armed policemen went towards him and held out a hand. He was ignored.

Cannon knew this could be a flashpoint in a difficult situation. It never took much, and these bikers could be unarmed — or could be the ones involved in the service station shooting.

The armed officer went nearer, still holding out his hand. The biker kept touching the screen, rapidly, expertly — sending a message where? Cannon glanced around for any other reaction and was just in time to see another biker push a hand into the breast of his leathers.

'Get everyone into the back,' he ordered, then as one or two of the boys looked likely to argue, answer back, as kids did these days, and he caught a glint of something metal in the biker's hand, he bellowed, 'Move! Now!' The children were moving, but some almost fooling about, and the shop windows were in the direct line of any fire from the revolver that now emerged from that breast-pocket.

'Get down!' he yelled and wished he could warn the policeman who stood with his back to the danger, hand still outstretched for the phone, but even as the gunman sighted the revolver he was in the sights of a police marksman who was lying prone on top of one of the police vans. Two shots rang out.

The shot from the policeman disabled the biker with the revolver, while his shot caught the policeman a glancing blow, spun him round but continued on its trajectory straight towards one of Russell's shop windows.

Cannon saw the toughened glass bend in as if in slow motion, give way and craze like a giant spider-web. He and Russell automatically stooped and covered their heads, but mercifully the glass stayed in place. The bullet travelled on to embed itself in the wall above a display of chocolates.

Inside and out, general mayhem broke out.

The children squealed, panicked and pushed each other through the door to the back of the shop. Outside, several bikers pulled guns, the police dropped behind their vehicles and a police loud-hailer ordered the bikers to throw down their weapons.

Some of the bikers revved up, crouched low behind their handlebars, drew guns, and drove at the police lines, firing. The police returned the fire and several bikes and riders were hit. Two fell from their machines, and the police increased fire to deter any rescue attempts.

The roar and smoke of exhausts and the mud, grass and gravel thrown up by the bikes increased as the remainder of the gang hastily circled away and rode after the main party — towards Snyder Crescent.

'What can we — ' Russell was asking but broke off as the shop door opened and a woman holding a small child's hand walked in. The normality of it was totally bizarre in the middle of such chaos — a woman with a child and a shopping bag, she was like someone from another world. Then both realized it was the woman who had come to meet her older child. She seemed to meet the shop-keeper's eyes then whatever control was keeping her on her feet deserted her. Cannon whisked the shop chair from near the counter and had it under her just before her knees gave way. Russell picked up the child.

'There's . . . shooting,' she said, but not as if she believed it, 'guns.'

'Where were you?' Russell asked, placing her child on her knee as she reached for him.

'Behind the jeep,' she said and looked at Cannon, 'but where's my David?'

'In the back with my wife,' Russell told her,

'all the children off the bus are safe.'

'But what shall we do?'

'Best for you all to stay here a little longer, then we'll make sure you all get home safely,' Cannon said. 'The police will have sent for help and ambulances. Even as he spoke there was the sound of a different siren in the background, but Stuart Russell nudged his arm and nodded over in the direction of Snyder Avenue. A line of black smoke was rising into the pale-blue afternoon sky and in seconds the line billowed into a cloud, the cloud became denser with sudden bursts of angry red lighting the centre.

'Something's well ablaze,' he said.

'24 Snyder Crescent,' Cannon said.

'You reckon?' Russell said.

Cannon nodded as they watched the remaining police tending to the injured, taking guns and knives from the prostrate bikers, waiting for ambulances so these men could be taken to hospital, kept under armed guard and, when they were fit, questioned.

Then there were other people hurrying across the green, coming from all directions. Some stopped to look or talk to an officer, most headed straight for the shop.

'Parents of the children, they'll have heard the commotion, bet they can hardly believe it either,' Russell said, with a quick glance at his splintered window with the bullet hole through the top left-hand corner, and the woman being reunited with her second son.

More sirens, very near this time. Two ambulances sped into the village and were soon tending to the injured and loading them into the vehicles. An armed constable ran across to the shop and asked all the adults and children to stay inside until they were told it was safe to leave. Cannon stationed himself near the door.

It was difficult to decide whether it was more gunfire he could hear, or the great crack and snap of house beams and timber in the flames that now rose many feet above the other house-tops in the direction of Snyder Crescent. Two fire engines followed. It would be a containment exercise, he thought.

Then a white van came speeding back into the village green. For a vital moment everyone thought it was one of the police vehicles, but this Mercedes van was unmarked — and it was away, out of sight, before the police could get back to their vehicles and manoeuvre around the ambulances, stretchers and equipment laid out alongside the injured. The number plate, Cannon noted as a police car gave chase, was completely obscured by filth and just like the vehicles used by the Jakeses to fetch and carry to and from number 24.

So had one of the Jakes family come back for something? And if it was a Jakes making a late escape, why weren't the Faima after him? A Jakes prisoner could be exploited, made to talk. Cannon remembered the stash of gold bullion, the enmity between the two gangs. If the Faima had a member of the Jakes family, there would be no holds barred. He'd talk — sooner or later.

One of the ambulances was preparing to leave and while the constable received several messages on his radio his face was grim and he shook his head at the questioning looks from the adults. Then he put his hand to his ear, holding the microphone more firmly in place, exclaimed, 'What!' and listened again. 'Right,' he said.

'So . . . ' a father holding the hands of a boy and girl, asked, 'can we go?'

'An inspector is on his way to speak to you all.'

There was some muttering from one or two of the men, but before mutiny could break out a police car came from the far side of the green, the first vehicle not to break the speed limit for some time, and stopped outside the shop. A uniformed inspector got out, spoke to the constable briefly, then turned to the adults and children now all crowded into the main part of the shop.

'The parents who are here may leave with their children, and if there are neighbours' children here they could see safely home that would be a great help. I do not want any child to leave here on their own. They will be taken home by a police officer as soon as possible, and I would advise that you all stay at home once you get there.'

'Are you expecting more trouble?' one man asked.

'Are those bikers still in the village?'

'We believe they are no longer a danger to you at this moment.'

'So have you arrested all the trouble-makers?' another asked.

'No, they've not,' a robust, middle-aged woman who had just bustled across the green and into the shop, red-faced and breathless, said, 'I can tell you, I live opposite 24.' She paused for breath and jerked a thumb in the direction of the pall of smoke behind her.

'I've seen it all but none of this lot wanted to listen to me and Mr Thompson.' The gesture now was at the policeman standing next to her.

'Come on, Mrs Brompton, this is not the time,' the constable said.

'Oh! Know me, do you?' she retaliated.

'Then you should know better than to try to shut me up.'

Big, Irish, red-faced, Madge. Cannon realized he knew her too, or knew of her. Her husband had been a regular for breakfast at The Trap, a lorry-driver who had transported Lincolnshire produce all over the UK and beyond. Cannon had heard he had died. So this was where Madge had finished up.

A paramedic came hurrying over to the inspector. 'We're ready to leave,' he said, 'and he's conscious.'

The inspector hastily handed over to the constable and, leaving the situation and his car in his care, went to climb into the back of the ambulance, which left immediately.

'Those bikers,' Madge continued, 'they were after something they didn't find. They went through that house like a hoard of rampaging elephants, but they didn't find the man — not at first. I saw him come earlier. He was loading things out of the garden shed — planks, signs and things. He must have managed to keep out of sight for a bit, and — cheeky bugger — he'd backed up on poor old Mr Thompson's drive.'

He remembered Thompson had talked about planks, supports and a 'Road Closed' sign.

'But next thing that happened, one came

out of the front door with a fur rug, a settee thing came hurling through the window. Another clever sod brought a can of petrol, doused the rug thing and threw it back in through the window, a lit match after it. The place went up in no time. Scary, that was. I'm getting a bloody smoke alarm, I don't mind telling you.'

'Mrs Brompton,' the constable tried to stop the flow, 'these people should be getting to their homes.'

'We want to hear this first,' one said.

'They *should* hear,' Madge asserted, 'don't you try to shut me up, this is still a free country.'

Somebody muttered a doubt and she rounded on him. 'It's what we make it,' she told the doubter and she was encouraged by several to go on. 'Anyway,' she continued, 'this bloke who'd been fetching things from the shed suddenly runs out and tries to get away in his van, but he'd no chance.' She blew out her cheeks and shook her head. 'They had 'im in a short time, and they thanked their God, I can tell you, you could see by their manner. I should 'ope he's praying to 'is 'cause I reckon he'll need divine intervention to save himself.'

'We saw the van race off across the green,' one said.

'So where are the bikers?'

'Oh!' she exclaimed. 'With the police all blocking the way out of the Crescent, they took off over the back fields, across crops and crashing through fences and gates like it was a bleeding rodeo.'

'Have you come here for a reason?' the constable asked. In spite of his riot gear, he was obviously feeling disadvantaged in front of this Irish virago.

'I've come to pick up my neighbour's girl, she stays with me until her parents get home from work.' A tall, intelligent-looking girl came to stand by her side, raising her chin as if defying anyone to contradict her parents' friend.

'And I can't stay here or at home, I have to go to work,' a man said, 'so if it's all right I'll . . .'

The constable stood back and it was the signal for all the adults to gather up their children and any others they knew and escort them home.

Cannon followed Mrs Brompton out of the shop. 'Mrs Brompton, I knew your Billy well. I'm landlord of The Trap public house. I was sorry to hear of your loss.'

'Ah!' she exclaimed. 'He loved your breakfasts.' She added with direct and honest sincerity, 'You never get over it, y'know, you just get used to it. Nothing'll bring m'dear man back.'

He walked a few steps with her and said, 'So did I understand you went to the police about the goings-on at number 24?'

'Nah,' she said, 'I waylaid some inspector in the street when I was shopping. I'd just been talking to Mr Thompson, and don't try to tell me *that* was anything other than bleeding murder, and he said this inspector bloke getting in his car was the man he had seen at the police station, who had more or less just shown him the door.'

'And?'

'And he did the same to me, just got in his car and drove off. We all knew something was going on there. If my Billy had been here he'd 'ave sorted him out.'

'The police will want a statement.'

'I know,' she said, 'I'll tell 'em, don't you worry!'

'We could do with a few more like you and your Billy about,' Cannon said, and she reached forward and laid a hand on his arm.

'Thank you,' she said and there were tears in her eyes.

He watched her go, straight-backed, and as she and the young girl walked back across the village green she paused and the two of them flattened any churned-up turf they came to.

He remembered Billy coming into the pub with an injured forearm where she had hit him with a shovel. 'I love her to bits,' he had said.

19

Maddern had heard of a listening silence. He had never known exactly what it meant until the moment he lay being watched, but unable to see, listening to the breathing of the man who stood looking down at him in the back of the Peugeot.

'It was recognizing one of your family that got me into this mess,' he said. 'It doesn't take much, does it?' There was the noise of a shoe scuffing, coming half a step nearer. 'And I really liked the lad, young Danny,' he said, 'and you'd be his uncle.'

He listened but could hear only the wind now, the noise of the ride had stopped. Perhaps it was only being tried out for later in the season. The wind was strong, would be whistling along the beach picking up dry sand. A memory of his young daughters trying to shelter from its sting came to him.

He felt he was poised to take a step into the unknown, and he wasn't sure it was the future, as he added, 'But I guess given the chance you would be a very different uncle to, say, your own Uncle Sean.'

No sound.

'Danny could do with a good uncle,' he said.

20

'So the London lot have a member of the Jakes family?' Liz's face was grave. 'Plus, Jones, his wife *and* the undercover officer on surveillance are missing.'

'Like Maddern and his car . . . ' Cannon muttered on his way up from checking the cellar. He paused at the top of the steps, viewed the new handrail and the very clean floor below him, and added, '*Still missing.*'

'If they make that man talk . . . '

'*When*,' he corrected.

'So *when* they make him talk, all the action is going to move to those three cruisers.'

After the trauma of finding Danny and his mother between Boston and the sea, he thought the action looked likely to be the *battle* of the River Witham in the opposite direction. He wondered if the Jakeses now would risk taking those slow-moving boats all the way to Lincoln? And were Jones and his wife on those cruisers with Godfather Jakes, heading — they hoped — for the old man Jakes's last, long-planned gamble for a life of Riley, for unlimited luxury and consummate indulgence?

Liz watched Cannon standing silent, motionless, but as if poised for immediate action, and knew that for the moment he would not hear anything, no matter what outrageous statement she concocted — she'd tried that many times. When he strode off to the kitchen, she followed.

She watched him rummage through the pockets of his outdoor coat and pull out a printed leaflet she saw showed the inland waterways of East Anglia. He seemed to be trying to judge the distance between Boston and Lincoln.

'What are you thinking?' Liz asked. She added his name when there was no response. 'What are you thinking, John?'

He looked up. 'Cruisers are slow. Can the Jakeses afford to travel in such a leisurely manner now? The pressure is on . . . ' he was saying when he was interrupted by a knocking at the front doors.

Both looked at their watches. 'Hardly time,' Liz said. 'Someone's got a thirst.'

'I'll go,' he said.

When he unbolted the inner doors he saw a white Mercedes van outside. For a second he was apprehensive, then swore at himself. He was in danger of believing every large white van was engaged in something dodgy. The young man who grinned at him through the panes of the outer doors certainly wasn't.

'Hi,' he called, 'hope you don't mind my knocking.'

'Not if there's a good reason, or your watch is fast,' he answered.

'You remember me?'

'Callum, from the boatyard,' he replied, looking down at the brace of rabbits he was holding.

'These are for you. I've just seen Mr Hoskins, he sent them,' he added, 'and . . . '

'And?' Cannon studied the sudden look of concern on the young man's face. 'There's something else.'

The youth nodded.

'You'd better come in.'

'I had a word with Mr Hoskins and he said it was best to talk to you.'

'He's usually pretty sound in his judgements,' Cannon said, 'but don't tell him I said so.'

Callum laughed. 'It's just that I know there's something going on, and he said there's been trouble in Reed St Clement — he heard it on the local radio. Shooting he said?'

Cannon confirmed it all with a nod, adding, 'so he gave you the rabbits as an excuse for the visit.'

'Something like that,' he was saying but

when he found himself in the kitchen with Liz, he seemed a bit embarrassed.

'Is this men's talk?' Liz asked.

'It sort of involves a girl,' Callum admitted.

'I think you can safely say we've both seen enough life to be very broad-minded,' Cannon said.

Callum still looked doubtful but, seeing the leaflet from the boatyard on the table, walked over and looking down at it said, 'The thing is I have a girlfriend who lives near Bardney. Her people run an art gallery combined with a restaurant, and most evenings I drive over there to see Cathy. Last night we went for a run in the car, then we walked through the woods to the river, and those three cruisers my boss sold were all moored up there.' He looked up now. 'They were the Boston side of the first locks going up towards Lincoln, and I wondered if they were in trouble. I brought . . . ' he pulled a folded map-book from inside his black jacket, 'to show you exactly where I'm talking about. Those men hadn't seemed very expert to go off with three boats in the first place, and in the hands of amateurs there can be problems navigating locks. Wouldn't be the first time a holiday-maker has got a boat too near the lock gates, flooded and sunk it.'

'So you went to the boats?' he asked.

'We just walked along the towpath past them at first.'

'So who was with them?'

'No one,' Callum said, 'and when we walked back we had a closer look.'

'Went aboard?'

'Yes.'

This answer was hesitant.

'There was, like, party food and wine, spirits, all kinds left there, doors all open and everything.'

'Did you go on all the boats?'

The young man nodded. 'I knew we shouldn't, but there'd been the money in the carrier-bags. I knew there was some kind of scam.'

The police would eventually need the fingerprints of this couple who had gone from boat to boat. 'So, three empty boats,' he said, 'and you saw no one?'

'Not then,' he said. 'This is where it gets a bit embarrassing . . . '

Cannon and Liz waited.

'Well,' he said, 'Cathy and I began to walk back through the woods. It was much later than we intended, but the sky was sort of light and Cathy's lived there all her life, never lost in that area . . . '

Another Brownie point for local knowledge, Cannon thought.

'And our eyes were used to the dark by then, so we could see quite well. We stopped after a time, you know and . . . after a while . . . '

In the real old films, Cannon thought this would have been where the camera would have switched to waves crashing up on a beach. It endeared him to young Callum that at least he was a bit embarrassed talking about it. 'You came back to this world and realized there were other things going on,' he suggested.

Callum grinned. 'Not far away from us, actually.'

He unfolded the map book. 'Here's Bardney and the lock; the boats were here. We left the car here,' he pointed to a spot where a minor road neared the river, 'and after we'd been on the boats, we must have walked to about . . . '

They bent forward to see that the immediate area was marked with the National Trust and picnicking symbols. Callum put his finger in the middle of an area marked 'Bardney Limewoods' and now the pause was more meaningful. 'It must have been because we were lying down that they did not see us, and believe me we stayed lying down, hardly dared breathe. But I recognized their voices, and once one of them came near enough for me to see him in outline. Looked like Shrek in the dark. They were definitely the men who came to the boatyard and paid in notes for those boats. But though they must have come quietly enough, we didn't have to listen long to know there was trouble. They argued in whispers for a start, but were soon shouting at each other.'

'You could hear what they said?'

'Some bits. At first it was more general impressions. Some thought it was 'all over', but an older man, you could tell by his voice, said it was only the timing that would be different. But one was furious, raised his voice, said if the moaner had talked the 'other lot' would know where they were going. The older man said the moaner didn't know where they were going, only the family knew, and once they got there they were safe. They could fly out whenever they wanted to. They only had to wait for the vans. Then they decided they'd move 'the stuff' nearer the road once they'd had a rest. We knew we had to move then. We slowly edged our way back until we were behind some thick bushes, then got to our feet and legged it as quietly as we could.'

'Would you be able to pin-point exactly where they were?' Cannon asked.

'Cathy's marked it.' He pointed to where a

faint dot had been inked in.

'And you came straight here, so how long ago was this?'

'I took Cathy home, we talked about it on the way, I decided to go to Mr Hoskins, then here . . . ' He consulted his watch. 'A couple of hours or more I guess.'

'A couple of hours or more!' Cannon exclaimed as he picked up his mobile phone.

'There's something else, I — ' the young man paused, then rushed at it, 'I took a bottle of wine and a blanket off one of the boats.'

Cannon frowned to hide his true feelings. There was always the little things, the stupid things people did on the spur of the moment. 'Where are they?' he asked.

'In my car, I thought I'd just throw them away.'

'No, leave them here, I'll deal with them.'

While he went back to his car, Cannon phoned Austin, told him briefly what he knew.

'Ah!' Austin exclaimed. 'Just what I needed. The man taken must have talked . . . '

'Poor sod,' Cannon muttered.

'The Faima bikers were heading in precisely the direction you've indicated and we've had reports of several large white vans leaving Lincoln in that direction. We're trying to seal them off. It looks like being a major operation. I just thank God that it seems to be in an isolated spot. Tell that young man, his young lady *and* their families to keep well clear. The next few hours are going to be very tricky.' Austin paused then added, 'And we've found our surveillance officer, the body of our surveillance officer — he was twenty-nine, just married.'

Cannon felt a burning anger knot his stomach.

21

Maddern knew he was dealing with the trickiest thing in the world, a strong, powerful man's emotions.

'Danny.'

The voice was thick, guttural, flat.

'Yes, Danny Smithson, he used to deliver my newspapers. I like the lad.' Bound, helpless, his voice his only weapon, he tried to keep it level, sounding as normal as possible.

'Carol.'

'His mum, yes.' Maddern's hopes soared ridiculously. 'A nice girl, she's done her best for him.' He listened intently, tried to gauge this brain-damaged man's reaction. 'It can't have been easy for her, in the circumstances.'

'Cir . . . cum . . . stan . . . ces?' Jockey climbed the word like it was a flight of steps.

'Family pressures, you know all about those,' he said, inwardly wincing, this was where it could all go wrong, 'being told what to do.'

'T-told what to do.'

'Even when you don't want to do it,' Maddern ventured.

'Yes.'

The agreement was like an electric shock. He forced his voice to stay steady. 'You could help save Danny from that. He's a good kid. Sean — '

'Sean!'

The name exploded out like a dull thud, a blow, a dum-dum bullet, and the next moment he sucked in air as hands fell on him, held him, shook him. 'What can I do? What?'

'Get free of the family, go to him, stay close to him and Carol. He's lost his father, he needs someone. They both do.'

The hands that had shook him gripped tighter and Maddern knew this younger man had a strength way beyond his own. Punch-drunk he may be but powerful he certainly was. 'Sean's at the house,' Jockey said.

'I'll do everything I can to help you, as I've tried to help Danny.'

'Got to go to the house,' Jockey muttered.

'I'll go with you,' he said, envisaging the former council house in Snyder Crescent. 'We'll deal with Sean, then help you find Danny and Carol.'

'He should leave her alone,' he said, 'she . . . '

'Let's go, then,' Maddern said, beginning to feel he just wanted an end to this — one way or another. In the distance, that ride started up again. 'You could bring Danny to Skegness when this is all over.'

'Over, yes,' Jockey mumbled. 'I've got a knife.'

22

The whole area was quiet as the grave — not the phrase Cannon would have wished to slip into his mind as he followed Callum back to his girlfriend's home. He wanted to be sure Cathy and her family understood that there was going to be a major incident not too far away — or even on their doorstep, he corrected, as he was alerted by the roar of bike engines.

They met on a bend and he saw Callum's vehicle rock with the shock of displaced air as twenty, perhaps more, huge motorbikes swerved and scraped past on the narrow road. Some blared horns but that was all. They were gone in seconds but Cannon was pleased Callum put his foot down after the encounter.

On the edge of the National Trust land, under a graceful sweep of trees, some already in bright green leaf, they reached a converted farmhouse. At the far side of the house were former barns — now shops and a restaurant — and tucked behind these, a car park. Callum signalled and stopped in front of the house. He drew in behind.

Almost at once, a petite girl, with long dark hair, part caught up on top of her head, ran out of the house. Callum put his arm around her and, when she would have drawn him straight into the house, indicated that they should wait for the driver of the jeep.

Cathy was there alone. Her parents had gone into a Lincoln wholesale outlet to begin stocking up for the Easter trade. Callum said he would stop at least until they got back.

'Will your parents worry?' Cannon asked him.

'They know I'll be here,' he said.

From the main road there came the sound of more speeding motorbikes.

'It's serious isn't it, what we saw and everything?' Cathy asked.

'Big time,' Callum added.

'Yes, and I think instead of staying here it would be a good idea for you to take Cathy to your home. You're in a village, not isolated like this. Phone your parents, Cathy, let them know they should also go to Callum's place, and stay there with you until the police, or I, can let you know it's all over.'

'You think so?' she said, giving him that doubtful look the young give the middle-aged they suspect of over-reaction.

'Mr Cannon was in the Met,' Callum told her, 'we should follow his advice.'

'OK,' she said as Callum took her hand.

Cannon went inside with them, supervised the locking of the house, personally checked doors and shutters on the shop and outbuildings, then saw them off. Cathy still looked doubtful until in the distance they heard a gunshot. They all stood still and listened, but it was a single shot.

'Could be someone after rabbits?' she suggested.

'Could be,' he agreed but stood stern-faced until she was in the car next to Callum.

'See you, Mr Cannon, and thanks,' he said.

They drove away and he stood with his hand on the jeep door, listening. He would have expected mayhem, an all-out gun battle if the groups had caught up with each other, not just one single shot. He wondered if some of the Faima had already found the empty cruisers. Following tracks of men carrying ingots as heavy as hefty babies would not be difficult with the ground as soft as it was. Had the single shot been to pinpoint where the Jakeses and the loot were? And every second, these bikers bent on revenge were closing in. He calculated that with a couple of ingots in each pannier they could about clear the loot — when they had disposed of the Jakeses.

He was about to climb in and head home — away from the action, which felt a strange thing to do — when the sound of a helicopter made him walk out into the road to check to see it was the police. He could imagine the great blob of glowing heat the Jakeses and the Faima would make on their radar.

He turned at the sound of more traffic and headed for the side of the road just as a police car, followed by a large police van, came around the corner. The car stopped next to him.

'Get in,' Austin said. 'We need to be out of sight, the air folk tell us a few stragglers on bikes are behind us; we need to let them get past.'

'Turn in behind the shop; there's a car park.' Getting in, Cannon waved his hand to the driver of the van to follow. Austin indicated and in a minute both vehicles were well out of sight. Even as their engines were turned off, the sound of the bikes came, grew louder and passed on.

A message came from above that they were clear now. 'Getting out?' Austin asked.

It was more a prompt for action than a question. 'I know the roads, can take you to the exact spot,' Cannon said.

'We have to save lives, be it one side or the other,' Austin decided and drove on.

'And there's the gold, they have it with 'em, they've sent for vans.'

'They won't be coming,' Austin said. 'Stopped those in Lincoln, and arrested some of the Jakeses' understudies.'

'Any of the family?'

'No, more's the pity, I want the arch-villains — the godfather particularly, Sean Jakes who's stepping into the old man's shoes, he . . . ' His radio sounded and he pressed the receiver more firmly into his ear.

'The helicopter reports a solid ring of men now around the group in the woods some miles ahead,' Austin said.

'I'll direct you. It'll be quicker than relayed messages. How near are you going?' he asked.

'We're the unit completing our own circle outside the Faima. We'll have cars, men and stingers on every road and two armed units on foot ready to go in.' He half-turned in his seat. 'What the hell am I doing taking you along?'

'Force of habit,' Cannon suggested.

'Keep behind me and don't get into trouble, or I may be applying to you for a job as pot-man.'

Cannon gave a grunt of laughter. Robert Auguste Austin, barrister father, French mother, collecting glasses in a pub!

'I could do it,' the other man said seriously.

'I'll give you a trial,' he promised, though infinitely grateful he did not have to account to Liz at that moment.

Cannon stopped the car and van at the edge of the field, on the far side of which were some very dense woods. The field gate was open and the ground churned into mud: very recent mud, for some still dropped from where it had been thrown up onto the hedge.

'Sit tight for a bit, will you,' Austin said, as he took some information over his radio then went over to the van. A dozen armed police came quietly from the back of the vehicle. This was not a sight he had wished to see repeated so soon in this green and pleasant land, Cannon thought, as he watched the men being deployed along two hedgerows and begin to move cautiously in towards the woods.

Caution did not last long, for mayhem did break out. From deep in the trees, the sound of rapid automatic fire could be heard — one gun, then more, interspersed with single shots. The police just walking in along the hedgerows now went at a run. A loud hailer burst into life somewhere and police emerged from other hedgerows around the area of the trees and closed in. Austin thrust the car keys at him and said, 'Stay here, look after the vehicles,' and followed.

Like bloody Nelson on his flagship in his full dress uniform, Cannon thought, and for the first time asked himself why his friend wasn't in combat gear like the rest of the unit?

There was more firing, spasmodic gunshots — more like shots aimed at targets, sniping shots at individuals, where assassination got personal, one to one. The armed police from the van reached and joined the circle outside the woodland. So far, he judged the police had not fired a single gun. Then a prearranged signal must have been given, for every man he could see lifted his rifle and shot up into the air, once, twice, three bursts of fire in quick succession — and a powerful loud-hailer announced the presence of armed police.

'You are surrounded. Come out with your hands in the air.'

Cannon heard that plainly enough across the field. He held his breath in the pause that followed, then let it out in a great exasperated sigh as the firing started up again with a new intensity. There was going to be no stand-off in this battle, the stakes were too high. The blood was up, it was kill or be killed — with the police the enemy of both. He hoped Austin kept his pips and braid well out of sight.

The heaviest firing now seemed at the far side of the wood, the river side. The Jakeses would surely not be going that way by choice; water at your back slowed you up and dispersed men along banks were easy pickings. The cruisers might provide a cover from fire for a time, but they were far too slow for escape. So were the Faima driving them that way, away from the bullion they had carried there? If so . . .

The idea beginning to form was confirmed as there was the sound of engines brought back to life, and from the trees straight in front of him a line of motorcycles burst out and headed for the gateway.

Now there was something he could do. He ran and closed the gate, then, getting into the car, drove it in front of the gateway. Through the metal bars he saw the bikes coming straight towards the barrier.

The first did not seem to see their entry point was now blocked, swerving away only at the last minute. The bike slewed from under him, it going one way and him the other with the speed of a rugger player going for the winning try. The second rider, coming too fast and too close behind the first to see the danger, came straight on.

Cannon jumped sideways behind a substantial oak post just as, with an almighty metallic clang, the bike struck. The bars buckled, but the gate held, rider and bike fell as if pole-axed. The man, part under his machine, lay very still, body at odds with the angle of one leg.

The bikes behind these two swerved away and headed towards an un-gated opening into the next field. By the alarming sway as they turned, their panniers were well loaded. Even so, while he was still crouching between car and gate, they roared out onto the road behind him. He hoped the police stingers were in place everywhere.

Overhead the helicopter droned, hovered over the wood, and just the other side of the buckled gate the man groaned. He could see the telltale bulge of a gun under his jacket, and beyond him the other faller was struggling to his feet.

He was over the gate and had the revolver in his hand before either man had realized what was happening. The man on the ground was going nowhere — he undoubtedly had a broken leg — but the other man had reached his bike and was trying to pull it upright when he saw Cannon, dropped the bike, and went for his waist.

'Don't! Don't try!' Cannon shouted. 'Put your hands high, right up above your head.'

In seconds he was by the man's side and had relieved him of his revolver. At the same time he saw several armed police escorting a small group of the men in biking leathers out of the woods. Some were already handcuffed, others had their hands above their heads. There was still a spasmodic shot or two from the far side of the area, the pungent smell of nitro-glycerine in the air — and no sign of Austin.

He waited for the group to come to him, urged his prisoner to join them, then indicated the biker by the gate. 'Broken leg. This is his gun and . . . ' he held out the two revolvers to the sergeant in charge.

The officer took one. 'Give the other to CI Austin. He's unarmed, and — ' he turned his head and indicated the formally uniformed figure watching from the edge of the wood, 'I was told to send you over.'

'Right,' he said and hurried towards his former colleague. Before he reached him Austin turned and walked back between the trees. He hurried after him. 'You OK?' he asked.

'You mean faced with murder, greed, and lack of respect for all things living?' He indicated a small, fawnlike creature lying in the shrubbery, its side ripped open by shots from an automatic. 'Tried to run at the wrong time,' he said.

'A muntjac,' Cannon identified, regretting the end of the creature's life.

'So did these,' Austin said, pushing aside a green-leafed hazel bush. It was as if the colour palette changed from green to red.

Cannon blasphemed quietly, awed by the scale of the bloody slaughter, bile rising in his throat — manageable, but only just — as his mind went from the torn, blood-stained fur of that wild creature to the blood-soaked coat and fur collar of Luke Jakes, godfather and grandfather of the clan. He lay face up, shot through the heart, over a low pile of bags, and around him at erratic intervals and angles lay at least seven of his gang.

'All family by the look of the build,' he said, 'from grandfather to grandson.' Criminals they were, but there would be overwrought mothers and partners some unfortunate sod would have to seek out and tell. No amount of training quite prepared you for that task.

'None of them identified yet, of course,' Austin said, 'but the bags — are these the same as you saw in that old council house roof-space?'

He walked to the body stage-centre in the woodland horror. The smell of wet earth and warm blood was overwhelmingly potent as he stooped. 'Yes, hessian, with as many gold ingots in each as a strong man could carry.' He straightened quickly, adding, 'Most of 'em now swaying about in motorbike panniers.'

'We'll get them,' Austin said with certainty. 'One by one, we'll get them. I'm going to walk through to the river. You never know, we might've got lucky and netted someone like godfather-in-waiting, Sean Jakes.'

'I'll come with you,' he said and offered him the gun. 'From one of the bikers,' he said.

'You keep it for now, you were always a better shot, I seem to remember. I might kill someone.'

'Or be killed. Why?' he asked, indicating the full uniform.

'Question of time, old boy,' Austin said, leading the way.

They met a line of police coming slowly back towards them, re-searching the ground, one carrying a Hessian bag.

'I think we've cleared between here and the river, sir,' one reported. 'The bank's a bit messy, though.'

'Well done,' Austin said, 'well done, I'm on my way there now.'

When they reached the river, Cannon realized it was more than a mere skirmish that had happened here. A blue-leathered biker, with yellow lightning flashes on his sleeves, lay dead on the towpath, as were three members of the other side — one across the bow of the furthest cruiser, two others, one half in and half out of the nearest boat, another half in and half out of the reed-edged water.

The Jakeses had been driven away from their loot and then ruthlessly slaughtered.

Further along the path, bikers were being held at gunpoint and cuffed. There would be nothing sweet about the revenge they had taken.

A smaller, separate group of four or five was being walked the other way. These were the solitary survivors of the siege.

'Do you recognize any of them?' Austin asked.

'The man in the black jeans and top is one of those I saw bringing goods to Snyder Crescent,' he said.

'You'll give evidence when the time comes.'

'Of course,' Cannon said, 'but Sean Jakes is not among them, I can tell you that.'

'I suppose that would have been too much to ask,' Austin said. 'We'll get back to the car.'

He handed over the revolver and the car keys as they walked back. There was the sound of many sirens and ambulances as well as police cars. The biker who had hit the gate had already been taken away, but his bike still lay there. 'You'll have to collect these machines pretty quick or some smart alec will be taking them into safe custody for their own use.'

'I thought we might . . . ' Austin took a pair of gloves from his pocket and stooped to open the topmost pannier, heaved out the bag that was in there, pulled the handles apart, then stood shaking his head. 'Why does it have such a look of pureness, cleanness — such desirability? Gold never seems to take up the filth around it.'

'The filth of man's greed, you mean,' Cannon said. 'With a bag in each side, about twenty-four kilograms in all, no wonder he was unbalanced.'

'I'll get a guard on this lot until it can be moved,' Austin said, struggling to lift the bag back into the pannier, before signalling to one of the men who was just coming back to the van.

Cannon, more used to awkward stiles, helped Austin climb the now unopenable gate. As he took his arm, Austin said, 'I don't think you should attempt to go back in your jeep until we have news from the road blocks. Do you want to phone Liz?'

Cannon said nothing.

'Do it,' Austin said.

She answered very quickly.

'Liz,' he said, 'I'm with Austin near Callum's girlfriend's house. You OK?'

'What are you doing?'

'Just sitting in the car, talking,' he answered.

'Has Austin any news of Jim Maddern yet?' she asked. 'Surely his car should have been sighted somewhere.'

He looked at Austin, who had clearly heard what Liz said. 'Tell her I'm going public on the car as of now.'

23

Maddern thought he'd lost his sight as the tape was sliced through near his ear and pulled away. He had trouble raising his eyelids. Desperate to blink he had to make a forceful effort to screw his eyes tight before he could open them again, and when he did for a few seconds all he could see was bright white light.

A few more blinks and the puffed, punch-damaged features of Jockey loomed.

Jockey had worked from his ankles up, knees, wrists, arms, slicing through rope and tape, rapidly, one, two . . . He tried not to think how sharp the knife must be.

As some feeling came back into his limbs and more sight to his eyes, he struggled to the edge of his car boot space and gingerly stretched his legs until he was sitting on the edge. Jockey stood, overshadowing him.

'Feel I've gone ten rounds with you, Jockey, and I lost,' he said. Words had got him this far, he knew he mustn't lapse into silence. 'You won,' he added, 'hands down.'

'Yes,' Jockey agreed.

'And now we have to go to the house,'

Maddern suggested, putting a little weight on his feet, wondering if he'd be able to stand — and then he heard voices.

It sounded like a family — children, adults, coming nearer — and he saw the knife, a nine-inch beast, slid into a sheath in Jockey's waistband. He had a choice here. He was pretty sure if he took Jockey by surprise he could knock him off balance, attract attention and be out of this situation. But he had been a policeman a long time, and he also knew that he was gaining Jockey's trust, that it was possible he was going to be taken to the place where all the Jakes clan were gathering before they left the country, where apparently the infamous Uncle Sean already was, waiting.

The voices — the family, calling to each other, laughing — came nearer. Then he realized what they were doing in the wide flat space of the empty car park. They were flying a kite.

'Daddy,' a young voice piped, 'I think that man sitting on the car is ill.'

'Is everything all right?' a man's voice asked, coming nearer. Jockey stood over him and he could see nothing, but felt the tension in Jockey's stance. He caught a glimpse of the kite, brilliant as a huge butterfly rising into the sky.

'It's up! Daddy! Look, look!' A child's voice

from further away.

Maddern put his head a little to the side. 'No, I'm fine,' he called, and in case he was bleeding anywhere they could see added, 'Just a tumble,' then added, 'nice kite!'

What kind of fool was he, he asked himself, as the family, the laughter of carefree children, moved away. There was his own family. He could have wished they had not accepted his explanation quite so easily, but they could see he was not alone. He had Jockey — or Jockey had him.

'We have to go now,' Jockey stated.

'In the car?' he asked.

'To the station.'

'The railway station?'

'Yes,' Jockey said and got back into the driving seat.

He glanced around. The sea was far out. On the windswept beach, there were just a few distant dog-walkers, looking like Lowry figures with long-trousered legs and big boots. The family were on the beach now, the children dancing along, exultant, their kite high and tugging behind them. In the distance that fairground ride stopped again. He took a lungful of the sea air — and went to sit in the passenger's seat.

He lifted his hand towards the vanity mirror, the slowness of the action asking permission from Jockey, who was watching him closely. He looked like death and there was dried blood in his hair.

'Perhaps I could have a swill at the station, if we're going on a train, and a cup of tea,' he said. 'Be good for both of us.'

Jockey did not answer, but started the car.

The streets were not overly busy but there were people about — shopping, strolling. What he needed was for a local copper to spot his car, make a report. He had no illusions about what he was getting into, knew there would be no sweet-talking Uncle Sean.

At the station they parked the car, and *surely* if there was a call out for it, it *must* be seen here. He had to concentrate to walk normally. Much of him hurt, particularly his side which had tangled with the doorframe. He pulled himself up straight and kept close to Jockey, who gave him no cause for concern. When Jockey bought the tickets for Lincoln Central he helped him out with the right change from his pocket.

The man in the ticket office glanced at a clock and said, 'Next train due in two minutes,' he said, 'you'll just make it.'

'Time to get a tea?' he asked a porter when they stepped out onto the platform.

'On the train, mate,' the porter answered indicating the train coming into sight, and

291

they were hardly in their seats and on their way before the trolley came. He supposed he was surprised there was still money in his pockets. Margaret always told him off for bundling the odd five pound note and coins all in together; now it stood him in good stead and he bought tea and bacon sandwiches for them both.

He tried to remember when he had last had a drink and eaten. He made himself sip his drink slowly at first, but then both food and drink were like nectar and he could have eaten four times as much. After they had both finished their snack, Jockey startled him by digging him in the ribs and indicating the end of the corridor. 'You're coming,' he stated.

'OK,' he said, rising obediently and walking in front of Jockey along the swaying train to the toilet compartment. 'You first?' he asked as they reached the no-man's land between carriages.

Jockey hesitated. 'No, you,' he said.

The biro he had in his inside pocket was broken in half, but he could make it work. He lost no time in writing on a paper towel. 'Police — please ring this number'. The number that came first to his mind, the one he could safely appeal to, was that for The Trap public house. 'Message: Sgt Jim on train to Lincoln.'

He folded the towel and put it in his trouser pocket, put the broken pen back in his top pocket, used the lavatory and went out. 'I'll go back to our seats,' he said as a woman with an anxious child came and stood behind Jockey. By the tut she gave she had expected Jockey to relinquish his turn.

He re-entered the compartment and looked for the most likely person to pass his message on. Then he saw the ticket inspector in the next compartment. He hurried to encounter him in the next section between carriages. The man was in his forties, smart, neat hair-style, clean-shaven.

'I need your help,' he said.

'Of course, sir,' and, looking at him more closely, asked, 'are you ill?'

He pulled the message from his pocket and opened it for him to read. 'It is important,' he said, 'but say nothing when you get to me in the next compartment.' With that he turned back and walked to his seat, just established by the time Jockey came swaying back to take the aisle-seat beside him. His face was impassive and he sat back down without comment. Even so, Maddern held his breath as the ticket collector reached them. The man looked down over Jockey's shoulder, took in his appearance, then, taking the two tickets for inspection, asked, 'Travelling together?'

Jockey glanced at him and took the tickets back. Maddern released his breath slowly and soundlessly as the inspector nodded and moved on.

He guessed the journey would take about another hour, too long to be silent, to let Jockey brood too much about things.

'Have we far to go when we reach Lincoln?' he asked.

'About twenty miles,' Jockey answered at once.

'Will someone meet us?' he asked.

'No, there'll be a car.'

'I could do with another sandwich,' he said; it seemed a safe topic.

'There's always food — and drink,' Jockey said. He leaned his head back and closed his eyes.

Where this food would be and whether there'd be any on tap for either of them he much doubted, but it seemed conversation time was over. He supposed Jockey had been up early, had a long day. He leaned back and tried to relax, rest while he could, no chance of him sleeping with so much on his mind.

As the announcer said they were nearing Lincoln Central station it did occur to him that he could feign sleep and they could both go by the stop, but he nudged Jockey, who woke with a start.

'We're at Lincoln,' he said. It took the ex-boxer a moment or two to realize where he was. They had to stir themselves, were last to alight and the doors were already being closed for the train to go on.

Jockey, who really did seem to need time to get his brain in gear after a sleep, now led the way out of the station. The station car park was right outside, very convenient, but Jockey led the way past the rows of vehicles and began walking along the road. Maddern kept pace with Jockey but his mind was riveted back in that car park. Near the exit he had glimpsed — thought he had glimpsed — a jeep, a Willy jeep. Cannon's pride and joy, or just another like it? Had there been time for Cannon to get here? If the ticket collector had phoned from the train and Cannon had been near his jeep, then yes, for he would have been miles nearer to Lincoln than a train just leaving Skegness.

He followed Jockey with his heart racing, but *if* it was Cannon, had he seen the two of them walking away? Jockey led the way into a side street and he turned to look back the way they had come. There were several people behind them on the same side, and on the opposite side, a man, strolling but taking long strides, covering the ground, glancing his way and then a bus obscured him from view. He could not linger as Jockey turned to indicate a Range Rover parked just beyond the regulation distance for a vehicle near a corner.

Jockey went to the far side and, stooping, retrieved the key balanced on top of the front wheel.

24

They were still sitting in the car talking when Liz called back with a message from a ticket inspector, who had begun by saying, 'I hope this is not someone messing about . . . ' She had told him he might well be saving someone's life.

'For Jim Maddern to resort to such tactics . . . ' Liz paused, 'he really is asking for your help now, John.'

A message for Austin had come hot on its heels. A large group of bikers had tried to bypass one of the roadblocks and, not having managed, were fighting it out, trying to remove stinger and police, who needed assistance. 'I have to deal with this,' Austin said.

'Get me back to my jeep, and through the nearest roadblock. The inspector said the tickets he inspected were to Lincoln and they were due to arrive in about an hour. I could be there by then. I'm miles nearer Lincoln here than if I'd been at home.'

'But what's going on?' Austin puzzled, as he started the car.

Cannon shook his head. 'But thank God it

seems he's still alive,' he said fervently. 'Whatever he's doing, or being made to do I could at least follow, keep in touch . . . '

'With me, top priority,' Austin said, swinging the car round. He consulted with his radio contacts. 'Nearest roadblock is on the B1190,' he repeated to Cannon, then listened intently, 'and the block needing reinforcements? Right, I'll be there.'

'And for the sake of your nearest and dearest get yourself some body armour,' Cannon advised.

'For the sake of your nearest and dearest I should be telling *you* to keep out of this,' Austin said as he dropped Cannon off outside the farmhouse, delaying only to tell him that the road stinger would be pulled aside when the jeep arrived, but he must stop to identify himself by giving CI Austin's full name.

'Well, it's like Rumpelstiltskin,' Cannon said, 'no one would guess it, would they.'

The momentary light-heartedness was gone in a second as Austin held out his hand and they shook solemnly, wishing each other 'good luck' and 'Godspeed'.

He reached the roadblock in less than ten minutes, saw the men were alert and on the lookout for him. He rolled down his window and said to the nearest man, 'Robert Auguste Austin.' The man grinned and signalled for the stinger to be pulled aside. 'And tell them wherever Auguste's going to provide him with some body armour,' he shouted as he drove on.

He reached the station minutes before the arrival of the Skegness train, parked near the exit to the car park, waited, and then very nearly missed the two men who walked away behind the ranked cars. He crossed the road and followed, saw Maddern turn to look back before being led around a corner to a side street.

A bus obscured his view momentarily and when it had passed he saw a 4×4 come out of the side street. His heart gave a great thump — that had to be Jim sitting in the passenger seat and the huge shoulders and bullneck of the driver must belong to a Jakes. He was going to lose them if he didn't look sharp, but he forced himself to stand still and register the number of the grey Land Rover Discovery 3. He pulled out his phone to call Austin as he sprinted back to the station car park, wishing for a lapel radio as he fumbled with a parking ticket, keys and phone.

'Are you in eye contact?' Austin asked.

'No, but he can't be far ahead — there's too much traffic.'

'I'll put out a call for the vehicle to be stopped and detained on sight. I've requested help from the Leicestershire force.'

So, he thought, dropping the phone on the passenger's seat, I'm on my own until the cavalry arrive.

25

The way the sun rose high over his left shoulder Maddern knew they were travelling north from the city, north and slightly east.

'You've driven to this place before?' he asked Jockey.

Yes.'

'By yourself?'

He saw the slight shake of Jockey's head. 'No, bringing Uncle Sean, he set it up. Everything.' The last word was accompanied by a hand lifted up into the air.

'Clever, then,' he commented.

'Says I'm stupid.' Jockey said the words, sounding like a hurt child.

'Clever but not kind, then.'

'Never kind to me.' The words sounded dragged from the depths of old hurts. 'He tore up all my boxing pictures from the newspapers, one by one, until I learned to drop.'

'Drop?' Madder queried.

'Pretend to be knocked out in the ring, fall down. He kept making me do it over and over.'

'And if you didn't get it right, he tore up — '

'A picture, one by one.'

'That,' he said quietly and with some feeling, 'was really spiteful.'

'Carol says he's a devil.'

'You like Carol,' he said, beginning to feel that this and Jockey's hatred for his Uncle Sean were the two things he could be sure about. Jockey nodded with great emphasis.

Maddern had seen what unkindness, cruelty and mistrust could do to people, but he was a fervent believer in the power of love, love that could move mountains.

'And Danny?' he asked.

'I could be his uncle, his kind uncle, like you said.' Jockey smiled, a heart-warming but grotesque sight on such a ravaged face.

'Jockey, when we get to this place, what are we going to do about Sean?'

The car slowed down as if Jockey had forgotten he was driving. Though they were now on a deserted country lane and hampered no one, it was alarming as he appeared to switch off completely. The 4x4 hit the grass verge, bumped in and out of a water gulley and back onto the road.

'Perhaps we should stop and talk about it before we get there.'

'Yes,' Jockey agreed, and stopped the car.

'I . . . ' Maddern began, startled at the

immediate reaction, then asked, 'so, are we nearly there?'

'Next turn.'

He could have wished it was further, given him more time for these next negotiations. 'First, Jockey,' he said, 'your uncle won't expect me to be with you.'

'No,' Jockey agreed, 'I should've killed you.'

'So we mustn't let Sean know you haven't . . . ' he said, and curved his mouth into something he hoped resembled humour, going on to ask, 'So what were you told to do?'

'No one to make any phone calls to or from the pad, phone calls can be traced. I have to come to be told,' Jockey said in monotone as if he had learned this by rote.

'Jockey, if you do what I say I'll help you to a life free from Uncle Sean and your family.'

'With Carol and Danny,' Jockey said, nodding.

'That would have to be for Carol to say.' His life might depend on this but he could not bring himself to give this man unrealistic unattainable hopes.

Jockey sat still, silent, brooding.

'I think, like you, she has been *made* to do things she did not want to do, live in places she did not want to live in. Carol must be given the chance to choose, as I am giving you the same chance to choose. Maddern sat quite still, waiting for some word, some decision, while at the same time watching Jockey's hand in case he went for the knife in his belt. There was no word, no movement.

'If you want to be free of Sean you must leave me here, go to the pad,' he used Jockey's word, 'then just do as your uncle tells you . . .'

'Keep him sweet,' Jockey stated.

'You've got the idea. Keep him sweet, until I have help to take him away.' He saw Jockey's chest rising and falling more rapidly as he thought about this.

'He won't know?'

'Not until it is too late — and I won't be far away.'

'You get out now,' Jockey said and with another of these surprisingly quick decisions restarted the car.

Maddern released his seat belt and got out, staggered by his sudden freedom as Jockey drove off immediately. He lifted his head skywards and felt a sense of deliverance. Deliver me from evil, he had prayed as a child. It felt like that.

There were two things to be done, one to locate exactly where Jockey had gone, two to make contact with Cannon or the police — that meant finding someone with a phone.

He stepped off the verge into the road as he heard a vehicle coming, a lorry or a tractor — or perhaps both — but someone he could hopefully ask for assistance. The engine noises increased and he stationed himself in the middle of the road, while reminding himself he was not in uniform and wondering whether anyone would stop for such a disreputable-looking individual.

The first vehicle was a milk tanker, and the driver did begin to slow — but then Maddern saw the vehicle immediately behind, and quickly waved the tanker by, indicating to the driver he really wanted to stop the jeep coming behind him.

Cannon made the worst emergency stop he had ever made in his life, stalling the engine and throwing himself forward hard into his belt. He truly felt he did not believe his eyes. 'Jim,' he mouthed to himself, 'it is you, isn't it?' He released his belt and got out calling, 'It is you, thank God.'

Maddern passed his knuckles hard across his mouth, emotional and knocked by Cannon's prompt arrival. 'So it *was* you in Lincoln,' he said as he walked towards him.

'You look terrible,' Cannon said as they made a fumbled job of a handshake then just gripped each other and embraced.

'Thanks,' Maddern said, 'always count on

your friends to tell you the truth.'

'So how come you're on your own? I was sure you were with a Jakes. He didn't just throw you out and drive away! How did you manage it?'

Maddern shook his head as if much more effort was beyond him, though he said, 'It's not over yet.'

Cannon saw his exhaustion, took his elbow and led him back to the jeep. 'Not sure if this is what a doctor would prescribe, but I think a little nip . . . ' He pulled a small flask of brandy from the glove compartment and handed it to Maddern, who took a couple of sips, handed it back and began to tell what had happened to him. He did it shortly, succinctly, like a report from a notebook he might produce in court. Cannon once more admired him for his constraint and dignity.

'So this Jockey has gone to his Uncle Sean, who is waiting for the arrival of the godfather Jakes, the rest of the gang and the loot?'

'That's right.'

'They're not coming,' Cannon said and now briefly related his side of the known events.

'So the old man, Luke, the grandfather, is dead?'

'Yes and a good few more, on both sides,' Cannon said, 'but some of the family may have slipped through.'

'Jockey said only the family know about this place,' Maddern told him, 'but I'd think any survivors might well try to make their way here.'

'So it'd be useful if we could have a look at the layout before we report back to the police,' Cannon said.

'Jockey said it was just around the next corner, and I heard him turn off very quickly after leaving me.'

'So I'll pull well into the side and we'll go on foot.'

When they were some hundred metres around the corner they could still see no building of any kind. The lane was narrow with a copse of silver birch trees to the left and shrubs to the right. They were under the birch trees when they heard the sound of a helicopter coming in low and loud above them. Instinctively they both stopped in the trees and saw the machine coming lower — so low they could hear the swish and slice of the rotors through the air. It dropped out of sight but they had no doubt it was landing.

'Jockey called the place 'the pad',' Maddern said.

'So *that's* the way they were going to get out,' Cannon said. 'No wonder they didn't allow phone calls, they wouldn't want this finding.'

They moved closer, much closer, in the shelter of the trees and undergrowth, and saw that the pad consisted of a low built farmhouse, with a huge, barn-like construction on the right and in the field immediately to the side of this was a concreted landing circle, where the machine had come to rest, its rotors still slowly turning.

They watched as the helicopter now trundled slowly forward until it disappeared into what was obviously its hangar. The pilot came walking out after a couple of minutes and was joined by another man who came from around the corner.

'Jockey Jakes,' Maddern breathed.

The pilot stood and watched while Jockey pulled the huge sliding doors closed. Then the two of them walked towards the house.

'So are they all here?' the pilot asked.

'Only me and Sean.'

'What the hell are they . . . ' the pilot began, then paused to listen. Another engine — a car this time — was on the lane coming towards the house.

'Sounds like some of 'em now,' he added, 'they're late!'

What came into sight was a taxi, but there was no passenger and the man who got out of the driver's seat was no taxi driver. He was certainly a Jakes, and by the state of his clothes, Cannon thought, one of those who had finished up in the river.

'What the hell?' a new voice shouted. Sean Jakes stood in the doorway of the house. 'Josh! What the hell are you doing here . . . in that?'

'First thing I could get into. We've got to go, Dad.'

'Go?' the man roared. 'Where're the others?' He advanced on his son, menacingly repeating, 'Where're the others?'

'The bikers got 'em, then the police had us all surrounded. It's all up.'

Sean seized his son by his jacket, shook him before he struck him twice across the face. Maddern remembered his father's and his grandfather's stories of Jakes children being thrashed by their own fathers. From one generation to another, he thought, as, once more, father struck son, shouting, 'Talk sense!'

'It's true,' he gestured towards the pilot, 'tell Jimmie to get the chopper out, let's get out while we can. If there're bikers following me, the police'll be following them for certain.'

'Get out! With nothing?' Sean exclaimed.

'With our lives,' Josh said, but stepping

309

back as if to be out of range of another beating. 'Grandpa's dead, Matt and Tony. I saw them.'

'And the gold?' Sean asked. 'The gold?'

'The police will have all that by now,' Josh said, making a last appeal. 'See sense, Dad, we can start again.'

'Christ!' Jimmie shouted. 'What're we doing standing 'ere chewing the fat, let's get out while we can. Come on, Jockey, get those doors open again.'

'Wait!' Sean ordered, drawing a gun from a holster under his armpit. 'We'll do it my way. You open the doors,' he gestured at his son, 'I want Jockey to carry some things out for me.'

'Then we go,' Jimmie said, 'so OK, why the gun?'

'Then we go,' Sean repeated and motioned Jockey towards the front door with the revolver.

Maddern watched and before the helicopter was once more rolled out to the take-off area, Jockey had already been out and put four bulging holdalls on the front doorstep. Sean obviously had some private loot he did not mean to leave behind.

They watched Jockey take the second two bags to the helicopter. Sean stood with just a single bag left at his feet. So why wasn't he carrying that over himself?

'What's he up to?' Maddern whispered.

'He's not got long, whatever,' Cannon assured him. 'The police are on their way.'

Jockey came back towards his uncle. There was something about Sean Jakes that reminded Cannon of the way a man stood waiting for the target at a shooting range to turn — poised and ready to lift the gun from his side to fire. Cannon drew the gun Austin had made him keep.

'Are we going now?' Jockey asked, as he neared his uncle.

'Yes, I'm going, you moron,' Sean said and raised the gun, 'but you're staying here.'

'Drop! Jockey! Drop!' Maddern roared, springing out into the open.

Cannon saw a kaleidoscope of rapid images: Jockey's startled face, him falling to the floor as if pole-axed; Sean Jakes fired twice, three times; Maddern fell; Sean scooped up the last bag and made for the helicopter, which looked ready for take-off, rotors whirling.

Cannon raised his gun and took careful aim. Overhead, he heard the sound of the police helicopter Austin had promised would be there in minutes. As he ran towards Maddern he saw he had hit Sean in the leg but the man was still trying to drag himself and his bag towards the helicopter. Cannon reached Jim Maddern and saw he was covered in blood.

'Hit in the groin,' Maddern gasped, his hand pressed deep into the top of his left leg, but the blood was bubbling through. In seconds, Cannon had ripped his jacket and shirt off, rolled the shirt into a compact pad then, as Maddern removed his hand, pushed this more firmly and effectively into the wound.

'It's bad,' Maddern said.

'You'll be fine, keep still.'

I'm not going to lose you now, he thought, and concentrated on keeping the pad hard down to stem the bleeding.

In the distance, they could hear the sound of a police siren and overhead the police helicopter loomed in and hovered menacingly above the revolving rotors of the one on the ground. There was no way that was going to be able to get airborne and the two men aboard abandoned it, running in opposite directions into the surrounding woodland. Sean emptied his revolver after his son and his pilot, but stopped neither of them. Cannon had no doubt the police heat-imaging cameras would keep them well in view and they would be picked up.

While Cannon steadfastly and motionlessly kept the right pressure on the wound to save

Maddern from bleeding to death, everything around him was action and movement. The men in the first police car which screamed into the arena radioed for the urgent attendance of the air ambulance. One man wanted to take over from Cannon. Maddern was alarming him by beginning to drift into unconsciousness and he thought they might lose him, fumbling about, changing over. 'We'll wait for the medics, won't we, Jim?' he said, demanding Maddern stayed awake and paid attention as he now talked to him, giving a running commentary of what was happening.

'They're attending to 'Uncle Sean',' he told him, 'not too gently; he's being cuffed, he's not co-operating. Jockey's already sitting in the back of the police car.'

There was a new roar above their head. 'Here's the air ambulance, Jim, soon have you up, up and away, you lucky lad. Margaret'll be pleased to see you safe and sound.'

At the sound of his wife's name Maddern opened his eyes, then frowned as he saw Cannon naked to the waist, and blood-splattered, bending over him.

The noise of this third helicopter landing on the grass next to the helipad — just as the police helicopter veered out of the airspace — drowned out all talk. In minutes, Maddern was being expertly attended to, blood transfusions were set up and Cannon found himself automatically included in the ride to the hospital — which was fine by him. There was no way he was going to leave Jim's side now.

26

In a sweater loaned to him by one of the air ambulance crew and with money obtained from the hospital shop after a call to Liz and relay of a card number, Cannon prepared to wait it out.

Somewhere in this complex, hushed world, Jim Maddern's life was being fought for, and his wife was on the way to his bedside.

He called Austin, who told him with grim satisfaction that they had many of the Faima and a few of the remaining Jakeses in custody. 'By the time we've interviewed, fingerprinted and DNA'd this lot we'll have the biggest clear-up rates of crimes in the history of the force,' he said. With the tone of a weary barrister refusing to defend a despicable wrong-doer, he added 'And we've got Jones — *who wept* — so whatever, we'll get no credit from the press, their focus will be all the bad apples in the barrel.'

Not all, Cannon silently resolved. Whatever the outcome he would make sure the part of a very special sergeant was told. Cannon knew some people on national newspapers;

he'd make certain the whole true story was printed.

He tried to settle to the job of waiting. One person alone in the midst of so many — their lives on pause, but nearly all supported by their nearest and dearest or by neighbours and friends. He shook his head a little, wondering at the importance of human companionship at these times.

His own thoughts turned back to Jim, Margaret and their three daughters, then to the family he did not know, the one whose daughter had been murdered in a midland park. He felt sure Katie Maddern would want to visit them sometime. Not an easy thing to do — and if Jim did not pull through . . .

He was reminded of an old Met constable who had spoken gently to a young Cannon, distressed by his first sudden death. 'It's our line of business,' the old hand had told him. 'People die. Our job is to find out why and make it easier for those left behind.'

'John,' a voice said. He looked up to see Liz standing immediately in front of him. A surge of gratitude and love for a moment made him incapable of speech or movement. Then he reached for her hand and pulled her down onto the bench next to him.

'Thanks for coming,' he said.

'How are things?' she asked, holding on to

his hand. 'What happened to your clothes?'

He shook his head. 'They've sent for Margaret,' he said. 'If Jim's brother set off with her straight away they should be here in about three hours; meantime . . . '

'It's just waiting,' she said.

'Coffee?' he asked.

They were two coffees and a snack into the waiting time when, alerted by a phone call relayed from Alamat at The Trap to Liz, they learned that Jim's brother, Mark, and Margaret were nearing Lincoln.

Liz and Cannon were in reception when they arrived.

'Have you seen Jim?' Margaret asked as she came towards them.

Liz took her into her arms as Cannon told her, 'Not since he went down to theatre, but we should let them know you've arrived. I'm sure they will come and talk to you as soon as they can.'

'I'll do that,' Liz said and went towards the desk, Mark Maddern going with her.

'He's not . . . ?' Margaret asked the worst outcome without putting it into words.

'No, no,' Cannon began, watching as the woman on the reception desk picked up a phone even as Liz and Mark talked to her. 'Here,' he said, giving her his coffee. 'It is hot, I've only just fetched it.'

Margaret took it, but just held it until Cannon gently lifted it towards her lips. 'Just a sip,' he encouraged, but the plastic cup never reached her lips as a nurse in white with blue plastic gloves, hat and apron over her uniform came over to them.

'Mrs Maddern?' she enquired.

'My husband, Jim?' she asked.

'Yes, would you like to come through to see him? He has been taken from recovery to intensive care.' She led the way through what seemed a maze of corridors at the quick nurse's pace they use to cover these distances, and all of them followed as best they could with their legs hardly feeling they belonged to them.

They all stood back as Margaret went into the intensive care suite first. Jim Maddern lay surrounded by monitors and drips, his face colourless. Cannon found himself looking at the repeating patterns on the screens for reassurance he was still with them.

A nurse placed a chair for Margaret near the head of the bed. 'You can talk to him,' she said kindly with a nod and a smile, 'it may help.'

Margaret sat down, lifted Jim's hand into her own. 'Jim, my love,' she said and her voice broke a little as she asked, 'what have they done to you?'

There seemed to be no perceptible change, and yet something did happen, they all seemed to sense it. Had Maddern heard his wife's voice? They said the facility of hearing was the last to go, that patients seemingly far gone could still show signs of responding.

Then Cannon saw his fingers close over his wife's hand; the nurse saw it too. 'Keep talking gently to him,' she encouraged, 'I'll tell the doctor.' She gently ushered the others outside. 'There's a family room,' she said, 'you can wait in here.' She opened a door at the end of the short corridor leading to intensive care.

Cannon exchanged glances with Liz, each knowing exactly what the other was thinking. This was a room which had subdued but definite opulence, deep armchairs and settee, a soothing dark-green and blue decor, a room to bring as much comfort as possible to those waiting on the life-and-death struggles of their dear ones.

'So what has been happening?' Mark asked in a low voice once they were seated. 'Damned if I understand half of it.' He was much like his brother — ruddier of complexion, a little shorter, but had that direct way of looking at you when he spoke.

'I don't know all that happened to Jim . . . ' Cannon said, but he told Mark and Liz the main outline as he knew it.

'And it all began because Jim recognized his paperboy as belonging to a local family, the Jakeses,' Liz said. 'He had the family face.'

'And build,' Cannon added.

Mark swore under his breath. 'We all knew the Jakeses, they were a blight on the landscape . . . ' he was saying as the door opened once more and Margaret came in.

'Margaret?' Liz rose to meet her.

'The doctor asked me to leave him for a few minutes while he made some checks, then he'll come to see us,' she said. 'Jim did hold my hand, didn't he? It wasn't just a reaction, a . . . '

Cannon wanted to ask if he had opened his eyes but thought better of it, instead he assured her, 'I think we all felt his reaction to you.'

'His fingers curled around yours,' Liz said gently, leading her to the sofa.

'And then there's the girls,' Margaret said, 'I must phone them soon.'

'Don't worry,' Mark said, 'when we have a bit more news I'll phone them and as soon as you want me to I'll drive back and bring them home to you.'

'Home,' Margaret said wistfully, 'I've almost forgotten what the cottage looks like, so much has happened.'

Liz and John exchanged glances. The state of the cottage was something they were certainly not going to divulge at that moment. Cannon was still pondering this question when the door opened again and a tall, young doctor came in.

'Mrs Maddern,' he nodded reassuringly at her, 'your husband is rallying. We were worried for quite a time. It wasn't just the groin. He has so many other injuries. I'm not even sure how your husband managed to walk about before he was shot.'

'He won't give in!' she said, shaking her head. 'He just won't.'

'It's probably the reason he's still with us,' the doctor smiled, 'and I think I can say he probably needs you sitting quietly by his side more than he needs us right now.'

Margaret was taken back to the bedside immediately and then, after a time, Mark was allowed to go to see his brother. Mark was a much-relieved man when he came back into the family room.

'He's opened his eyes, looked at Margaret and winked at me.' He shook his head and tutted as if it had been an outrageous thing for Jim to have done. 'He's going to be all right, and Margaret wants me to go back to the farm as soon as I can.'

Liz asked if he would like to go back to the

pub with them and stretch out on a bed for a few hours, but he refused. 'I'll drive straight back, reassure those girls, and tell them some of what their father has been involved in.'

'I'd keep the detail to a minimum for the time being,' Cannon advised. 'Katie, in particular, has been through a lot.'

They saw Mark off then went to the doorway of the intensive care suite and were allowed to the bedside for a few moments. Maddern's eyes brightened as he saw Cannon. 'Thanks,' he managed in a gruff croak. Margaret beamed; it was the first word he had managed.

The nurse moved in again and once more they were gently shepherded out.

'We've got to do something about the cottage,' Cannon said as they walked to Liz's car. 'I'll have a word with Austin and the local boys.'

'Yes, but not tonight,' she said.

'No,' he agreed.

It was only when they were climbing into bed that she asked, 'By the way where's the jeep — and Jim's car?'

'I hardly remember,' Cannon said, his head sinking gratefully to his own pillow.

'Never mind, we'll sort it out tomorrow,' she said, 'they're not that important anyway in the order of things.'

There was no answer. She studied his face, lined and sallow with exhaustion. 'You needn't do any of this,' she silently harangued him, 'you crazy ex-policeman, you!'

His head fell slightly towards her as he slept and a wing of his black hair fell over his forehead. She instinctively and gently pushed it back away from his face, and remembered Margaret doing a similar thing for Jim's hair as he lay in intensive care.

Margaret Maddern had come near to losing her man. John had undoubtedly saved him from bleeding to death. How could she wish him any different? She leaned over to touch his forehead with her lips, switched off the bedside light and slid down beside him.

27

'At least they left the garden alone,' Margaret said, staring steadfastly out of her kitchen window. Liz wondered at her control, wondered if she had turned away to hide tears, but when she turned back she was dry-eyed, her face quite resolute.

Margaret had arrived by taxi from the hospital and walked in on Liz and John organizing the beginning of the clean-up operations. She had been shocked and appalled but insisted on seeing everything — and as she went from room to room had become stiffer-backed and tighter-lipped.

'So Jim knew all about this and he never said a word.' She shook her head. 'No, he wouldn't. Knowing him he would have been more upset for me when he saw my Beatrix Potter figures,' she said, 'but I am not having his dream retirement home ruined. I presume forensics have finished here and I can go ahead?' She opened a kitchen cupboard and took out a broom and dustpan. 'No time like the present.'

'Why not come back to The Trap with me,' Liz suggested. 'John's got several off-duty policemen coming in about an hour to help clear things up. You won't want to stay here . . . '

'Won't I?' Margaret said, and there was a set about her chin that made Liz realize that was just what she intended to do. 'They said Jim could come home by the end of the week, so I'm having this place ready for him.'

None of them spared themselves. Cannon organized the working parties of off-duty policemen to clean and redecorate and when Margaret insisted on sleeping in her own home, police wives made a rota of sleeping over, shopping and taking Margaret to and from the hospital every afternoon. Too impatient to wait on official sources, Cannon put a collecting box on his counter to help towards decorating materials. Then money from police sources replaced destroyed appliances and the damaged back door.

Cannon took special pleasure in seeing the threatening messages scrawled on the bedroom walls obliterated and did the 'Wreaths for All' one himself.

Margaret became notably more cheerful, as each day she went to tell Jim news of how the renovations were going and how Mark was bringing the girls back a day or two after he was home. 'Give you time to settle in,' she told Jim, adding that the one good thing that had come out of it all was that the dinner service she had always described as 'bile-yellow' which his great-aunt had given them as a wedding present had been broken and she would be able to buy one she really liked.

Austin appeared on television giving guarded amounts of information about the rival gangs and the recovery of gold bullion hijacked by one gang from the other immediately after the original robbery — and then the local press came to the house. Pictures of the remains of Margaret's collection of figures resurrected by the photographer from the refuse bin were taken in close-up and appeared on the front page.

The 'Bad Apple' headline appeared on the third day, when a local reporter made himself a nice little profit, having seen Inspector Brian Jones in handcuffs and selling the story on to the nationals.

The 'Family Face' revelation and the name of the sergeant observant and dogged enough to follow his instincts was reported the next day — Cannon made sure of that.

A few days later, Maddern rang The Trap. 'You two,' he said in mock tones of severity, 'had better come over for tea and see what your actions have done.'

★ ★ ★

'They started to arrive yesterday,' Margaret said, leading them into the dining-room where the table had numerous small boxes on it. Jim followed, putting his arm around his wife's shoulders. 'Some are addressed just to 'Sergeant Maddern, Lincolnshire'. Others have come via the police station, or police headquarters.'

Margaret displayed the contents and Liz and John soon realized they all contained Beatrix Potter figures, everything from Squirrel Nutkin to Jemima Puddle-Duck, Hunca Munca to Mrs Tiggy-Winkle — often with notes wishing them both well and saying they had seen the broken pieces of the figure they enclosed in the picture of the fragments published in the newspapers. They hoped their contribution would be some compensation.

'People are so kind,' Margaret said, 'and some of these are quite expensive figures.'

'Ah! But I've got something far more valuable here,' Maddern told her and sat down at the table. 'You haven't seen this yet. He held up a reproduction of a rabbit which looked as if it might have been picked up at some rather downmarket car boot sale.

She frowned at him

'Read the note,' he told her.

In a round boyish hand, it said: 'I read

about it in the paper, Sarge.'

'Oh! That's what Danny Smithson used to call you.'

'That's right,' he said with a humph of ironic laughter, 'and I used to call him Young Jakes.'

'Oh, Jim!' Margaret went to stand behind him, ran her hand gently down over his shoulders and put her cheek on the top of his head. 'I wish you'd take early retirement if they offer it to you.'

'We'll see,' he said, 'we'll see. I need to speak up for Jockey Jakes. Danny might have finished up being used as he was. I'm hoping he can join up with Danny and his mother eventually.'

'Is he hoping for a fairy-tale ending?' Liz asked, as they drove back to The Trap.

'Stranger things than that have happened,' Cannon said. 'You never know.'

'So do you think Jim will retire?'

'He's lost weight, his uniform will hang on him for a bit,' Cannon said.

★   ★   ★

A month later Jim Maddern was back on duty, after he, his daughter, Kate, and Cannon had all been to Cardiff to see the family of her friend. It had not been an easy visit, but it had been right, and Amy Congreve's mother had given Katie her daughter's favourite 'whale-tail' necklace. 'We bought it for her when we all went to Canada on holiday before she started uni; she'd like you to have it.' She had taken Katie's hand. 'You, my dear, must go back and finish your course,' she said. 'Don't let these evil people win.'

There was a photograph of Sergeant Jim Maddern in the newspaper when he received a police commendation and alongside it . . .

Cannon exploded with anger.

'They had to do it, didn't they!'

Liz came back into the kitchen from the bar where she was cleaning, to find him furious about an inset picture of 'ex-Inspector Brian Jones'.

'It's as if they glory in the bad news,' he went on.

'Jones will be in for a rough time in prison,' Liz commented. 'Neither the officers nor the prisoners will have any time for him. He'll have to watch his back.'

'Tell you what,' Cannon said with a grin, 'he'd better not suck his teeth.'

A WATERY GRAVE

Jean Chapman

Out on a morning run, ex-Met officer John Cannon vaults a stile, becomes ensnared in a discarded fishing line — and entangled in trouble. For there is a macabre discovery at the far end of this line, leading John into a search for a missing au pair, which puts him into conflict with the local police and involvement with international crime. He discovers that the local health spa has much to conceal, with its security guards and dogs patrolling the grounds. But the Portuguese owner is a ruthless business-man, and Cannon faces danger every step of the way . . .

THE BELLMAKERS

Jean Chapman

A heart-warming historical novel. Country life in the 1880s is difficult for three women without a man between them — and a living to make. As Leah seeks out her grandfather's debtors she encounters Ben and Nat Robertson, the bellmakers, and soon she and her faithful friend Ginnie become involved in a delightful summertime romance. But prejudice, superstition and gossip threaten to come between them, and the lust of a rich and determined man endangers Leah and those she loves.

A WATERY GRAVE

Jean Chapman

Out on a morning run, ex-Met officer John Cannon vaults a stile, becomes ensnared in a discarded fishing line — and entangled in trouble. For there is a macabre discovery at the far end of this line, leading John into a search for a missing au pair, which puts him into conflict with the local police and involvement with international crime. He discovers that the local health spa has much to conceal, with its security guards and dogs patrolling the grounds. But the Portuguese owner is a ruthless business-man, and Cannon faces danger every step of the way . . .

THE BELLMAKERS

Jean Chapman

A heart-warming historical novel. Country life in the 1880s is difficult for three women without a man between them — and a living to make. As Leah seeks out her grandfather's debtors she encounters Ben and Nat Robertson, the bellmakers, and soon she and her faithful friend Ginnie become involved in a delightful summertime romance. But prejudice, superstition and gossip threaten to come between them, and the lust of a rich and determined man endangers Leah and those she loves.

PSYCHO

Robert Bloch

She was a fugitive, lost in a storm. That was when she saw the sign: MOTEL — VACANCY. She switched off the engine and sat thinking, alone and frightened. The stolen money wouldn't help her, and Sam couldn't either, because she had taken the wrong turning. There was nothing she could do now — she had made her grave and she'd have to lie in it . . . She froze. Where had *that* come from? It was *bed*, not *grave*. She shivered in the cold car, surrounded by shadows. Then, without a sound, a dark shape emerged from the blackness and the car door opened . . .

THE SACRIFICE

Mike Uden

When private eye Pamela Andrews and her daughter, Anna, are chosen to investigate a high-profile case concerning the whereabouts of a missing girl, they wonder why. They're hardly household names and no one really expects them to succeed. Then the penny drops — they've just been cast as headline-grabbing eye-candy. With no help from the police and nothing much to work on, it soon becomes a daunting mission. Hunting down an abductor is one thing. Becoming the next victim is quite another . . .

THE ONE A MONTH MAN

Michael Litchfield

Thirty years ago, Oxford was a city of fear for female students, terrorized by a killer dubbed 'The One-A-Month Man' due to the ritualistic regularity of his crimes. Advances in DNA profiling since the time of the murders have identified Richard Pope, son of a US senator and now a frontline CIA operative, as the killer — and survivor Tina Marlowe finds herself in danger once more . . . The bad but brilliant detective Mike Lorenzo, exiled from Scotland Yard, is assigned to trace Tina before she is tracked down by her lethal enemy — just the challenge he needs to redeem himself . . .

AN INVISIBLE MURDER

Joyce Cato

When travelling cook Jenny Starling starts her new job at Avonsleigh Castle, she is thrilled. She envisions nothing more arduous than days spent preparing her beloved recipes. But when a fabulous bejewelled dagger, one of the castle's many art treasures, is used to murder a member of staff, the Lady of the House insists that Jenny help the police with their enquiries. But how was it done? The murder was committed in front of several impeccable witnesses, none of whom saw a thing. It seems the reluctant sleuth must once again discover the identity of the killer in their midst . . .